Jeune Amour

By: John Sterling Bridges

Jeune Amour
By: John Sterling Bridges

KDP ISBN 9798714962912

To the young -- and forever -- love of my life
Lorraine Estelle

JEUNE AMOUR

CHAPTER 1

"This has to be one of the most spectacular views I've ever seen. I mean, look at this! It is 360 degrees of gorgeous cityscape! The history here dates back over a thousand years to the kings and emperors, the church, the artists, the revolution, the pride and glory, the tragedy, the occupation, the devastation, the rebirth, the beauty, the perfection, and the romance. It's all here, all of it, and we are standing here, having just climbed the most iconic tower in the entire world. This has to be the ultimate bucket list item ever. Thanks for forcing me to fight off the jet lag and get up so early this morning to join you, Mark. To think I might have chosen to sleep in and miss this. Wow!"

"Yeah, I've wanted to climb the Eiffel Tower ever since I was a kid," Mark Tanner replied while gazing out over the Seine River below. "I remember seeing it in a movie once when I was about eight. I don't even remember what the movie was about. I just remember this building and thinking how cool it would be to climb someday. It's been on my bucket list ever since.

And actually doing it is way cooler than I ever imagined. I don't know all that much about Paris's history like you seem to, but I do know that this view is to die for. It was well worth the climb. Here, let's take a selfie together with the river in the backdrop. Everyone back home is going to be so jealous."

"This is the perfect way to start our great France adventure," Mark's best friend and traveling companion, Joshua Morgan, said with a hint of awe still lingering in his voice. "If this is hour one of morning one, I can't wait to see what is going to unfold for us over the next two months. This is going to be one epic summer!"

***

Mark and Josh had been friends since high school. After growing up as neighbors in the small Sacramento, California, suburb of Orangevale, the two went to college together at U.C. Davis. Mark studied viticulture and Josh oenology, and both graduated with their degrees in five years. They had talked many times about venturing together into the wine business and had dreams of someday buying a small parcel of land in Napa or Sonoma or maybe even Lodi, with hopes of eventually becoming wine kings. Both had graduated at the top of their respective classes and were celebrating their degrees and hopeful future by visiting France to see first-hand the place where the history of wine began.

Their direct flight from San Francisco had landed at Charles de Gaulle airport north of Paris the night before, around 5 p.m. Paris time. Having left the west coast on a redeye at 9 p.m. California time the preceding day, their bodies lost nine hours, which was tough on anyone, even strapping twenty-something young men. A friend's father knew a winemaker from Lodi who owned an old riverboat that was permanently moored on the left bank, the La Rive Gauche, of the Seine River near the Pont Neuf Bridge, between the Louvre and the Notre Dame Cathedral. Appreciating the boys' intentions to explore the history of wine, the barge owner had invited them to sleep on the boat in return for handling a few repair jobs that needed doing. Mark and Josh had been quick to accept the offer realizing it provided the perfect opportunity to hang out in the center of Paris and to save their limited budget for things far more important than a comfortable bed, such as wine tasting.

From the airport, they caught the train into Paris and arrived at the station Gare Saint-Lazare about an hour later. They had planned to catch the subway, locally known as the Metro, to the downtown train station. The place was buzzing with travelers, and due to the Friday evening commute and the weekend tourist crowds arriving, all the information booths were burdened with long lines.

"Man, this is frustrating," Mark said as he squinted at the large display map on the poorly lit subway wall showing myriad different colored trains that criss-crossed through Paris and it's outer reaches. "I can make out where we are, here at the train station, thanks to the 'you are here' dot, but everything else is in French, so I can't make any sense out of the directions. Do you have that French language translation app on your phone handy?"

"I do, but my phone battery is shot," Josh replied. "We need to get to the hotel, eh, I mean the barge, to recharge it. Maybe we should take a cab."

"No way, man. And drop 20 euro on a ride? Nope, we'll figure this out, or we'll hitchhike to the downtown," Mark insisted. "All we need is a little help from someone who speaks English."

Then, turning away from Josh and raising his hands in the air, Mark called out boldly to the passersby, "Does anyone here speak English?" Most of the busy commuters ignored him, but two young French girls in their twenties stopped, looked at each other, and giggled.

Then one of them waved toward Mark, "We do!"

Josh's mouth dropped both at Mark's bold display of ugly Americanism and the fact that it worked so well.

"Ah, merci, mademoiselle," Mark replied in a false accent that sounded more British than French. "Uh, we are trying to get to the Point New-eff station in downtown Paris," he said, pointing to a paper map he'd extracted from a Rick Steves guidebook back home.

The pretty brunette looked puzzled for a moment. "Pardon?" She then looked at the map, "Oh, Oui, you mean Pont Neuf, yes, we can help you find it."

She pulled out her cell phone and deftly opened an app specially made for the Paris Metro System. She typed in Pont Neuf and within seconds had an itinerary showing the four stops between Saint-Lazare and the selected destination, the precise time each link in the trip would take, and the start and stop times of each train involved.

"Do you have a phone?" she politely asked Mark while eyeing Josh.

"Uh, yeah, sure," Mark said, as he fumbled in his pocket for his cell.

"Okay, take pictures of these pages on my phone, and then you'll have your directions." Addressing her next words to Josh, the girl then asked, "First time to Paris?"

"Yes, it is. Your English is very good," Josh replied, somewhat surprised by the follow-up. "Have you been to the United States? We're from California."

"Oui, I mean yes, my friend and I both studied at Georgetown for a semester abroad last year, and I stayed over during the summer and served as an intern on your Capitol Hill while living with my aunt. She has a place on the Potomac. Her lineage is from France and dates back to your revolution in the 18th century. Are you boys in Paris for long?"

"Not for too long, but first things first, I'm Joshua Morgan," he said, holding out his hand.

Smiling demurely, the girl accepted Josh's hand and gripped it firmly to shake.

"Hello, Joshua Morgan. My name is Noelle LePage, and this is my friend Elise Gerard," Noelle said, nodding toward her strawberry blonde companion. "It is a pleasure to make your, uh, your acquaintance, yes?"

"Yes, indeed, but the pleasure is all ours. Noelle, that's a pretty name; were you born at Christmas?"

"Thank you. Actually no, I was born in February. But during the Christmas season, when my mother was pregnant with me, my parents visited my grandparents in Lyon, and as the story goes, my grandmere started referring to me in utero as her little Noelle. My mother liked the name, and it stuck.

"So," Noelle continued, "back to my question, how long will you guys be in Paris?"

"We're not entirely sure," Josh answered. "We're planning to explore France, especially the wine regions, for about eight weeks, but depending on what we find, we might stay all summer. The only real limit on our time is the 90-day maximum visit rule. We don't have work visas to be able to stay any longer. So, we could be in Paris for up to a week. Do you and Elise live in the city?"

"We will soon. Right now we're staying with Elise's family in the village of Versailles about 28 kilometers west, but in two weeks we're scheduled to move into a small flat we've rented in the seventh district, near the Rodin Museum; you've heard of it?"

"Oh, yes. He was a great sculptor, no? He created The Thinker."

"Oui, and The Kiss," Noelle said with a flirtatious sparkle in her eye.

"Hey, you two," Mark interrupted, "before you go scheduling a date at some cute sidewalk bistro, Josh, we should get going. We need to settle in if we're going to get any rest before tomorrow's big climb."

"Big climb?" Elise asked, finally joining the conversation. "What are you going to climb? Are you going to hike up to Montmartre to see the Basilica of Sacre-Coeur? The views of the city from the top of the hill are breathtaking."

"No, actually, we're planning to climb the Eiffel Tower in the morning," Mark said proudly.

"Ah, Gustave's folly," Noelle said matter-of-factly. "But of course, everyone must see the tourist highlight on their first visit to Paris. The view's not too bad from there either if you don't mind fighting the crowds to buy a ticket to climb a thousand stairs."

"It doesn't sound like the Eiffel Tower is one of your favorite places in Paris," Josh replied.

"No, not so much. But, you do need to visit it at least once, and I don't mean to discourage your adventure. You'll have fun, I'm sure. There are just so many other worthy places to visit in Paris that are not, how do you say in English ... tourist traps?"

"Yes, tourist traps," Josh chuckled. "Perhaps you've also heard of bucket lists? Climbing the Tower is on Mark's bucket list."

"So, anyway," Noelle said, intending to redirect the conversation, "we didn't have any certain plans for tonight and were just coming into the city to catch a movie at the cinema unless something else caught our attention, and you've caught mine, Joshua Morgan. Why don't we ride the metro to Pont Neuf together and we can show you my favorite cafe near there? Would you like to enjoy a little unplanned Parisian adventure on your first night in La Ville Lumiere, the City of Lights?"

Before Josh could answer, Mark took Elise's hand and began swinging it playfully. "Well, sure we would! Sleep is overrated anyway. One double espresso, and I should be good for a few hours."

Josh looked at Mark with an expression that said: Are you kidding me?

"Josh, what do you say?" Noelle asked softly, suddenly abandoning her earlier flirt.

Her dark brown eyes melted any resolve Josh might have been harboring, and he smiled.

"Yes, that sounds fun. Spontaneous adventure is really what this trip is supposed to be about anyway, and a favorite local cafe with two lovely ladies such as you showing us around sounds like the perfect beginning to our discovery of France."

"Okay, then follow us, and we'll show you a sunset in Paris," Noelle said as she grabbed Elise's hand and the two girls began skipping toward the escalator leading to the Metro's purple line.

Mark looked at Josh with a smile on his face and wide eyes. Josh shrugged his shoulders, "Well, when in Paris," he said, as they started after the girls.

**

Twenty minutes later, they stepped off the pink line at Pont Neuf. During the journey, the four had briefly exchanged stories about their respective post-college plans. The boys learned that Noelle, who was from Avignon on the Rhone River in southern France, was staying with Elise over the summer. The two had recently graduated from Sorbonne University, both having majored in history. Elise's emphasis had been French history, and Noelle's degree was in art history. Both were in the process of looking for work in Paris and planned to go to grad school eventually. Like the boys, their plans for the summer centered primarily around adventure and exploration, although it would be in their own country for the girls.

After the subway doors whooshed closed behind them, the four stood together momentarily on the concrete platform outside the train while the girls got their bearings. In comparison to the crowds at Saint-Lazare, the Pont Neuf station seemed relatively abandoned. Noelle then signaled to the left, and they headed toward the stairs.

When they emerged from the underground labyrinth into the warm summer evening air on the street, Noelle asked, "So, why Pont Neuf? Do you have a hotel reserved in this district or something? I only ask because this tends to be a bit on the expensive side in terms of places to stay in Paris, and for a couple of college boys on a post-graduation jaunt, I would have expected you to be staying in a hostel somewhere."

"Well, let's just say we are fortunate," Mark answered. "We know a guy whose father knows a guy," Mark stopped himself, "Wow, if that doesn't sound weirdly American, huh?" The group shared a chuckle. "Anyway, that guy is a big-time winemaker from Napa, California, and he owns a boat that is permanently tied up on the south side of the Seine River just over the bridge."

"Yeah," Josh jumped in, "and he invited us to stay on it while we're in Paris in return for doing a little painting and some other odds and ends type maintenance. He usually rents the boat out to tourists, but he said because they tend to be hard on the vessel, every once in a while, it needs a little TLC."

"TLC? What is that?" Elise asked with a scrunched up nose.

"Oh, I learned that saying when I was in the states," Noelle offered. "It means, uh, tender, uh loving …."

When she hesitated with the last word, Josh came to her rescue. "Care," he said.

"Yes, that's it, tender loving care. So, you two are the tender loving type, eh?" Noelle teased.

"Maybe, I guess. Heck, for a free week's stay on a riverboat on the Seine in the middle of Paris, I can be whatever I'm asked to be." Josh teased back. "So, where is the favorite cafe you promised?"

"While we'd love to take you to a cafe, there are lots of those, practically one on every other corner," Noelle said, "but your mention of the barge on the Seine where you're staying sounds far more interesting. Would you mind if we went there first? I'd really love to see it."

"I agree," Elise added. "And I know of a cute little wine shop near the hotel Saint Germain, which is less than a block from the bridge. You said that you're interested in wine. We can pick up a bottle and sip while we watch the river traffic. It's a trendy thing to do, sit on the river banks, that is, especially on Fridays. It'll give you a good feel for Paris on your first night here."

"That's an excellent idea, Elise! Josh, Mark, I know you'll love it. Please, let's go visit your barge," Noelle pleaded.

"Well, sure," Mark agreed. "That sounds great, though I do need to grab a coffee of some kind along the way. We've been awake for over 24 hours, Paris time anyway."

The three paused to gauge Josh's sentiment, and after he offered a quick grin and nod of the head, they were off.

The bustle of Paris on a Friday night was nothing less than sheer excitement, especially for a group of four footloose twenty-somethings. Noelle led the way across the bridge, coaxing the others to keep up. Elise was more interested in playing tour guide, and her stories kept the boys from running ahead. Realizing their natural inclination to hear about Paris, rather than run straight away to a wine shop, Noelle smiled to herself. She skipped back to join the group as they huddled at the north point of the bridge that crossed over the small island in the river called the Ile de la Cite, which was, for all intents and purposes, the epicenter of Paris.

"What does Pont Neuf mean?" Mark curiously asked as the group leaned over the bridge's west side to watch a boat float by underneath them.

"Well, interestingly," Elise began, "the name means new bridge. What's interesting about it is that Pont Neuf is actually the oldest standing bridge in France that crosses the Seine. It was built between the years 1578 and 1607."

"It took almost 30 years to build this bridge?" Josh asked incredulously.

"Yes. You must remember the state of technology back in the 16th century was basically zero. This bridge was an engineering marvel at the time and, frankly, still is. We are so fortunate it was not destroyed during World War II."

"Did the Germans bomb Paris during the war?" Mark asked.

"A little bit, but fortunately not too much -- some say it was a miracle -- as if Providence saved all the beauty here. So much history and architecture could have been destroyed but wasn't," Elise answered quietly.

Looking to lighten the subject, Josh asked, "I don't see any locks on this bridge. Where is the love-lock bridge? You know, the one where lovers attach a padlock and then throw the key into the river as a symbol of their forever commitment to each other."

Before Elise could answer, Noelle stepped in to take a turn playing tour guide. "Oh, that would be the next bridge downstream. You can see it just over there. It's called Pont des Arts. My high school boyfriend and I put a lock on it once. It didn't end up being a forever thing, but it was fun anyway."

Elise then added, "I did that with a boyfriend once, too. Of course, with Paris being known as the City of Love, there is a lot of romanticism here. But, sad thing, about four years ago, a portion of the parapet on the Pont des Arts collapsed from the weight of all the padlocks, so the Mayor ordered them all removed. They cut off over a million locks weighing nearly 45 tons."

"That was a lot of love," Mark quipped.

"We now have a new saying for the bridge," Elise continued, "Love without Locks. People are encouraged to take selfies and post them on Instagram instead. It hasn't exactly caught on yet, but I thought it was a clever idea."

"The locks are gone, but all those keys remain in the river, so the testimony to love is still out there," Noelle said somewhat dreamily.

"Noelle, you are always such a romantic," Elise teased her friend. "You should write a novel someday."

"I just might do that," she said in a quick fun-loving retort. "And maybe I'll make 'you' the main character. Wouldn't Mark love to read about all your secrets!"

A momentary pause in the banter followed when everyone, including Noelle, realized she had just inadvertently coupled Elise with Mark, leaving herself to be Josh's unofficial date for the evening.

"I mean, Mark and Josh, and the rest of the world for that matter," she quickly followed with an embarrassed giggle.

"I, for one, think I'd enjoy learning more about Elise," Mark said, sensing the awkwardness of the moment.

"And I, about you, Noelle," Josh said, smiling at the brown-eyed beauty. "Come on, let's keep walking. I think I'm going to need some French caffeine, too, if we're going to fully enjoy our first night in Paris."

CHAPTER 2

After they crossed over the bridge to the south side of the river, what Parisians call the left bank, Elise once again stopped to get her bearings and check her phone app for precise directions to the wine shop she was thinking of. While she did, the other three took in the sights and sounds of early evening in Paris.

"What are all those street vendors selling?" Mark casually asked Noelle.

"They are called the bouquinistes," Noelle replied. "They sell mostly second-hand books, but some sell small paintings and even some tourist trinkets. They've been a fixture on the left bank for many years. You can spend hours browsing the books. It's really quite fun."

"Okay, I've got directions to the wine shop; are you all ready to go?" Elise interrupted.

"Yes, but before we do, I was wondering if maybe we might go to a different wine shop," Josh said.

"A different one?" Elise queried. "You know of a wine shop in Paris? I thought this was your first time here."

"It is, but I do know of a wine shop. It's rather famous, at least in the United States, but I don't know if it is here in Paris. It's called Caves de la Madeleine. I think it's on a street called Royal Street or something like that. I know of it because a man named Steven Spurrier once owned it. Have you ever heard of the Judgment of Paris?"

"The Judgment of Paris? Do you mean the famous mosaic work that is displayed on the main floor at the Louvre and tells the story from Greek mythology about Zeus choosing the fairest Goddess of Olympus?" Noelle asked.

"Huh?" Josh uttered.

"Yes, as the story goes, Zeus didn't want to offend any of the Goddesses. So he assigned the task of choosing the most beautiful to a Trojan man named Paris. Paris chose Aphrodite because she promised to give him in return the most beautiful woman in the world who happened to be named Helen of Sparta. Paris's affair with Helen eventually sparked the famous Trojan War, with the horse and all. You know the story?"

"Well, yeah, I've heard of the Trojan horse and Helen of Sparta, but that's not what I'm referring to," Josh continued. "The Judgment of Paris I'm talking about had to do with wine."

"Wine? Oh, you mean the blind wine tasting that George Taber made famous in his book. Yes, of course, you do. You said you're from California, and that so-called 'judgment' made your Napa Valley quite famous, didn't it," Elise said knowingly.

"Yes, that's the one," Josh answered. "Anyway, the Brit who put the event together had a wine shop somewhere near Royal Street, I think somewhere near the river. I thought it would be interesting to visit that wine shop, but we don't have to do it tonight if it's not close by."

"Oh, we can go there tonight," Elise said. "The night is young, and I know where Rue Royale is. It's just off the right bank, back on the other side of the bridge, and down a little ways past the Louvre. It's only about ten minutes from here, and it's a beautiful night for a walk. I think we should go so that you can visit your famous wine store, and we can enjoy the streets of Paris for a while before the sun begins to set. Then we can come back here to watch all the boats go by."

"Josh, do you know which barge you'll be staying on?" Noelle asked.

"The address we were given was just the number 35," Josh said. "We were told if you look down to the southern shoreline from the statute of Henry IV on horseback, you can't miss it. It's made of mahogany wood with green trim and has very tall sailing masts."

The group walked back to the statue near the middle of the bridge. Together they then looked down to the water's edge on the south side.

"There it is; that must be it," Josh exclaimed, pointing to a boat that fit the general description. "Well, that shouldn't be any trouble getting to; look over there near the wall, some steps lead down to the landing area. Let's find the Madeleine Wine Store and then come back. Maybe we can pick up some bread and cheese along the way and have a little snack with our wine while we watch the night float by."

Rue Royale was a reasonably short but prominent street that ran from the Place de la Concorde on the right bank, north to the Catholic church known as L'eglise de la Madeleine, thus the shop's name. The actual storefront was located on a small side street called Cite Berryer, which was easily missed by the casual tourist. Elise knew of it because her older cousin, Marie, who lived in Paris, attended the church, and just last summer, they had visited the wine shop together. The storefront was made of rich, hand-oiled walnut, and an inviting French oak wine barrel with two small chairs was out front on the sidewalk. When they arrived, Josh stopped to absorb the scene in his mind.

"It is different than in the movie," he declared as they peered through the street-facing window. "I thought it would be a lot smaller. This is actually a pretty big store."

"What movie?" Noelle asked.

"Oh, it's an American film called 'Bottle Shock' that was made back in 2008," Josh continued. "It told the story of one of the wineries in Napa that won the blind tasting at the Judgment. The winery was called Chateau Montelena. I've been there, too. It's kind of a part of wine history in California. I don't know how accurate the movie was. It was probably mostly fiction laced with bits of fact, as most Hollywood productions are, but it was a fun story nonetheless. Anyway, the promoter of the famous wine tasting, which I do happen to know actually took place, owned this wine shop back in the 70s. It's not all that important; I just thought it would be kind of cool to see it, so thanks for bringing us here. This is a real highlight for me."

The variety of wines available inside the shop seemed almost endless. It was as if all of France's 27,000 wineries were represented, but for sure, all 300 appellations were somewhere on a shelf. Josh recognized many of the more famous areas, including Burgundy, Bordeaux, Beaujolais, and Cotes du Rhône, with its most famous Châteauneuf du Pape appellation. The thought of such famous places urged Josh's mind to want to strike out on the train right then and there.

His musing was interrupted when Mark suggested the girls pick out a bottle for the evening that would pair well with the cheese they had bought at a small fromagerie they had passed on the way from the bridge.

"Hey, while you guys shop, I'm going to wander around a bit," Josh said as he strayed from the group and headed toward the back of the store.

Josh knew that the best wines were often kept in the back of a market so as not to dissuade the casual customer with high price tags. Sure enough, the further back he went, the higher the prices rose until he finally found a small display in the corner where the Grand Cru wines were kept. There the prices peaked.

Josh picked up a bottle of Chateau Latour and caressed it as if it were a newborn. He knew Latour was one of the finest Grand Cru clarets in Bordeaux from his history classes at Davis. It attained that coveted moniker even before the famous 1855 Exposition that established the modern-day French classification system for wine. He studied the bottle, noting the vintage and the varietals used in making the particular blend he was holding. Because Latour was on the Gironde River's left bank, the primary grape used was, as he expected, Cabernet Sauvignon. The second most used was Merlot, and this bottle included a splash -- five percent -- of Petit Verdot.

Josh's mind and memory raced as he perused the wines until he saw what many considered the holy grail of French wine. He gasped, almost audibly, as he touched the bottle of red nectar, careful not to pick it up lest he risk accidentally dropping it.

"Domaine de la Romanee Conti," he whispered to himself. "Oh my, gosh, there it is, right in front of me. I'm touching a bottle of DRC."

He carefully turned the bottle, out of curiosity, to check the price tag. "Huh, only 450 euro, that's a bargain," he again whispered to himself.

I remember reading that a 1990 vintage bottle of this wine was once priced at over $11,000. Someday, Josh, you'll go to this vineyard, and when you do, you will have found paradise.

"Come on, Josh, we're ready to go," Mark hailed from the cash register near the front door. "The sun is dropping fast, and we don't want to miss the red sky."

"Yeah, I'm coming," Josh replied as he removed his fingers from the dark-colored bottle. As he slowly walked back to the storefront, Josh's eyes continued capturing everything he saw for his memory. He then suddenly stopped in his tracks and was drawn to an old black and white photo on the wall. It was of a smiling man wearing large rimmed glasses, probably in his mid-thirties, holding a glass of red wine as if toasting to a friend. Underneath the image was an inscription: "Steven Spurrier - Owner 1976."

Spurrier ... he was here, Josh mused. *He walked these aisles and stocked these shelves -- the man who changed the world of wine forever. Huh, what a trip that I'm standing here, in his store. This is so cool.*

"Dude, come on, hurry up!" Mark implored.

"Yes, come on, Josh; we don't want to miss the sunset. And you won't believe how many boats we'll see cruising up and down the river," Noelle chimed in.

The route they took back to the barge passed by the giant glass pyramid outside the Louvre. Even though they were in a hurry to get to the river, the sun was still well above the horizon, and Mark couldn't help but ask the group to stop for a moment to view the superb piece of architecture.

"This is amazing. It's obviously fairly new. Do either of you know anything about its history?" Mark asked.

"The pyramid was built in 1983," Elise answered. "So it's not at all historical. In fact, by Paris standards, that is practically yesterday. But, of course, it does have a story. President Mitterrand decided they needed to freshen up the museum with a new entrance for some reason. The Chinese-American architect named I.M. Pei, designed this pyramid. As with most newer things in Paris, it was controversial at the time. I mean, to put something so modern and so different than the classic French Renaissance style at the entrance to the Louvre, in the Cour Napoleon, was considered sacrilegious and even heresy by some. A few early articles went so far as to link the work to Satan, claiming it had 666 glass panels; the mark of the beast mentioned in the final book of the Bible called 'The Revelation of John.' But the museum claimed it had 673 panels, and that settled the debate for a while. The 6-6-6 notion then resurfaced again a few years ago when the popular novel called The Da Vinci Code came out. Of course, fiction writers will say anything to sell a book."

"Wow, you girls are a veritable fount of information. Any chance you could tag along with us as tour guides when we explore the Loire Valley next week?" Mark asked hopefully.

"Yeah, that's a fun idea," Josh added. "You said your only plan for the summer was to explore things close to home. And we wouldn't necessarily have to, or even want to, for that matter, only do tourist stuff. I'd like to get off the beaten path and get a glimpse of 'real' life in France."

"Interestingly enough, working as local tour guides was one of the jobs we were planning to apply for this summer. Let's talk about the idea when we're on your barge sipping wine," Noelle suggested. "Come on; you don't want to miss the river."

The foursome crossed back over Pont Neuf and turned right on Quai de Conti. After another block, they walked down a steep set of concrete steps, which dropped them onto the 30-foot wide boat landing and pedestrian way that stretched for miles in both directions along the river.

"This area is really hopping," Mark noted with excitement. "There are lots of young people. I like the vibe down here."

"This neighborhood is known as the Latin Quarter. It is my favorite place to experience nightlife in the city," Noelle said. "So, there's your boat, I can tell by those huge masts, but the gangway is up, so we can't get on. What's that about?"

"Oh, yeah," Josh stepped forward, reaching into his pocket. "Security -- I have the code here somewhere."

Leafing through his wallet, Josh found the slip of paper with directions to the boat and instructions on accessing it. He walked over to a small box mounted on a wooden post and tapped in a five number combination. The gangway pulley system sprang to life, and all four jumped back and watched the large access ramp slowly drop to the edge of the landing.

"After you, ladies," Josh said, bowing as if to royalty.

"Pourquoi, merci monsieur," Elise said with a cute curtsy.

As predicted, the river traffic was heavy, and people were lined up along both banks of the river to watch it. Mark found a narrow staircase that led from the upper deck down into the vessel's hold, and a few minutes later emerged with four wine glasses, a cheese knife, and a corkscrew.

Meanwhile, Josh found four folding chairs beneath a tarp and set them up on the boat's bow. After everyone was seated, Mark opened the wine, and Josh sliced the cheese. The girls just sat reveling in the moment.

"Umm, this wine is good," Josh exclaimed after tasting it. "Left bank Bordeaux has always been one of my favorites."

"Mine too," Noelle agreed. "I've visited this winery, Margaux. Will you boys be visiting Bordeaux during your travels?"

"Absolutely," Josh replied excitedly. "We want to explore all of the famous wine regions.

"So, back to Mark's idea about you two accompanying us. I know it's sudden, and you hardly know us, but I promise we're both consummate gentlemen, and if you could show us around, even for a weekend or two, we'd be very grateful. I honestly can't think of anything better than having two locals like you showing us the 'real' France."

"Well," Noelle said hesitatingly while looking at Elise, "it does sound fun, but I do need to work this summer."

Elise jumped in, "Yeah, me too, but I suppose maybe we could take a few long weekends and meet up with you a couple of times."

"I think something like that might work," Noelle concurred. "We could take the train on a Friday night and stay until the following Monday. Maybe we could meet in Bordeaux? We have a friend from college who lives there, and maybe Elise and I could stay with her. And maybe Lyon too; remember, I mentioned my grandmere lives there. She has a lovely home, and it's large. In fact, I'll bet she might even be able to put all four of us up for a weekend."

"That sounds awesome," Mark said excitedly. "Let's exchange phone numbers before the night is over, and we'll follow up after you've thought about it a bit more. Meanwhile, tell me about all of these boats. It looks like some of them are floating restaurants."

Mark tore a piece of bread off the baguette they'd purchased and handed the hunk of the dough over to Elise.

"Ooh, it's still warm. Now that's what I call good," Mark said as he inhaled the aroma of the remaining portion of the loaf in his hand.

"Many of them are dinner cruise boats," Noelle said. "They run pretty much constantly from 6 p.m. to midnight. They head up-river to the far end of the island and then loop back around. They pass by Notre Dame, which is spectacular when it's lit up at night, and then they pass beneath the famous Pont Alexandre III Bridge, and then the river gradually winds around to the south, and they pass right by the Eiffel Tower. If you time it right, you can catch the Tower 'sparkling' as they say. It's lit all night, but for five minutes, at the top of each hour, the lights all twinkle. Even though it's kind of touristy, it's still pretty to see."

"You referred to the Eiffel Tower as Gustave's folly earlier. What was that about?" Josh asked.

"Gustave Eiffel is the man who designed and built the tower. It was constructed for the 1889 World's Fair and to commemorate the centennial of the French Revolution. It was controversial and supposed to be deconstructed shortly after the Fair, but it eventually won Parisians' hearts. It was the tallest building in the world until sometime in the 1930s.

"Eiffel was also connected with your Statue of Liberty. There is a smaller version of the same statue a bit further down the river from the Eiffel Tower. So, as you can imagine, there is a lot to see on a river cruise. That's why they're so popular."

They continued to watch the river activity until long after the sun was down. The city lights were magical, and the sounds of late-night bars and bistros along with the smells of summer, wine, and cheese filled the air. Slowly the crowds that lined the river began to dissipate, and the steady buzz of noise around the boat subsided.

"So, you said you're going to climb the Eiffel Tower tomorrow morning, right?" Elise asked as she sat up straight to stretch her back.

"Yep, that's the plan, as long as we get some sleep before then," Mark replied. "Speaking of which, it's getting kind of late. Can we walk you girls back to the metro station?"

"Thanks, but we'll be fine," Elise said. "This part of Paris is very safe, and we're together. No, you boys should unpack and get some sleep. We've got each other's phone numbers, and we'll call you later in the week. Maybe we can get together again before you leave Paris."

"Thanks for a fun evening, guys. It was totally unexpected and far better than a movie, that's for sure," Noelle added as the four stood from their chairs. "I agree with Elise; it would be nice to see you again before you strike out on your grand adventure. And, we'll talk some more about the possibility of serving as your tour guides some weekend. We'll definitely call you."

After a few more minutes of small talk, the guys watched the girls leave. When they had walked out of sight, the boys lifted the gangway and headed down into the bottom of the boat, where both fell asleep in a matter of minutes.

"That was fun tonight," Elise said as the two girls walked back across Pont Neuf toward the metro station on the right bank. "Are you serious about meeting up with them in Bordeaux or Lyon? I mean, what about your condition? Aren't you afraid you might have another episode?"

"Hey, stop that," Noelle chastised her friend.

"Remember, you promised we would treat this summer like any other summer, and we weren't going to talk about that. The doctor said there isn't anything they can do about it anyway, at least not now, so we'll just leave it be. Carpe Diem, my friend; that is my new mantra and the way I am going to look at this summer."

"I know what I promised," Elise said with resignation. "But I didn't expect there would be boys involved in our summer. I thought it might be fair if we warned them, but I understand why you'd want to keep things private, and if that's what you want, then that's what we'll do. It is, after all, your life we're talking about here."

"Thanks, Elise. I appreciate your understanding. And besides, I think those boys are nice, and it would be fun to explore some with them. We'll be together, so we'll be safe. But, like you, I want to be smart and cautious, so I thought that before we commit to anything, we should probably get to know them a little bit better."

"How do you propose we do that?" Elise asked.

"Well, what better way to learn about the depths of someone's personality than to invite them to church? So I thought we should invite them to church with us on Sunday. They'll want to see the

Notre Dame Cathedral anyway and there is an international service there at 11 a.m. I'm sure they'll come along if we invite them. What do you think?"

"I think that is an excellent idea, that's what I think. Noelle, you are brilliant sometimes, you know that."

"Thanks. I guess I do have my moments."

CHAPTER 3

"That was definitely worth the effort!" Mark exclaimed as the two men walked away from the great tower through the very long park that extended to its east. "Hey, I'm thirsty. I know it's too early to get a beer, but I read about this French drink called panache that is kind of a beer spritzer of sorts. You know, beer mixed with Sprite or 7-Up. I don't think ten-thirty is too early for a spritzer. Do you?"

"Well, let's walk down to the river at least, and then we'll look for something there. That'll give us another half hour and then, I agree, that should be fine. After all, the bars are still open in California, and my body is still in the home time zone. I tell you, I don't know how pilots and flight attendants do it. The time change is wreaking havoc on my brain."

Looking at a pocket map as they walked, Josh continued, "Hey, on the way, we'll go by the Army Museum where Napoleon is buried. Let's stop in there if it's open. After all, we don't have any agenda today, do we?"

"Nope, that sounds great to me. I also thought I'd like to ride around on one of those double-decker buses with the open top. You know, kind of take in all the sights via a drive-by and get our bearings. We can then go back to those places that seem most interesting later in the week," Mark suggested.

"Perfect," Josh agreed. "Let's hop on a bus right after we get the ... what did you call it in French ... panosh?"

"Ha, no -- panache. Dude, you've got to work on your accent if you want to get around this country for two months without constantly being labeled as a lazy American."

"Yeah, maybe Noelle and Elise can teach us some French. Oui?"

"Maybe," said Mark. "I hope they call us. I liked both of them, especially Elise."

"What about Julie back home? You can't go hustling a French girl when you've got a girlfriend back home," Josh admonished his friend.

"Well, about that, I don't think Julie and I are going to continue dating. She's headed to Texas for grad school in August, and we won't be home until after she leaves. She and I have talked about it, and we agree that a long-distance relationship is probably not the best thing for us. So, we decided to consider ourselves single for the summer, and I expect we will likely break up and pursue our own paths. We'll still be friends, there is no acrimony, but to be honest, there wasn't really any love there either. It's all good. So that means I'm actually not dating anyone right now. For a change, I'm the unattached bachelor like you always are. And watching you over the years, I'm looking forward to being available to play the field a little."

"Funny, I always envied you for having a steady girlfriend," Josh replied. "I guess the grass always seems greener on the other side, huh?"

After a quick stop at the museum, the two sat down at a small deuce table in front of a cafe to people-watch and refresh for the next segment of their day's adventure. They each ordered a panache, and because they were thirsty, each asked for the large size.

"What in the world!" Josh exclaimed, "I asked for the large size, not gigantic. This glass is the size of a small keg. It's a good thing half of it is soda; otherwise, I might need to stop off at the boat for a nap before we start exploring." He took a long draw from the mug and, licking his lips, said, "But I will admit it's pretty tasty. I could get used to drinking French beer coolers."

The on-off bus was the perfect choice for day one in Paris, and the boys rode all four of the different colored bus lines, which exposed them to the majority of central Paris and Montmartre. The tourist lines to visit some of the more popular attractions seemed daunting, so they spent the vast majority of the day "on" rather than "off" the bus. They returned to the barge around 6 p.m. after grabbing a sandwich for dinner from a street vendor.

"I am exhausted," Mark said, yawning, as they plopped down into the lawn chairs on the boat deck. "This is a massive city, but I think we got a good look at it today, at least a cursory view. What do you want to do tomorrow?"

"I don't know," Josh replied. "But since its Sunday, I'd like to go to church somewhere. That's always a fun thing to do when traveling. Did I ever tell you about the time, during spring break of junior year, I went to Hilton Head, South Carolina, with some buddies? We were there on a Sunday, and I got it in my mind that I wanted to visit the oldest church on the island. So, I did some Google research, and we ended up at the First African American Baptist Church. Since we were in the South, I didn't give a second thought to the name, and the website only told about the history of the place. It was one of the first churches built after the Civil War. Anyway, when we arrived, we immediately realized that we were definitely in the minority, at least in terms of ethnicity. It was no problem, though, just different for me. And the church was traditional gospel, with the choir moving and swaying as they sang old-time gospel songs. It was amazing. We were welcomed with open arms, and I really enjoyed the different style of worship there. We even stayed for a potluck lunch after the service. It was a blast."

"I didn't know you're Baptist," Mark said.

"I'm not; that's the point. The name on the door doesn't always tell you what goes on inside the building. I've seen all kinds of great worship in many different kinds of churches. Around here, it seems the vast majority of the churches are Catholic, so maybe we should go to a mass somewhere -- maybe in one of the big fancy cathedrals. That might be cool."

Their conversation was interrupted when Josh's phone pinged.

"What? I wonder who is texting me?" he asked himself, reaching into his pocket.

"I guess it could be someone from back home since it's nine o'clock in the morning there," Mark replied.

"You really have to stop doing math all the time regarding the time zones, dude. You're starting to drive me crazy, and every time you do it, you remind me about how tired I'm supposed to be," Josh joked.

"Well, I'll be," Josh said, reading the message on his phone. "It's not from back home. It's from our friends here in Paris, and you won't believe what they just suggested."

"You mean the girls from last night?" Mark asked. "Wow, that was quick; I must have made a good impression."

"You? They texted me," Josh said with one raised eyebrow. "Anyway, what were we just talking about?"

"Church, why?"

"Well, this is from Noelle, and they're inviting us to church of all things."

"No way, that's a bizarre coincidence," Mark replied.

"Not only that, but they are also suggesting a way we can avoid a huge line to see one of the most important attractions in Paris."

"Josh, slow down; you're confusing me. What are you talking about, church or a tourist attraction? Let me see the phone."

Mark took the phone from Josh and read the text message from Noelle:

-- Boys. Hope you had a great day in Paris. Elise and I are going to church at Notre Dame tomorrow morning at 11 when they have their international service. They translate the message into English for visiting tourists. By going to service, you also get to skip the line to get in. Interested in joining us? Noelle --

"Wow, that line was more than three blocks long when we drove by on the double-decker bus," Mark recalled. "I think we should go, don't you?"

"Why not, I just suggested almost the same idea, didn't I? Only I wasn't thinking about THE biggest cathedral in all of Paris -- how cool."

Josh texted back:

-- Noelle. Thanks for reaching out. We are a yes! See you outside the entrance around 10:45. Lunch will be on us afterward. Josh --

***

The boys finally caught up on some much-needed sleep and stepped off the boat at ten o'clock the next morning. They stopped at a corner bakery for espresso and croissants before walking across Pont

Neuf and then to the vast courtyard in front of the Notre Dame Cathedral. The girls were sitting on a bench off to the right waiting for them.

"Hi, Mark," Elise called out. "Over here."

"You two are sure punctual," Noelle said, smiling. "That's nice for a change. Most guys I know are kind of slackers when it comes to that."

"As I told you," Josh responded with a grin, "we are consummate gentlemen. And besides, I assumed there would be some kind of line. I hope it's not that one," he said, pointing to a queue that had already wrapped around the corner of the massive structure.

"Nope, we get to walk right in through that special entrance over there," Noelle said, pointing.

She grabbed Josh's hand and started pulling him along. Mark and Elise quickly fell in step behind them. The greeter at the gate handed them a service program and bid them welcome in French: "Bienvenue dans la maison du Seigneur."

"What did he say?" Mark whispered as they walked up to the massive front doors of the church.

"He said, 'welcome to the house of the Lord,'" Elise explained. "Apt for a Sunday morning worshipper, don't you think? Do you guys go to church often?"

"Josh goes all the time," Mark replied. "I'm kind of hit and miss, to be honest. But I don't have anything against church. I'm just not as disciplined as I probably should be. How about you two? Is this a regular thing for you?"

"Yes, we were both raised Catholic. When I was little, it was mostly just a family thing, you know, what you did on Sunday. I never really questioned it. But then, three years ago, during the summer between our freshman and sophomore years, Noelle and I attended a week-long church camp near a little town up north called Giverny. My cousin suggested it, and it sounded fun, so we went. In addition to being fun, it was pretty profound for both of us spiritually. Since then, going to church has been by choice rather than just routine."

"Do you come to church here often, Notre Dame that is?" Josh asked.

"Oh, no, just once in a while, usually when we have friends or family visiting from away. In addition to enabling you to skip the long lines to get in, it is a beautiful church to worship in. You'll see."

Josh stopped before entering, to marvel at the stone carvings of scenes from the Bible above the door. The detail of each story portrayed was a masterpiece in and of itself, and Josh wanted to ask about each scene but found himself standing alone outside as the others passed by to go in.

In stark contrast to the hustle and bustle outside the church, inside, it was hushed, almost stoic. The cathedral was certainly grand, but Josh was a little surprised that it seemed less so than he'd expected, at least in comparison to the many pictures he had seen of other great churches in Europe. It was, nonetheless, awe-inspiring and spirit-lifting. The soft golden hues cast by the marble, stone, and wood interior elicited a sense of almost heavenly calm. At the front were three tall stained-glass windows reaching, it seemed, perhaps 60 feet in height. On the sides were countless other ornate multi-colored windows, again, as above the door, portraying various Biblical scenes. The group gathered for the service sat in the pews on the right-hand side, while the tourists meandered along the left side.

"This is beautiful," Josh whispered to Noelle. "But it seems strange to be in church while tourists are milling around taking pictures."

"Yes, it is a bit different. That is why not many locals attend church here regularly. But I find if you focus on God, the distractions tend to fall away. Do you attend church at home, Josh?" Noelle asked.

"Yes, I do. I attend what we call in the states a non-denominational church. It's pretty down to earth, with modern worship style and more teaching of the Bible than preaching. It's a popular church with college kids. It's very different from this, but I'm liking this. The awesomeness of God somehow seems more celebrated in a place like this."

Noelle smiled to herself when she heard Josh's answer about church. She had hoped he would know something about God and the fact that he did set her mind at ease a great deal regarding the prospect of meeting up with the boys in Bordeaux and Lyon.

The service began with a traditional hymn sung in French. However, many in the crowd sang along in their own languages since most recognized the familiar chord progression of Amazing Grace. The mixture of languages all singing the song together caused Josh to think that maybe this was the kind of joyful noise God hears in heaven. The priest then offered a welcoming invocation in French and then repeated it in English and one other language that sounded like an Asian dialect.

The mass, which formally began at eleven o'clock, lasted precisely 50 minutes and ended with a magnificent doxology played on a grand pipe organ. The group was once again outside the cathedral when the noon hour arrived. Bells rang out from atop the two giant fortress-looking gothic wing-towers on the building's west side. Everyone standing in the square stopped what they were doing to listen, not that they could have continued their conversations over the din. Following a thunderous melody of praise, twelve separate and distinct gongs rang out.

As he peered up into the sun at the north tower, amidst the glory of it all, Mark's mind randomly wandered to recall the famous hunchback called Quasimodo, who cried out in anguish from high atop the north tower.

Such a sorrowful story to be set in such an amazingly beautiful place, Mark thought to himself, as he craned his neck to look up toward the bells and soak in the beauty of the moment.

"So, what did you think?" Elise asked as she sidled up to Mark. "Wasn't the mass just beautiful?"

"Yes, everything about it was beautiful: the cathedral, the music, the windows, the message, and even the bells at the end. I'm so glad you brought us here. Thank you, Elise. This is exactly why we want you two to join us elsewhere if you can. You know about things that we would surely pass by. While we are here to learn about the history of wine, we also want to learn about France; as Josh put it, 'real' life in France. Have

you and Noelle talked any further about the idea
of meeting up with us?"

"No, not yet, but I'll make sure we do over the next
few days. I know I'm leaning toward a yes, and I
think Noelle is, too. I think it would be super fun."

Noelle interrupted the conversation. "Hey, I'm
hungry. What do you say we walk through the
Jardin des Tuileries and grab a bite along the way,
and then we can sit by the pond at Grande Carre
and watch the tourists."

"I'm game," Josh said enthusiastically. "And lunch
is on us. It's the least we can do to thank you for
your excellent tour guide service. Church was an
absolute ten for me. It will be a forever memory."

Two blocks west of the Louvre, the group bought
Croque Monsieur Sandwiches and sodas from a
mobile vendor cart set up in the park.

"Let's sit over there in the shade," Elise suggested,
walking away from the group toward a grassy area
shaded by mature Linden trees. "This is perfect.
It's getting warm out here."

"It is," Noelle agreed. "The temperature is
supposed to reach 31 degrees later this afternoon."

"That would be, what," Mark paused to calculate,
"around 85-ish Fahrenheit?"

"I think that's about right," Noelle said, "very good."

"Yeah, math is just kind of a thing with me. I'm always calculating. While we were climbing the Eiffel Tower yesterday, I couldn't stop thinking about the 2.5 million rivets used to build it."

"Ha, I'm not sure how all those math skills are going to help you grow grapes for our winery someday. Maybe I'll put you in charge of accounting, too. That way, you can count all our profits," Josh said in jest.

"Your winery," Noelle pursued, "you own a winery?"

"Oh, no, not yet, but maybe someday -- that's our plan anyway," Josh answered.

"Mark's degree is in viticulture, that's the farming side of the wine business, you know, growing the grapes. And my degree is in oenology, which is the winemaking side of the business. Our dream is to team up to make great wine, maybe even in the French style, in California."

"Wow, that sounds pretty exciting," Elise chimed in. "Now your trip to explore the French wine regions makes a little more sense to me. You're not just on a binge trip; you actually have a real purpose."

"Yep, and my binging days are over," Mark assured. "I left them far behind when I quit fraternity life after my sophomore year. I still enjoy wine, just in moderation. All things in moderation, you know?"

"I do," Elise said quietly. "My father was an alcoholic before he became a Christian. Those were dark years for our family, but all is good now. He's been sober for almost ten years."

"Hey," Noelle said, changing the subject, "let's wander down to the pond. It'll be fun today with so many folks milling about. And the chairs there are interesting. They lean way back, almost like a lounge chair. I've dozed off to sleep in them more than once."

They walked another quarter mile beyond the Maillol sculpture garden before coming to the Grande Carre pond. It was a large circular body of water not more than a few feet deep. Lovers of all ages and families with children made up most of the crowd, with the little ones splashing along the edges.

"This pond is also popular for little wooden sailboat races," Noelle offered as she took in a deep breath and exhaled with a sigh of satisfaction. "I just love this place."

Nestling down into one of the reclining chairs, she continued, "So, what weekends do you think you'll be in Bordeaux and Lyon? We need to know, so we can see about reserving some time off from our jobs that is, assuming we get jobs."

"Oh, we hadn't planned that far out to tell you the truth," Mark admitted.

"But if you need to know, then we can figure it out, for sure," Josh jumped in. "Our schedule can be flexible, so we can be in those towns pretty much any time you can be. Does this mean you two will be able to join us?"

"Uh, maybe; we still have to check on some details. But I do plan to call my grandmere tonight."

***

The girls bid Mark and Josh goodbye around 4 p.m. and then caught the train back to Versailles. The above-ground tracks followed the Seine for a few miles from the Saint-Lazare station, and the Eiffel Tower was visible on the distant horizon. The train wasn't crowded because of the hour, and the girls could stretch out and relax on seats that faced one another.

"That sure was fun," Elise finally said. "So, what are you thinking about in terms of meeting up with them?"

"I liked what I saw today," Noelle answered. "I get the sense they are both Christians, and their story about why they're here in France seemed to hold up. They're both very polite, and I don't have any uneasiness around them whatsoever. What do you think?"

"I agree. And I kind of like Mark."

"And I think he might kind of like you, too," Noelle said with a wink. "I'll call Grandmere tonight. Maybe you can call Andrea in Bordeaux and ask if we can stay with her for a weekend. If everything comes together, we'll see if we can set some dates."

***

"That was a pretty spectacular day, eh?" Josh said with a satisfied sigh as he took a sip of wine while the two sat on the barge looking out over the river. "As fun as Paris is, though, I think that as soon as we finish up the work we have to do on the boat, I'd like to start our trek right away. We've already got our France Eurail Passes, and I'm anxious to see the Loire Valley."

CHAPTER 4

Four days later, the boys finished all the projects on the boat and decided to go out to celebrate their last night in Paris. Having thoroughly explored the Latin Quarter, they decided to take a walk on the City's wilder side, and after the sunset, they took the metro to the Blanche station near Montmartre.

"So this is it, eh?" Josh mused aloud, "the infamous Moulin Rouge and its red windmill. I've heard quite a few tales about this place. To be honest, I'm not exactly sure that I'm all that comfortable going in."

"Yeah, but hey, it's our last night in Paris. Don't you want to be able to tell your grandkids someday that you saw an original Parisian cancan?" Mark encouraged. "Come on, if it gets too rowdy or risqué, we can just leave."

"I don't know," Josh hesitated. "This whole neighborhood seems kind of, well, I don't know, a little bit like a red light district."

"Ah, just ignore the ladies of the evening. And don't worry, this place is safe. The businesses are not going to risk their reputation by letting a tourist get mugged. Come on, chicken, live a little," Mark coaxed.

Together they cautiously approached the front door and waited a few minutes while they sized up the clientele. Mark was right; it seemed pretty touristy and safe enough. People were laughing and happy but not raucously so.

"Okay, I guess we'll give it a go," Josh finally relented. "But if it gets weird in there, we'll leave, right?"

"Sure," Mark said. "You say the word, and we'll bug out. This is going to be great!"

The music was loud, and the air was heavy with smoke as they stepped into the ticket queue in the ornate lobby. The line wasn't too long since they had arrived between shows.

"Do you want to get a drink before we go in?" Mark asked.

"Uh, oh," Josh uttered in response.

"What? What's the problem?" Mark said nervously.

"I think our decision about whether or not to go in and watch the burlesque show has just been made for us. Have you looked at the prices?"

"Where do you see that?" Mark said, glancing around. "Oh, no, bummer!" he followed up, shaking his head. "120 euro! That's insane just to watch girls in frilly dresses dance around. Geez, I guess these must all be 'rich' tourists—no way we can pay that freight. Oh well, at least we made it into the lobby. Come on; we can go. I'm sure we can find somewhere a little more affordable to celebrate our last night in Paris."

Once outside again, the two followed their instincts and wound up at a small pub about five blocks away. The atmosphere was much more in keeping with what they were used to, young people talking and drinking beer while snacking on free pretzels and peanuts. By ten o'clock, the place had packed out, and the crowd was spilling into the street. The group seemed to respect that they were outside, though, and kept the volume down to a reasonable level. The guys met a few other students from America and spent an hour sharing stories about their respective Paris adventures.

On the way back to the Pont Neuf station, Mark asked, "So, do you think we should try to call the girls, Elise and Noelle, before we leave town tomorrow? We're going to be out in the countryside on bikes for several days, if not a week, and who knows what kind of cell coverage we might have, or not, out there. I'd kind of like to know if we're going to be able to meet up with them at some point. Agree?"

"I don't know. I guess you can call if you want, but I don't want to come off as being pushy, you know? But, then again, you do have a point about the cell coverage issue."

"Okay then I'm going to call them in the morning. What's the worst that can happen? They say they can't meet up with us in the other cities." Mark concluded.

***

Looking at the caller I.D., Elise answered her cell phone on the third ring,

"Hi, Mark. How is Paris treating you?"

"Great, Elise. We've finished our work on the boat and are thinking about leaving for Loire in the next day or two. I wanted to touch base before we go because I don't know what kind of cell service we'll have while on our bike tour. We're going to be cycling through the valley and will probably be in some pretty small villages. So, have you girls decided about meeting up with us later in the summer?" Mark asked expectantly.

"Well, first, some good news on my end," Elise said. "I got a job leading tours of the Versailles palace and gardens. It's the perfect job for me right now. I'll be able to walk to work from my parents' house."

"Wow, congrats! That sounds amazing. Hey, can I put you on speaker so Josh can hear the good news, too? He's standing right here."

"Sure. Hi Josh," Elise continued. "I was just telling Mark that I got a tour guide job at Versailles. I start on Monday, but I'd like to practice one more time before then, so I wanted to ask if you two could maybe come to Versailles for a day before you leave for Loire. I heard Mark say you'll be cycling. Well, the company I'm working for offers ... wait for it ...," Elise paused for effect, "bike tours of the gardens! The company is called Big French Tire Tours. It's a blast. We have loaner bikes and everything. Please say you'll come."

Mark looked at Josh, shrugged with a nod, and then mouthed the words, "why not?"

"Elise, that sounds great. We'd love to volunteer to be your practice tourists. Any chance Noelle could join us?" Josh asked hopefully.

"Absolutely! It was actually her idea."

The guys raised their eyebrows and smiled at each other.

"Look," Elise continued, "why don't you two catch the 9 a.m. train in the morning, and Noelle and I will meet you at the train station in Versailles. There's a little farmer's market that you'll love,

61

and we can buy lunch before we head out. How's that sound?"

"Like a perfect plan," Josh replied. "We'll see you then. And thanks again. Bye."

"Bye," Elise concluded the call and hung up.

"Wait," Mark said, grabbing for the phone. "Elise, Elise, are you still there?"

The line was silent.

"Dang, she never answered my question about getting together later in the summer."

"Well, I'd say based on this invitation, the answer is probably yes, but we'll find out for sure tomorrow. No worries, man. This is going to be cool. I've always been intrigued by the stories of Versailles -- Louis XIV, the Sun-King, and all that, and then Marie Antoinette, of course. So we'll just have a slight diversion from our wine history plan and absorb a little royal history for a day."

***

Compared to the thousands of frenetic travelers swarming the Saint-Lazare train station in Paris, the Château-Rive-Gauche station in Versailles seemed practically asleep. When they left Paris, the train was packed to the gills, every seat was occupied, and people were standing shoulder to shoulder in the isles. But by the time the train reached its final destination in Versailles, there were less than a dozen people still on it.

"Wow, this is weird," Mark said as the train door wooshed closed behind them, and they stood alone on the abandoned train-side landing. "It almost feels like we're in the middle of a spooky Twilight Zone episode or something."

"For sure," Josh echoed in a questioning whisper. "But I have to admit I kinda like it. After a week in the city, I'm thinking village life is going to suit me just fine. Come on, let's go find the girls."

Noelle and Elise were waiting on the public side of the turnstiles. Both shot up quick hello waves as soon as the boys acknowledged them. Josh's eyes went straight to Noelle, and a broad smile creased his face. Mark called out a greeting to both, though his eyes were firmly fixed on Elise.

"Excusez-moi mesdames. Nous cherchons nos guides touristiques." Mark said when they were within ten feet of the girls.

"Bien, monsieur, nous sommes au service," Elise replied.

"Huh?" Mark said.

"Well, when you begin a conversation in French, you'd better be prepared to continue it," Elise chuckled. "But nice work with the translation app anyway, you silly American, you."

"Oh, ha, yeah, I guess one sentence isn't going to fool anyone. Good advice, Elise. From now on, it'll be strictly English for me. Anyway, it's so good to see you two, and thanks for inviting us to the booming metropolis of Versailles," Mark said as he held his arms open wide in jest about the smallness of the place.

Josh then stepped in. "He's just kidding, of course. I love small towns, and we really can't wait to experience this aspect of France. Paris was great, but I've got a feeling village life is going to be even better."

"Well, let's go find out!" Noelle said. "The market we told you about is just a few blocks from here. It's a classic little village place, and besides, I'm starving. I missed breakfast this morning."

The market was located four blocks from the train station. As they walked, the boys continued commenting on the relative tranquility of what they were seeing. The group walked down a partially sunlit alley and then sat at a small table outside a quaint cafe nestled in an open-air courtyard on the south end of the market. The smells were fresh, especially the warm baguettes, and the steady hum of market customers was polite and subdued. It was apparent most of the shoppers were locals just doing what they did every day, picking up the necessities for the next two or three meals and catching up on the latest gossip.

When the waitress arrived, each ordered a coffee and a pastry. Elise also asked for a bowl of fresh-cut fruit for the group to share.

"The cherries are wonderful this time of year, as are the melons," Elise said.

"The raspberries are my favorite," Noelle added. "So, boys, what are your expectations for Versailles -- I mean the palace and gardens?"

"I, for one, am expecting big and grand," Josh answered. "Kind of the opposite of what we're experiencing here, right now. I had no idea there was even a town called Versailles."

"Oh yes, this village has been around since the 17th century," Elise explained. "I'll tell you more about the town during our tour. I'm so excited to share all the history I know with you. I know you're interested in that kind of thing, and that makes it even more fun for me."

"Yes, and we should probably get started," Noelle encouraged. "The day will fly by far faster than you can imagine."

The group walked from the farmer's market several blocks toward the main palace gate. They then turned down a narrow alley and stopped in front of a large roll-up garage door. Elise pulled a key from her pocket and opened the door. Inside were dozens of bright orange bicycles emblazoned with the name Big French Tire Tours on the baskets affixed to the front of each bike. Elise deftly pulled out four bikes, and everyone quickly adjusted their respective seat heights. After closing the garage, Elise led the group down a cobblestone street toward a side entrance to the palace grounds.

"I'm sure glad we have 'fat' tires on these bikes," Josh remarked. "I think regular width tires would have gotten caught between those cobbles. Man that was a rough ride."

"Are you complaining, Josh?" Elise said with a chuckle. "I thought you were an experienced cyclist."

"Oh, yeah, I am. I'm just saying my butt wasn't quite prepared for that bumpy a ride in town. I mean, that was rougher than some single track mountain bike trails I've ridden on."

After Elise explained her new job position to the gate guard, he let the four pass with a wave and a smile. They rode down a tree-lined street until they came to a placard with a sitemap on it. Elise pulled over and stopped. The others followed suit.

"Okay," Elise began with a deep breath. "There is so much to tell you, but I don't want to bore you. One of the things I learned in training was to cover just the basics and then let the guests' questions guide the tour.

"The basics then ... to begin, Versailles comprises over 800 hectares, which equates to about 2,000 acres, and includes approximately 230 acres of formal gardens. The palace started as a rural hunting lodge built by Louis XIII in the early 17th century. Following a failed coup attempt by Cardinal Richelieu -- you may remember that name from the Three Musketeers story -- the king decided to turn the lodge into a chateau to have a safe place to get away from the rigors and politics of Paris. Later, Louis XIV built a major expansion of the palace and the grounds, including constructing most of the famous gardens we see today. Here on this map, you can see the general lay of the land, and this," she said, drawing a line with her finger, "is the path we'll follow today on our bikes. We'll ride completely around the mile-long reflection pool called the Grand Canal, and then we'll stop to enjoy lunch on the lawn at the far end. Any questions?"

"Do we get charged extra for having such a wonderful tour guide?" Josh asked, smiling.

"And one so pretty, too," Mark added with a fun wink.

"Well, I'll have to ask the management about that. But compliments are encouraged when you fill out the 20-page survey you'll get at the end of the day," Elise responded with a return wink. "Just kidding. Okay, let's mount back up and get going."

After stopping to take a few pictures of the palace from the east end of the Grand Canal and marveling at the artistry of several of the ornate fountains, the group veered off the paved road and onto a comfortable gravel pathway that was wide enough for them to ride easily two abreast. Mark quickly maneuvered to be next to Elise. Josh was content to ride slightly behind Noelle while absorbing all the historical scenery.

The path took them along the south side of the mile-long Grand Canal, where rowboats and gondolas frequently played. In the 17th century, Louis XIV commissioned the construction of life-size warship replicas that would engage in mock battles on the Canal for the royal court's entertainment.

They rode through an area the sitemap referred to as a park, but which resembled more of a forest, with trees as high as 30 meters. Topiary shrubs were precisely interspaced between the giant and perfectly straight rows of beech trees that lined the water's edge, standing it seemed, as sentries to protect the sanctity of the place. The symmetry and perfection of it all reminded that this place, as robust and wild as it appeared, was all part of a very carefully crafted garden.

The sun's reflection off the Canal's still water was almost blinding until the path angled away from the water, and they began riding through a more densely forested zone where giant yew trees and other wild species had randomly filled gaps that, over the ages, the rows and rows of planted chestnut trees had seen fit to allow.

As mesmerizing as the water on their right had been, the view to the left was equally enchanting. Vast expanses of "hunting grounds" lie as far as the eye could see. Josh let his mind imagine that instead of sitting atop a bicycle, he was riding a horse in the company of a royal contingent on a fox hunt. His nostrils swelled with the sweet smells of the forest, which were amplified by the mid-morning heat. In his mind, he could hear the baying of the hounds and the roar of scores of galloping hoof beats giving frenzied chase to an innocent red-tailed prize.

Then, suddenly the view changed from open expanse to a man-made barrier, a wall standing twenty feet high that seemed to be protecting some ancient secret that it concealed from view. The stones had been so tightly placed and had weathered for so many years that they almost seemed like concrete. Ivy lazed over the top at random places and fell to the forest floor, seemingly inviting the curious to attempt to climb the wall and take a peek.

Josh sped up to catch Elise and asked, "What's behind the wall, a secret garden?"

"Actually, that used to be the royal menagerie, or what we would call a zoo today," Elise said with a broad grin. "Louis XIV developed it and kept many wild and exotic beasts back there, including tigers and elephants. The wealth of French royalty back then knew no limits. What the king wanted, the king got. I'll tell you more about some of their excesses later. In part, those excesses were what triggered the French revolution."

The marvel of the area and the multiple stories satisfied Josh's thirst for history as they continued to ride westerly out and around the south arm of the cross formed by the Great Canal and then on toward the far western shoreline. A big smile crossed Josh's face as he reveled in the moment, the breeze, the sunshine, the fragrance of the Linden trees, and the new friendships.

This is precisely what I hoped I'd be able to do while here, he mused silently. *This place is so amazing, so vast, and so full of history. It's almost funny how back home, a track house that has reached 50 years old can be considered historic and worthy of preservation. We don't know what real history is in California, except maybe for the Missions. I am so glad to be here riding a bike through Versailles ... who'd have ever dreamed?*

Elise stopped and dismounted when they reached the westerly most point of the canal. They laid the bikes on their sides in the tall waving grass, grabbed the picnic items they had purchased at the market, and walked down the gentle grade toward the water's edge. As they thrashed through the tall grass, scores of bugs were stirred and began swarming around their knees, but the repellent Elise had insisted they apply before they started worked like a charm so that the flying pests seemed to add to the enchantment rather than spoil it.

After spreading a light tarp to sit on, opening the wine, and slicing the salami and cheeses, the four commenced to eat and chat.

"Man, I didn't think I'd be so hungry," Mark noted. "This ride seems so flat, and it's not all that hot today, so I'm surprised I'm feeling it."

71

"We've ridden over five miles already," Elise answered, "and that pastry we had at the market, was probably well spent by the time we left the fountain area."

"So," Josh interjected, "any chance we can rent a canoe and paddle out on the water later? That looks like it would be fun."

"There is a concession that rents boats, but to be honest, we're not likely to have time today. Noelle and I have a little dinner surprise for you two after the tour, you know, to celebrate the start of your travels through France. So we'll need to leave the grounds here around six o'clock," Elise said.

"But there is a legend having to do with the boats I can tell you about. It is said that when a boy invites a girl for a canoe ride on the Grand Canal at sunset, it means he intends to express his jeune amour -- that is his young love. The expectation is that he plans to ask for her hand or make some other important romantic gesture. The reason for the boat ride was to protect against any third party hearing a possible rejection. Boys are so funny that way. I'm not sure how that legend got started, but I know it is taken very seriously, at least by the youth in this town. When we were in high school, whenever a canoe trip was suggested, the guys would either flat out refuse or demand it be a morning excursion. So, we should probably not go out at sunset anyway," Elise teased.

"That's a true story," Noelle added. "Two girlfriends of mine have gotten engaged in a canoe here. It's kind of a funny tradition, but I like the romance of it," she said, clasping her hands and raising them to her heart.

CHAPTER 5

After they finished eating, Mark asked Elise if she'd like to walk around the lake edge.

"Sure, that would be fun," she replied. "Do you two want to come along?" Elise asked, nodding toward Noelle and Josh.

"No, I'm content to sit right here. How about you, Josh?" Noelle answered.

"Yeah, me too, I'm good. You guys go on, just don't fall in, Mark," Josh said with a chuckle.

"You will never let me live down that one time slip, will you?" Mark parried.

"Nope. It's not every day your best friend falls off a perfectly safe dock into the San Francisco Bay for no reason."

"Yeah, yeah, I've told you a dozen times there was a harbor seal on the dock that I didn't see, and it startled me."

"Uh, huh, oh yeah, that's right," Josh said skeptically while rolling his eyes. "Well, Elise, would you please help my friend keep an eye out for hidden harbor seals along the lake edge?"

Mark smiled and waved his friend off playfully as the two turned to leave.

"You and Josh seem like very good friends," Elise said as she and Mark walked away together. "How long have you known each other?"

"Since the second grade," Mark answered. "We lived about a block apart in a little town in north-central California. My folks moved there from Oregon when I was six. Josh and I became best friends because of football. Josh is a big football fan. Do you know much about football?"

Elise nodded.

"His favorite team is the San Francisco Forty-Niners. Oregon doesn't have a pro football team, so I didn't follow it much when I was little. Anyway, the Niners were always doing battle with their arch-rivals, the Dallas Cowboys. They're from Texas.

"Oh, I know of the Cowboys," Elise said, excited to be able to relate. "They're 'America's team,' right? They played an exhibition game in London once at Wembley Stadium."

"Well, some call them that, at least folks from Texas do," Mark said smiling. "Anyway, Josh always rooted hard for the Forty-Niners, and being competitive little boys, of course, we had to be rivals, which was true in pretty much everything. So naturally, I had to root for the other team. His colors were red and gold and mine became Cowboy blue and silver. It's funny how a rivalry like that can bring people together. We were inseparable as little boys and became best friends in high school. Then after graduation, we decided to go to college together. Now we're here exploring France, and someday we are hoping to start up a winery in California. Big dreams, I know, but what's life if you don't dream a little?

"Do you have any dreams for the future?" he asked.

"Not too many," Elise said quietly. "I've always been pretty content living here. I love Versailles. But I'd like to travel some, maybe even spend more time in the United States and see some of your national parks like Yosemite and Yellowstone. I've read a lot about them, and from the pictures I've seen, I think your country may be the most beautiful on earth.

"As you know, I also love history, so I think I might want to teach someday. Not at the college level, but maybe children. And, as old-fashioned as it may sound, I'd like to be married and have a family someday. I've been blessed to grow up in a very loving home, and I think that is something I'd like to emulate.

"It's not too exciting, I know, but that's just who I am. Noelle is the more exciting of the two of us. Her spirit is so alive with adventure, it's sad ...."

Elise suddenly stopped mid-sentence, realizing she almost said something she shouldn't.

"What's sad?" Mark asked.

"I, uh, I mean, it's sad I don't have that same spirit. Sometimes I think I hold her back, you know? But like you and Josh, we've been best friends for a long time, and I'm glad she puts up with boring old me.

"So, what do you think of the palace grounds so far?" Elise asked Mark, intending to shift the subject in hopes her feeble cover-up would be overlooked and forgotten.

"I think it is spectacular. Just like the Eiffel Tower, coming here to Versailles was also on my bucket list," Mark said, smiling. "I'm just a big tourist at heart, and I'm a lover of history, too. I appreciate all the stories you are sharing with us. I could listen to them all day and never get tired. And, hey, I don't think you're being fair to yourself when you say 'boring old me.' I think dreaming of having a family someday is a good dream. I grew up in a good family, too, and I think that is important. I don't think enough people our age appreciate the value of family, you know? So, anyway, thanks for sharing that with me."

***

Josh took his shoes off and dangled his feet in the cool lake water. Seeing the relaxed look on his face, Noelle followed suit, but rather than relax like Josh seemed to be doing, she took the opportunity to splash him with water.

"Hey there, whoa girl, that's cold. The water feels good on my feet but not on my face," Josh said, laughing. He then gently splashed her back.

"It is peaceful here," he said, leaning back on his elbows. "I could almost take a nap, but I wouldn't want to sleep the day away."

Noelle put her hands behind her head, laid back into the grass, and closed her eyes.

"I don't know. I think a nap sounds kind of nice," she sighed. "Here, lay down with me in the grass and close your eyes. Tell me a story about a king in a palace."

"Okay, hmmm, let's see. Once upon a time … how's that for a start? Don't all great 'king in a palace' stories start that way?" Josh teased.

"Oh, yes, they always do, at least the ones my dad used to tell me when I was a little girl. And I was always the princess in his stories. I loved him so much."

Noelle's playfulness subsided, and she became quiet.

Josh could sense the sudden change in her mood and figured it had something to do with her father, so he said nothing and let the moment linger, not wanting to presume or interrupt.

"He passed away eleven years ago," Noelle said softly, finally breaking the silence.

"I'm so sorry," Josh said.

"Thanks. I don't think a day goes by without me thinking about him. He was the best father ever. His name was Paul. He was in perfect health until one day he started getting these headaches and dizzy spells, and then, when he started having trouble with his eyesight, he finally went to see a doctor. They said he had some kind of rare disease in his brain that they couldn't cure. A month later, he started having some pretty bad seizures, and sometimes he would hallucinate, so he had to

80

quit work. About two months after that, he died. At least we had him home full time during those final months. He managed the headaches pretty well with medicine, and aside from the occasional seizure episodes, everything was pretty normal at home. He did some writing, and we spent a lot of time hiking together. I miss him."

"How is your mom doing?" Josh asked.

"Oh, she's doing okay. I think she would prefer that I move back home rather than live in Paris, though. I think she's lonely. My older sister, Margareet, moved away a few years ago. She lives up north in a city called Rouen. It's only a day away by train, but she's busy with her career and doesn't get home to visit very often."

"Where is home for you?" Josh asked.

"Oh, I grew up in Avignon. It's in southern France on the Rhone River. It is a charming little city. It is near a famous wine area called Chateauneuf du Pape. You should consider visiting that region on your travels."

"I know of Avignon, and yes, we are planning to travel in that area. Hey, maybe that could be another place you might be our tour guide? Speaking of which, have you and Elise talked any more about that idea? It would be so great if I, uh, we, could see you again."

"Elise and I have talked about it, and we were planning to tell you at dinner, but since you asked, I'll tell you now. Yes! We would love to meet up with you two a couple of times this summer. A few key things have come together that will allow us the flexibility to do this. First, Elise got this job here in Versailles. She's already asked and learned she could schedule around weekends as she pleases. Her new employer is very flexible on hours and scheduling. Second, because she got the job here, her parents have invited us to stay with them the whole summer rather than commute back and forth to Paris. So we let the flat in the seventh district we were going to rent, go, the one I told you about before. So that means we won't have to pay rent, which frees us up on the budget side of things to take a few long weekends off. Plus, our friend in Bordeaux and my grandmere in Lyon both said we can stay with them whenever we want. So, it looks like everything has fallen into place for us to do a little exploring with you and Mark. I think it's going to be way fun."

"Noelle, that's excellent. Wow! I'm stoked about all of this. We should sync calendars tonight and set some dates -- Bordeaux and Lyon, for sure. I'd really like to meet up in Avignon too, now that I know that's where you're from. I'd love to walk the streets of your childhood and see the place through your eyes."

"Okay," Noelle replied excitedly. "I'll call my mother tonight. I'm sure she'll be thrilled at the prospect of a visit from her beloved Noelle. She might be a little leery of American boys, but I'll assure her that you are, as you said, consummate gentlemen," she said with a playful wink.

"Come on let's go catch up with Elise and Mark so we can fill Mark in on the news!"

Noelle went to pop up from her lying position in the grass, but as soon as she got to her feet, she began to wobble and immediately sat back down.

"Hey, are you okay?" Josh asked with concern. "You look a little pale."

"Ha, I just stood up a little fast. Too much excitement, I guess. And I don't usually drink wine this early in the day either. I'll be fine; just give me a second."

Noelle knew it wasn't the wine that was causing her to see stars and feel disoriented. She knew it was likely a precursor to a possible episode associated with her condition.

Lord, she prayed silently, *not here, not now. Don't ruin this moment with Josh. Please, Lord, just help me clear my head.*

Not knowing quite what to do next, Josh looked to see where their friends were. He relaxed when he saw they had turned around and were already headed back in their direction.

"No worries," he said to Noelle, trying to sound as casual as he could. "They're coming back this way anyway."

He sat back down on the grass next to Noelle, hoping she wouldn't feel awkward about the situation. She smiled at him as he did.

"Maybe next time, I'll just do a light white rather than a heavy red for lunch. Sorry about being a wimp with the wine. I'm feeling fine now, though. Let's try this again," she said while rising more slowly this time.

Then, trying to prove to Josh and herself that she was better, Noelle called out energetically to Elise and Mark, "We'll meet you two at the bikes.

"Come on, Josh, let's pick up the lunch leftovers and tarp and head toward the bikes. We've got a lot more adventure in store for you to see."

"Thanks, Lord, for the reprieve," she secretly whispered as she walked a few steps behind Josh, who was leading the way back to the bikes.

During the ride back toward the palace, Noelle shared with Mark the news she had relayed to Josh. Elise was beaming and expressed enthusiastic support for the idea of adding Avignon to the list of meeting places.

After a quick tour of two homes the French royal family frequented to escape the rigors of palace life, Grand and Petit Trianon, and their bountiful gardens of pink roses, the four rode a short distance farther to the Queen's hamlet.

"What is this place?" Mark asked. "A quaint farm village in the middle of the palace grounds seems kind of strange."

"It is," Elise answered. "It was ordered to be constructed by none other than Marie Antoinette. It is said she never really enjoyed the trappings of being queen, and she called them that quite literally, 'trappings.' She said she desired a more tranquil life, so she had this little hamlet built as an escape. Most of the buildings are a facade. Only that one there," Elise said, pointing across a pond, "is real. The queen would spend days here self-sequestered from all the politics of the royal court. I've read quite a lot about her, and to be honest, I feel sorry for her.

"She was taken from her home in Austria and forced into marriage at the age of only 14. Her marriage to Louis XVI was purely political, and he

85

was only 15 at the time. Can you imagine being taken from your home and thrust into having to manage an entire foreign country as a teenager? No wonder she sought to escape to this quiet little getaway."

"That is kind of sad," Josh agreed. "And then to eventually lose your head over it. Ouch!"

"We could all probably learn a lesson from those two," Elise continued. "People always think wealth and power are the answers to everything when in reality they can be a far more strangling thing than a freeing one. Like I told Mark earlier, a simple life is all I really aspire to.

"Of course, having friends who will someday own a famous winery in California won't hurt my feelings any, and I promise I won't let the success of my friends go to my head ... lest I lose it."

"Ugh," Noelle moaned, "bad pun, girlfriend."

"Yeah, I know. Sorry," Elise countered with a sheepish smile. "I guess it's a good thing I got this tour guide job since stand-up comedy isn't in my future.

"So, are you boys ready to go see the palace? We've saved the best for last."

They rode their bikes back past the fountains where they began and then across a vast open paved expanse leading up to the foreboding palace walls. Admission was through a side door in the wall, and just before they stepped in, Elise took charge.

"Okay, so here's where I really earn my money as a tour guide ... the palace. Are you ready?"

Knowing this was her last practice before taking on real paying customers, the other three dutifully nodded assent.

"Okay, take a deep breath and open wide your eyes," Elise said poetically with her hands and arms spread as if greeting the place. "This is Versailles!"

She said nothing more, nor did she need to. Stepping out of the shadow of the wall and into the sun-drenched cobblestone courtyard was like stepping 300 years back in time.

Josh loved the drama of it all and slowly turned a full circle imagining the courtyard full of royal guests buzzing about, buying and selling, gossiping, and plotting. He then stopped and faced the colossal U-shaped structure. It was everything he had dreamed it would be and more. Designed in the classic French Renaissance style, it was three stories high and had countless windows all encased in gold.

Elise led the way as they walked through various rooms, including the king and queen's private chambers. They were surprised to learn how public the monarchs' daily lives were, having to endure audiences during even the most mundane activities such as dressing.

The ceilings in almost every room were adorned with spectacular paintings, each unique and jaw-droppingly beautiful. Indeed, the ceilings seemed to be the centerpiece of each room, and more heads were tilted upward than outward as people milled through the spaces.

The sun's symbol was everywhere, testimony to Louis XIV's fascination with it, to the point of calling himself the Sun-King. Gold, silver, bronze, marble, and finely carved wood were everywhere. The opulence exceeded their expectations.

For the most part, Elise was quiet while the small group walked through the rooms of the estate, offering only small tidbits of information and answering questions when they were asked. She had modeled her tour guiding style after one of her instructors, who said less is usually more and that listening rather than always speaking was the key to being a useful guide. Her approach, however, shifted when they arrived at the famous Hall of Mirrors.

"This place is pretty fantastic, isn't it," she asked as the group paused to view a courtyard outside and below them. "The room we're about to enter deserves a little introduction, so please indulge me for just a moment.

"This is called the Hall of Mirrors. It contains over 350 floor-to-ceiling mirrors. In the 17th century, mirrors were among the most expensive items in the world to possess. Louis XIV was always about showing the world the wealth and preeminence of France. Many of the paintings you will see, on the walls, as well as the ceilings, depict great military victories. Through the windows, you'll also enjoy beautiful views of the famous gardens, which we will walk through afterward. It will be crowded in here, so if we get separated, let's plan to reconnect right here in, say, 30 minutes."

Elise was right about the opulence which reached its zenith in the room. While she and Mark wandered off to the left to focus on a painting, Josh was drawn to the right toward the gardens' window views.

"I just can't get over how perfect this place is," he whispered to Noelle, who had stayed by his side.

"I know," she whispered back. "I've been here probably a dozen times, and it still takes my breath away."

After spending an hour walking through the manicured gardens outside nearest the palace, Elise led them all out a back gate to where their bikes were parked. They then rode back to the alleyway garage. While Elise locked everything up, Noelle and the boys sat on a park bench and chatted about the day's adventure.

"Okay, everything is put away," Elise said. "I'm famished. Is anyone else interested in dinner?"

"I sure am," Mark was quick to answer. "I know you said you had something special planned, but I hope not too special. We don't need anything fancy or expensive. And besides, to be honest, my few formal French dining experiences thus far have left me a bit wanting on the quantity side of the equation."

Elise looked over to Noelle with a knowing grin and then nodded.

"Well, it's not too expensive, but I don't know exactly how you define 'fancy,'" Noelle said. "As far as quantity goes, that shouldn't be a problem where we're going. I hope you like tavern food."

"As in bar food?" Josh said. "You bet we like bar food. It's the best food in the world. Are we going to a French bar? That sounds like a lot of fun!"

"Yep, and it is fun, a whole lot of fun," Elise interjected. "The tavern is called Bon Temps, and it lives up to its name. It means Good Times. A neighbor of ours owns it, and they have live music tonight that starts in about a half-hour. So, if we hurry, we should be able to get good seats and order food before the band starts. Once they start, it's kind of hard to hear sometimes. I think you'll really like it. We won't stay forever, just an hour or so. Then we thought we'd go somewhere quiet so we could talk about summer plans over dessert."

"Sounds like a perfect evening," Mark said.

"Yep, Bon Temps, here we come," Josh added.

CHAPTER 6

The place was not much more than a glorified hole in the wall, but the vibe inside was electric funk. A makeshift stage, elevated just one foot off the floor, was tucked into the far right-hand corner of the room, and on it rested an electric keyboard, a small drum set, two guitars, and a bass guitar. Three mic stands were positioned at the front of the riser. Fewer than a dozen rough wood tables with chairs were randomly scattered throughout the room, and several standing drink tables lined the right wall. A long, colorful bar with an impressive array of wine and liquor offerings lined the entire left side wall. Two young cocktail waitresses were busy serving customers. Instead of crown molding, the top of the walls were lined with old vinyl record jackets, a few recognizable from America, but most were French and European. An ancient lava lamp from the sixties illuminated the corner behind the bandstand, and low hanging orange-glow orb style lights hung from the ceiling. Red string Christmas lights dangled from above the windows on the street side of the room. One string was flashing while the others were not. Over the bar hung dark red lampshades that looked like something from Marrakech or the Grand Bazaar in Istanbul. The wall art was a combination of garage-sale mirrors and old sepia photos of partially nude cancan dancers. It was a flash from the past, the distant past, to be sure, and the term eclectic was an understated adjective for the place.

"Oh good, look over there; my friend saved us a table like I asked him to. He's such a sweet guy. This place packs out early, and I've heard the band playing tonight is very cool. We should count ourselves lucky to have scored a sit-down table," Elise said excitedly.

"As they say, it's not what you know; it's who you know," Josh said, offering Elise a tip of an imaginary hat. "Yet another thing for us to be oh so thankful to you for. You girls are really making this a special day."

They ordered a pitcher of beer, a favorite local IPA according to the waitress, and snacked on mixed nuts while waiting for their sandwiches. The band arrived and started setting up about the time the food showed up.

"What do you know about the band?" Josh asked. "You said you'd heard they are good."

"I heard they do a unique mix of covers of old 60's rock and roll, mostly American. That's why I was so excited to bring you tonight. I thought maybe the music would help you feel a little bit like home." Elise answered.

The lead vocalist/guitarist was dressed in classic European flair with tight-fitting navy blue suit pants that were short enough at the bottom to reveal wildly colored striped socks reminiscent of the wicked witch from Oz inside his pointy-toed leather shoes. He also wore a matching navy blazer over a white linen button-down shirt with the top three buttons strategically left undone. The keyboard player was dressed in a billowy, almost clown-like, bright red ensemble and wore an odd black wig that fell over his face to completely obscure his identity. The drummer wore sizable dark aviator-style sunglasses and sported a purple Mohawk haircut. The electric bass player had long blonde hair tied back in a ponytail and wore clothes that looked like he had just beamed in from Santa Cruz, California. The female backup vocalist was the only normal-looking person in the group. She wore modest, comfortable clothing and was pretty enough to grace the cover of any magazine in France.

The opening number was a fast-paced and raucous cover of Blue Suede Shoes. It quickly became apparent that the five-some was an exceptionally talented and professional team despite the mismatched look. The set continued seamlessly, and the songs flowed one right into the next without so much as a breath. The key changes were perfectly choreographed, and each of the musicians took turns playing solo riffs, which tended to elongate each number by at least two minutes.

Noelle surreptitiously glanced over at Elise and winked approval, not only of the band but of the fact that Mark had lightly placed his hand atop hers on the table. Elise smiled back, and then while Noelle was watching, she turned her hand over, so it would be palm up, and she took hold of Mark's. Mark glanced at Elise and smiled while giving her hand a gentle squeeze.

Conversation was nearly impossible without yelling, so nothing was said until the band finally took a break after 30 minutes of steady, hard-driving rock and roll.

At the break, Josh excused himself and stepped away from the table. He returned two minutes later with a second pitcher of the IPA and two bags of hot buttered popcorn.

"I've been eyeing that popcorn machine since we first walked in," he said as he sat back down. "This place is an absolute blast! I only wish it wasn't quite so loud so we could talk.

"We will during dessert," Noelle reminded him. "We'll leave after the next set. Until then, let's just sit back and enjoy."

The band opened the second set with the night's first slow song, and both girls immediately stood.

"Come on, boys," Elise said, "show us how Americans slow dance."

The tune was instantly recognizable, and soon half the people in the room were swaying to the popular cover. While Mark and Elise were enjoying the moment, Josh was feeling strangely cautious about dancing too close to Noelle. As they danced together, he questioned himself.

What is wrong, dude? Normally you'd be all over this. But you're holding back. He glanced down at Noelle, whose head was resting softly on his shoulder. She neither held back nor pressed in. She was just comfortable and seemingly enjoying the moment for what it was rather than worrying about what it might or might not be. *You should lighten up, Josh. There is nothing to be afraid of here. She's a sweet girl, beautiful to be sure, but you've dated lots of pretty girls.*

As they had done during the first set, the band's transition to the next song was perfect and without a moment of silence. The pace picked back up as the lead vocalist growled out another old school rock favorite. Josh looked at Noelle to gauge whether she wanted to continue dancing. She put her hands up to her ears, signifying she didn't like the volume, and pointed to the door to suggest they step outside. Josh smiled and nodded while raising his eyebrows and tipping his head toward the door in agreement. He then tapped Mark on the shoulder to let him know they were going to step outside, and Mark waved them on.

"We're going to keep dancing," Mark yelled to Josh though he was standing less than three feet away.

Josh offered a thumbs-up signal and then took Noelle's hand as they exited.

Outside, the din diminished enough to enable conversation, and the two sat on a stone bench next to a small coy pond home to two orange fish and a fountain feature. The sun was setting, and the sky cast a warm hue of crimson and orange.

"That band is terrific, especially the lead guy," Josh commented. "They could go somewhere. Pretty cool we got to see them tonight. But, truth be known, that slower song was a little more to my liking than their pounding rock tunes."

"I agree completely," Noelle said, "and I enjoyed the chance to dance with you. But, I'm pretty sure we're not going to get another danceable song in this set, at least not one that doesn't involve jumping up and down and head banging."

She laughed out loud, and as she did, she tossed her hair back casually. She then reached up and quickly fashioned a ponytail knot to tie her hair up off of her shoulders.

"It was getting stuffy in there. Thanks for coming outside with me," Noelle offered.

"I can't imagine any other place in France I'd rather be right now," Josh said warmly. Then realizing his tone might be interpreted as romantic, he quickly added, "with you and Elise in this wonderful village of Versailles."

Noelle caught the follow-up cover but didn't say anything. She just smiled on the inside to know that Josh was having feelings similar to the ones she was.

Over dessert, the four decided on which weekends they would try to meet up -- the first in Bordeaux, in three weeks. The second would be in Lyon, a week after that. And the final visit would be to Noelle's hometown of Avignon, sometime after that. The last connection's date remained up in the air because Elise had not been aware of a possible third meeting, so she still had to clear it with her work.

"Would you mind if we stayed in touch by text while we are in Loire, that is, when we have cell service?" Josh asked.

"That would be great!" Elise replied, though his question had been more directed at Noelle. "Send us pictures of what you're seeing, and we can be your remote tour guides. You're going to love Loire, especially the chateaus. You really must plan to see Chateau Chenonceau. It is, in my humble opinion, the most beautiful and romantic in all of France. There are two exquisite gardens that rival, in a small way, what we saw today at the palace. One garden was created for King Henry II's mistress Diane de Poitiers who lived in the castle until the King's death. After that, his queen, Catherine de Medici, who despised Poitiers, forced her out. Medici, the queen, then developed her own separate but equally beautiful garden. Still another famous woman who lived in the chateau years later was Medici's daughter-in-law, Louise de Lorraine. When her husband was assassinated, de Lorraine went into mourning and became a recluse in the castle for over ten years. Interestingly, back in those days, the color the French wore while in mourning was white, not black like today, so she became known as the white queen."

"You see," Mark said with a grin, "that is exactly why we so need you to come with us during our travels. I just love that you know something about everything. And while I'm happy you got such a great job at Versailles, I'd be lying if I said I wasn't just a little bit jealous. Especially when I think about all those young American cyclists you'll be

100

leading around the grounds and wowing with all your history expertise. Noelle, you have to promise me that if Elise begins swooning over anyone, you'll call me. I'll be back in a flash to challenge the nave to a French duel or something."

Elise blushed at the expression of endearment and bravado. "Never fear, oh fair Marcus de California, I will wait for you. At least for three weeks when we meet up in Bordeaux."

The four shared a chuckle, but at the same time, all felt a tinge of regret that their day together was coming to an end.

"I'll protect her from other suitors, Mark. You can rely on me," Noelle said.

While another good-natured laugh ensued, Josh thought to himself, *but who will protect you for me?*

***

The next three weeks flew by for all four. Elise led tours of Versailles almost every day. Noelle picked up a waitressing job at a popular cafe near the farmer's marketplace with no other employment prospects coming to the fore. The hours were flexible, and in anticipation of the planned weekends away, she too opted to work almost every day. Meanwhile, the boys cycled through the Loire Valley. In addition to Chenonceau, they saw several other famous chateaus, including Chambord, Brissac, Amboise, and Villandry. They also made it a point to visit several wineries in the regions of Nantes and Anjou-Saumur. While Mark regularly texted Elise to ask history questions about the places they were seeing, Josh's daily text messages to Noelle were more on the personal side, having little to do with France or their travels. Though enjoying the trek, Josh found himself preoccupied with the thought of seeing Noelle again in Bordeaux.

***

"That was an amazing adventure," Josh said as they stepped out of the shop where they returned the bikes they had rented for the Loire tour. "Between Loire and Versailles, I'd say bikes are definitely the best way to see France, eh?"

"Totally," Mark enthusiastically responded. "The only trouble was the lack of space in the panniers to bring along all the wine I wish we could have purchased."

"Yeah, but that just meant we had to drink it instead, and I didn't mind that at all," Josh laughed. "But tonight we arrive in serious wine country. Bordeaux is perhaps the most famous of all the French wine regions. The Garonne River valley is the ultimate place in terms of French reds, and I'm anxious to explore and compare French Bordeaux to the blends we taste in America. I hear they are very different here in France, and I'm curious to see if that's true."

"And seeing the girls again will be fun. Maybe even more so than the wine," Mark added expectantly. "I have the address of the place the girls will be staying over the weekend. Elise said there is a hostel about three blocks away that we can stay at. She said it's nice, too."

"It'll be great to sleep on something other than the cots we've been enduring while on the bike tour. Some of them were only one step above lying on the ground as far as I'm concerned," Josh moaned.

From the Bordeaux train station, Josh and Mark made their way to the meeting spot with the girls, an area called Place des Quinconces. Elise had told them it was one of the largest squares in France and that they should plan to see the girls sitting on a bench near the monument placed in memory of Girondists who fell victim during the French Revolution's Reign of Terror. She said they couldn't miss it as it had two fountains decorated with bronze horses and a tall column in the middle, which represented the spirit of liberty.

Elise's directions were perfect, and the boys saw the girls from a distance.

"Hey, let's sneak up from behind and surprise them," Josh suggested.

The boys walked the long way around the square and then quietly approached their waiting friends. Simultaneously put their hands over the girls' eyes Mark whispered, "Guess who?"

The girls giggled.

"Hmm," Noelle was the first to reply, "I'm going to guess maybe some cute American boys looking for some free tour guide services."

"Bing, bing ... you are correct!" Mark said in his best game show host voice. "Josh, tell these fine ladies what they've won for giving the correct answer."

Picking up on the joke, Josh replied in his own version of a radio DJ voice, "Well, Mark, these two beautiful girls have won the grand prize, an all-expenses-paid night on the town with two future California wine kings. Their evening will begin with pizza and salad, American style, followed by wine, Bordeaux style, and then wrapping up with gelato, Italian style. But wait ... there's more. Depending on how they are feeling after all that international cuisine, they'll have the opportunity to go dancing in a local club followed by a leisurely stroll home under the romantic lights of the left bank quayside."

"Ooh, that sounds like a wonderful grand prize," Noelle said playfully as she grasped Josh's hands and squeezed them. "And once again, you guys are right on time. More evidence of the consummate gentlemen that you two are."

After gelato, the four emerged onto the quayside. The lights were amazing as the old historic structures seemed to dance with illumination almost as literally as a group of young people who were dancing on the beach near the water's edge.

"So, are you girls up for some clubbing?" Mark asked. "This city seems even more alive than the Latin Quarter of Paris, and I think we should be able to find someplace fun to dance."

"Sure, we're game," Elise said, speaking for the two. "There's a fun bar down this way, a block or two. Come on, follow me."

The sights and sounds of the evening were electric, and by merely following their ears, they arrived at the nightclub Elise was thinking of. Inside it was standing room only, and the dancing had spilled out into the adjoining alleyway. Noelle spied a table outside about thirty feet from the main door, and they all sat down together.

"This is better than being inside, much better," Noelle said. "We can listen to the music and talk at the same time. Plus, the breeze out here is nice; I'm sure it's stifling hot inside."

"When the waitress comes by, what would you two like to drink?" Josh asked.

"Just water for me, thanks," Noelle said.

"Me too, that pizza made me very thirsty," Elise followed.

"Hey, do you want to dance?" Mark asked Elise.

"Sure, but we should probably take turns, so we don't lose this table," she suggested.

"That's fine with us," Josh said. "You two go on ahead; we'll take the first watch over our stuff."

When they were alone, Josh began, "I can't tell you how excited I am to be here. Not because of Bordeaux so much, but mostly because of, well, because I missed you, Noelle. I hope that doesn't sound too awkward, but I'm just saying."

"I missed you too, Josh. But I think texting every day helped. Funny, sometimes I feel like you can get to know someone better through writings, you know?"

"Yeah, my folks always used to talk about how they wrote letters to each other via regular mail every week during the year they were apart attending different colleges. I used to think that was incredibly lame, but now, well, for our generation, I guess texting is kind of like letter writing, minus the postage.

"Speaking of parents, did you get a chance to talk with your mom yet about us maybe visiting Avignon?"

"Yes, and she's one hundred percent on board with the idea. She says she wants to meet my new mystery man from America as she calls you. I told her you're no mystery at all and that she's going to love you. Besides, she's made me a doctor's appointment for when I'm there, just routine stuff, so I'll be able to kill two hens with one rock."

"Birds with stones," Josh quietly said while smiling at the failed interpretation and innocence of the girl.

"What?"

"Never mind," he said. "I can't wait to meet your mom and your grandmere in Lyon, too. I want to meet them all.

"Do you have any other siblings, besides your sister in Rouen that I will get to meet when we're in Avignon?" Josh asked.

Noelle's demeanor dampened at the question, and she pursed her lips. "Yes, I used to. I had a younger brother, but he died several years ago."

"Oh, I'm so sorry, Noelle."

"That's okay; you had no way of knowing. His name was Michael."

"An accident?" Josh carefully asked as he reached across the table and took Noelle's hand.

"No, an illness, but he believed in Jesus, so I know he's in a better place, and that I'll see him again someday."

"Yeah, that reality can be a huge comfort," Josh said. "I just can't imagine losing a brother and a father. Your faith must have really been tested."

"To be honest, it was. Michael wasn't just my brother; he was seriously my best friend. When I said he was my younger brother, I didn't tell you the whole story. You see, he was younger, but only by 35 minutes. We were twins. And all those stories you've heard about twins are true. We were inseparable. We often thought the same things, and we would even finish each other's sentences sometimes. It wasn't weird at all; it was completely natural. I loved him more than anything or anyone in the world. When he died, I wished I could have gone with him. I was devastated for months, almost a year. Going away to college is what helped me start getting back to being myself. And then I think the camp experience we told you about in Giverny is what finally brought me back to joy. I'm thankful to have weathered that whole storm. Without God, I don't think I'd have been able to.

"I don't usually share about this with others, and I'm sorry to burden you with it, Josh. But for some reason, I just feel like you're the kind of friend I can share intimate things with. I know that's a little strange since we hardly know each other, but I figure if I can't be totally honest with someone, then a friendship with them probably isn't worth pursuing. And I'm hoping our friendship will come to be worth having to wade through the baggage of the past.

"But if not, and if I'm stepping over the line or maybe going too fast, please tell me. Honesty in all things, speaking the truth in love, and all that, you know?"

When Noelle paused, she felt a slight pang of guilt; *if speaking the truth in love is so important to you, girl, then why are you holding back from him about your condition?*

Josh paused before responding. He could sense this was a pivotal moment in their fledgling relationship, and he wanted to be similarly honest in his reaction, even if it might mean pushing Noelle away. He'd had lots of girlfriends in the past, but none of the relationships had ever seemed to go any deeper than the wading pool they'd sat next to in the Tuileries Garden in Paris. Noelle seemed different somehow. At least he wanted to believe she was.

"Noelle, I," he paused again while continuing to hold her hand. "I can't, in my own experience, personally relate to what you're saying, but I can appreciate the truth of it. I've been fortunate never to have lost anyone close to me, except my grandpa years ago when I was eight. But back then, I didn't have much concept of God or heaven or salvation. I just knew I missed playing with the old man. To lose a twin like that must surely have been impossibly sad, and I'm so sorry you had to suffer that loss. But, I believe that somehow God works everything for our good, and maybe someday you'll be a comfort to others because of your experience. Thank you for trusting me enough to share this with me. I'm, well, I'm not sure it's the right word, but I'm honored to be counted as one of those kinds of friends, and I hope I can live up to what that means."

CHAPTER 7

On Saturday, the foursome rented a car, and for the next two days, they drove around the left bank countryside visiting and tasting at several winery operations. Josh was pleasantly surprised to see how welcoming the French winemakers were and how freely they shared stories about their experiences and techniques. They also discovered that what they'd been told about the taste differences between French Bordeaux wines and American blends was true. The simplicity of the French offerings was stark and surprising. Both Josh and Mark agreed that while they were still partial to the more complex American blends, there was something special about the purity of the French flavors. As interested as the boys were in hearing about the French history Elise and Noelle shared with them, the girls were equally enthralled by the boy's stories about wine. The interests between the two couples, men and women, were similar enough to invite stimulating conversation during the drives between wineries.

Vines covered the gently rolling hills as far as the eye could see. The only interruption in the vineyard landscape was the occasional oak tree and the even rarer farm building. Tiny village clusters also dotted the countryside, remnants of the long-ago feudal state that once was France. And just like they had been hundreds of years before, the villages were still home to the field workers. As they drove by scores of workers toiling in the fields, Josh had to remind himself that what he was seeing was work, hard work, and not just some romantic vision of the birth of wine. He was also reminded that his future would hopefully someday involve such work, and he prayed it would never become just a job.

Monday morning, the four met early for breakfast at a cafe near the square that was called La Boheme. The temperature was already in the 70's which indicated a very warm afternoon on the train. The excitement and adventure that infused the previous two days had waned as each recognized the end of their time together was fast approaching. Mark and Elise seemed relatively light-hearted as they chatted while awaiting their food selections, but Josh and Noelle were more reserved.

"Hey," Elise broke into the quiet with an enthusiastic comment directed to everyone, "so in just a couple of weeks, we'll be together again in Lyon at Noelle's grandmere's house. Boys, you're going to love her place. I've been there, and it is amazing, especially her garden out back. Her collection of roses will stop your heart. What does she have, Noelle, forty or fifty different varieties?"

"Yeah, something like that," Noelle responded in a far less energetic tone. "I think she lost a few to a late frost this spring, but Grandmere is never deterred. She cares for those plants better than some people care for their children. She speaks to them each by name as she waters and tends to them. I've even seen her shed a tear when she prunes them back in the early winter. She calls it 'putting her girls to sleep.' She really is a sweet old lady. Grandmere has been the cornerstone of our family since I was born."

"Is your grandfather still alive?" Josh innocently asked.

"No, he died in a farming accident a long time ago … when my mom was only nine years old."

"Your grandparents were farmers then?" Mark cautiously joined in.

"Not exactly," Noelle continued. "Grandpere was a vine keeper for a very famous winery called Domaine de la DuBois-Estelle. Maybe you've heard of it? It's about a half-hour northwest of Lyon, in the middle of Burgundy country."

"I've heard of it, yes," Josh answered. "Please go on about your grandfather."

"Well, I know very little of the accident as it wasn't talked about much by my mother or Grandmere. I

113

do know, though, that my grandpere was very beloved by everyone in the area. He grew up in a small village called Arney-le-Duc. He was born just after the end of World War II. Aside from stories I've heard from the family, all I know of him is the epitaph on his gravestone. He's buried behind Saint Paul's Church in Arney-le-Duc."

"What does his epitaph say?" Mark asked.

"It was a line from an American poem, actually. Grandpere loved poetry. He was a romantic and a dreamer. I'm told he often dreamed of visiting the United States. Grandmere said he felt a deep sense of gratitude to the Americans for rescuing France from the clutches of the Nazis. Sadly, that sentiment seems to have faded over the generations, what with modern politics and the global economy and all. But my mother insisted on carrying that torch for Grandpere, so I was raised to honor and respect America. My grandmere has still never been to the United States, and I think that may be one reason she is so excited to meet you two.

"Anyway, the poem was by a man named Sam Walter Foss. Grandpere's epitaph says, 'Laisse-moi vivre dans ma maison au bord de la route et sois un ami pour l'homme.'

"In English, that translates to, 'Let me live in my house by the side of the road and be a friend to man.'

"From what I know, that was an apt saying for him as he truly was a friend to everyone."

Changing the subject to something lighter, Noelle continued. "Did either of you have a favorite place we visited while here in Bordeaux?"

Both boys paused to think, and then Mark spoke first.

"I think my favorite was that chateau where we had lunch after tasting. What was that place called, um, Pichon Baron?"

"Very good memory, Mark," Elise commended. "I liked that place a lot, too. The history there was amazing. Remember how they said Joseph Pichon took over the winery at the age of 19 and then ran the place until he was 90! Do you think you guys will still be running your winery when you're that old?"

"I don't know about that," Mark responded with a chuckle. "I hope I'll be retired before then, and maybe I'll have a summer home here in France. Then we could galavant through the countryside together like old friends. Wouldn't that be fun?"

The food finally arrived, and while Mark and Elise continued their banter about the wineries they had visited, Josh and Noelle spoke together in softer tones.

"Is the cafe you work in like this one?" Josh asked.

"A little bit. Most cafes are somewhat similar. The work itself is kind of mundane, but meeting the people is always fun. For a small town, Versailles actually gets a pretty diverse group of visitors. Of course, the palace is the big attraction, but I've been surprised at how many people I've met who aren't really there for the big tourist experience. They're more interested in just experiencing French life. Like you said when we first met in Paris. What did you call it, the 'real' France?"

"So, how about you, Josh -- did you have a favorite place?" Elise interrupted, harkening back to her earlier question.

"To be honest, I loved all the places we saw," Josh replied. "Bordeaux is way more than I had hoped for in terms of the experience, both wine and personal."

"Personal?" Noelle asked, smiling.

"Yes, and that means 'you.' I'm trying mightily to stay focused on my reason for being in France, you know, learning about wine. But, and I'm not ashamed to admit it, my mind has been thinking about you, Noelle, as much as it has wine these past few days. So, I'm feeling kind of distracted and don't take this the wrong way, but I'm second-guessing our plan to meet up in Lyon. Noelle, you are distracting me ... in a good way, so I'm not really complaining, but I feel like maybe I need to be more focused on what we came to France for."

The other three stopped cold and stared blankly in response to Josh's revelation and the abruptness of its delivery. Noelle's eyes betrayed both her acknowledgment of what Josh had just said and its pain.

Seeing her friend's reaction, Elise reached over and took Noelle's hand. She then glanced at Mark for some sign of understanding, but his face was as empty as theirs were.

"Really, Josh?" Elise hesitatingly said. "I mean, that's sweet how you feel about Noelle, but you honestly don't think you can achieve your travel objectives and enjoy our company at the same time?"

"Yeah, dude, that's, like, kind of harsh, don't you think?" Mark finally gathered himself together enough to speak. "I mean, come on, I like Elise too, but I'd never think of avoiding her just to focus more on wine. Frankly, that sounds kind of nuts, Josh. Come on, man, really?"

Josh looked deeply into Noelle's eyes, and she into his. For a long moment, they sat there, motionless, seemingly pleading, both of them, for an alternate choice.

"Josh, please," Elise whispered.

Noelle then broke character and winked at Josh, who immediately sat back in his chair and laughed.

"Gotcha!" He chuckled.

"Yeah, gotcha," Noelle repeated as she playfully squeezed Elise's hand.

"What?" Elise reacted.

"We're just kidding!" Noelle exclaimed. "We're teasing you. We wanted to find a fun way to let you know how we feel about each other. I didn't think you'd take it quite so seriously. It was my idea. By the way, Josh, you are quite the actor, I must say."

"And you, fair Noelle, you set that up like a total pro. Maybe we should go into the grift business together."

"Ha, that was, uh, funny ... in a mean kind of way, but I have to agree, Oscar-worthy performances by both of you," Mark replied, still showing a hint of confusion on his face.

"Well," Elise said, taking a big breath, "I'm not so sure about that being very funny, my heart stopped there for a second, but it is nice to know you two like each other. That makes me less self-conscious about pairing up with Mark all the time."

Elise let go of Noelle's hand and took Mark's instead. Noelle, in turn, reached over the table to hold Josh's.

"So, now I guess we're officially couples! That should make our time together in Lyon even more fun!" Noelle announced as the four collectively relaxed in their chairs and laughed together.

***

Lyon is the third-largest city in France, next to Paris and Marseilles, and it is the hub of the wine region called Burgundy. The boys arrived a day before the girls and stayed the night in a small hotel near the Rhone River. At least down by the river, the city's pace was somewhat similar to what they had experienced in Paris. The night temperature was warm, so they had slept with the windows open. Consequently, the two were

119

awakened by a man playing the accordion outside on the sidewalk. Josh crawled out of the small twin bed and pulled the window sash aside to greet the morning. He looked up and down the street from their fourth-floor window, inhaled deeply, and then sighed and smiled. Next, he focused on the older man making the music across the narrow street in front of the hotel. He was dressed in shabby clothes and wore a red neck scarf and a tattered black leather beret. He sat on a rickety wooden stool, and his accordion case was propped open next to the wall beside him, awaiting hoped-for consideration from passersby.

"It is beautiful out this morning," Josh said aloud while continuing to watch the old man. "I think we are going to have a perfect day, Mark. Rise and shine, buddy. Let's not sleep the day away. We've got to get rolling; we're supposed to meet the girls for lunch in less than two hours."

Because they had a car and the boys didn't, Elise and Noelle picked the guys up from their hotel at 11:30 a.m. sharp. Noelle's grandmere's home was in the older section of town, east of the Rhone River near the Saint-Jean-Baptiste Cathedral. Due to her familiarity with Lyon, Noelle did most of the tour guiding as they drove across the river and up into the section of the city called Vieil Lyon. They arrived at Grandmere Celeste's house just a few minutes after noon.

The large home was situated in a cul-de-sac, of sorts, at the end of a long winding lane. The lot, a good two miles removed from the city center, was nearly a hectare in size and was covered with mature landscaping and trees. After passing through an old gate, the car rolled down a long tree-lined driveway and then around a slight bend before the house came into full view. It was in need of paint, and the surrounding forest floor had not been tended to for quite some time. While it wasn't exactly a chateau, it was nonetheless an impressive structure, and the original owner had apparently been a person of means. Once again, Josh allowed his mind to drift back in time, and he imagined what the place might have looked like in its heyday.

A single small car sat on the circular part of the driveway that provided access to the house's front door. Inside the small circle created by the gravel drive was an ornate fountain surrounded by an array of roses that were meticulously maintained, unlike much of the surrounding landscape. Celeste was sitting in an old rocker on the veranda, awaiting the arrival of her granddaughter and her friends. When she saw them, she slowly rose from the chair and walked down the four veranda steps to greet her guests.

"Noelle, Noelle, ma belle Noelle," Celeste exclaimed as she hugged her granddaughter.

"Bonjour, Grandmere. C'est tellement bon de te voir. Ce sont mes amis mais ils ne parlent que l'anglais."

"Ah, but of course, English, yes," Celeste responded cheerfully. "Welcome to my home," she said to the three following Noelle. "I am Celeste Moraine, but please feel free to call me Grandmere if you would like."

"It's a pleasure to meet you, Grandmere Celeste; I'm Joshua Morgan," Josh said, extending his hand and stepping forward ahead of Mark.

Celeste smiled broadly as she playfully swiped the boy's hand away and stepped in for a hug instead. She then dutifully kissed him on alternate cheeks three times.

"It is I who has the pleasure, Joshua Morgan. My little Wello has told me all about you, and I can already see much of it is true. You are quite handsome, as she reported, and you have the manners of a gentleman. I look forward to learning about your heart over the weekend," Celeste responded with a wink.

"Wello?" Josh echoed questioningly.

"Oh, that's my nickname, but only within the family," Noelle scoffed. "I don't remember it, but apparently, my brother struggled to pronounce my name, and Noelle somehow became Wello, and I guess it stuck because Grandmere thought it was cute."

"It is cute, Wello," Celeste followed. "Just like you have always been, though I have to admit I think beautiful is perhaps a better description for you these days."

"Aw, thanks, Grandmere," Noelle blushed.

"And you must be Mark," Celeste continued, "the other half of the future Wine Kings of California. I've heard good things about you as well, young man. I am very much looking forward to our time together. Come, I have some nice cool lemonade ready in the back garden."

After a quick and familiar cheek to cheek hello to Elise, Celeste turned and led the group of four into and through the house to the garden.

As soon as they stepped from the foyer into the living room, Josh's senses were struck by several things, all of which threatened to transport him back in time to the tiny cottage in the northeast section of Portland, Oregon, where he had spent many summer weeks as a boy visiting his own grandparents. First and foremost was the smell of the place. It was old and musty, but not in an off-putting way, more in a familiar, cozy, loving, cocoon kind of way. Next was the distinct

123

squeaking of the old and scarred hardwood floors. Each step brought with it a different sound in tone, quality, and volume. The boards were like the instruments of an orchestra tuning to play. There was no discernible rhyme or reason, but to the knowing ear, it was the prelude to a beautiful song. Then Josh's eyes were filled with the myriad stories told by the ornate wall hangings and paintings and the trinkets that, along with an impressive array of old books, adorned the built-in shelves and coffee table.

Josh's focus was gradually drawn to the fireplace, which was the natural centerpiece of the room. An elaborate tri-fold metal ember screen sat on the hearth in front of the opening. On it was etched a vineyard scene depicting workers in the field. On the wall above the opening was a painting of a cityscape that appeared to be Paris on a rainy day with a shadowy hint of the Eiffel Tower hidden in the distance. Then, in the center of the gnarled wood mantel made of a twisted collection of old vines topped with polished glass, sat a photograph in a sterling silver frame. It was a black and white photo of a handsome man sporting a dark mustache and a grayish French beret. His smile glistened, and his eyes spoke of love for whoever had been behind the camera taking the picture. Josh walked over and gently traced the outline of the slightly tarnished frame with his finger.

"Is this your grandfather?" he asked Noelle.

"Yes, it is," she beamed. "Wasn't he just the most fetching man?"

Celeste's eyes grew soft watching the exchange between the two of them, and she involuntarily clasped her hands and raised them to her heart, just like Noelle had done at the Grand Canal. Josh glanced over and smiled at the senior, and he saw in her eyes the same look of enduring love he had noticed in the photo.

"Yes, fetching indeed. Celeste, I'll bet you took this photo, didn't you?" Josh asked.

"Why, yes I did," she replied. "Robert was 29 years old in that picture. We were on our way to Sunday service. It was Easter Sunday. Next to Christmas, that was Robert's favorite time of year. He always loved celebrating our Savior's resurrection, which he insisted was indisputable proof of the gospel and the assurance of eternal life through grace."

Her moving words hung in the room like a sweet fragrance.

Noelle took a deep breath of knowing agreement and then said, "Okay, let's go out back, we can tell stories about Grandpere while we sip on the lemonade," Noelle prodded. "Josh, you're going to love Grandmere's garden!"

CHAPTER 8

Walking into the backyard garden was like walking into a dream. The group gathered at a round patio table with six chairs under a teal colored umbrella to protect from the noon sun, where a glass tray with silver handles held five crystal tumblers and a matching pitcher filled with ice, which contained a light-colored liquid with fresh cut lemons floating on top. Next to the table were several porcelain pots of different shapes and sizes, each stuffed with an array of flowers like one would see in a florist shop. The combination of colors and smells was sublime.

As had happened while walking through the house, Josh was again reminded of his boyhood days in Portland. Maybe it was something about the way older people took care of things, precisely - just so, that struck him as being so consistent, or perhaps it was just the numerous similarities he saw in the homes and landscapes.

"Oh, my, this is beautiful," Josh uttered to Noelle as they stepped outside. "It so reminds me of my grandparents' home in Oregon. I haven't thought about that place in years, but your Grandmere's house is flooding my memory. Even though we live across the world from each other, our histories are similar, it seems, at least concerning our grandparents' homes. It's cool that we have that kind of connection. Maybe it's one of the reasons I'm attracted to you."

Josh paused and looked directly at Noelle.

She smiled at him.

"Maybe, Joshua Morgan, maybe."

"Celeste, would you mind if we strolled through your garden for a few moments before sitting down to lemonade?" Josh asked. "My grandparents in the United States had a backyard similar to yours, not quite as large, but full of roses and flowers like you have. I'm sure there are stories behind some of your roses. I love a good story. Would you share one?"

"I'd love to, Joshua. Come, over this way."

Celeste led the four along a cobblestone path, around the huge shade tree in the middle of the yard and then toward the garden's left back corner. They approached a stone pedestal surrounded by three lush rose bushes, each displaying scores of vibrant pinkish-purple roses. As they got closer to the pedestal, Josh could see a poem entitled, 'Unfolding the Rose,' expertly carved into the top of the rock. Celeste paused in front of the piece of marble garden art and looked up to heaven. She then turned to the four.

"These three roses have a story," she began. "Robert was the head vine manager for a winery near here called DuBois-Estelle. He died in an accident in the vineyard, and the owner of the estate, a wonderful man, named Aubert DuBois, gave me these roses. They were just little bare roots at the time, but over these past, what, nearly 40 years now, they have flourished here. Roses seldom live beyond 35 years, but some have been known to last up to 50 years or more. The incredible thing about these three is that they continue to flourish like you are seeing. The bloom count on these beauties has been relatively consistent over the years.

"Anyway, Aubert was a very kind man. He knew my passion for roses and said the three bushes celebrated three time frames: Robert's life and his service to family and friends; to comfort me in my present and provide strength to go on without him; and finally, to look forward to the future when I will see him again in heaven."

"What kind of rose is it?" Josh asked respectfully.

"It is called Rosa centifolia. It is one of France's most famous roses. It is cultivated in a small town called Grasse on the French Riviera. A very famous and world-renowned rosarian named

Georgio Chuvault called it the perfect rose. I'm told its fragrance is the model for several fine perfumes, including Chanel and Dior. Here, smell them; they are truly magical."

Josh bent down and inhaled deeply with his nose mere inches from a large bloom. He withdrew with a smile on his face and a knowing nod toward Celeste.

"Magical indeed," he said.

"Mark, you really should smell these. Smelling roses is good practice for us. The depth and intricacies of God's work in flowers can train us up to be more aware of the complexities we will want to create someday in our wines."

"Well said, Joshua," Celeste commended. "I think you will enjoy meeting my friend Aubert."

"Meeting Aubert -- do you mean Mr. DuBois? We will meet him?" Josh responded excitedly.

"If you'd like, yes," Celeste said. "When Wello told me of your interest in wine, I thought it would be fitting to introduce you to my friend. He can tell you much about French wine, at least the Burgundy perspective about it. He is a very generous man, and I'm confident he will make time to see you if you would like."

"Oh, that would be spectacular, Grandmere Celeste, thank you!" Mark chimed in.

"Good, I'll call him this afternoon, and perhaps we can schedule something for tomorrow. Now, come, let's enjoy that lemonade."

While the five relaxed under the shade of the umbrella and enjoyed the cool drink and the breeze that was sweeping through, Celeste casually asked, "So, Wello, how are you feeling these days?"

Noelle did her best to allow the question to glance off the conversation, hoping no one would notice. "Oh, just fine, Grandmere, perfectly fine. I think staying in Versailles this summer has been good for me. Did you know we are planning a visit down to see mother soon? She has expressed interest in meeting the boys as well, and I can't wait to show them Avignon. Do you have any other plans for the summer?"

Celeste accepted the response without further inquiry, and the two began chatting about their respective plans for the balance of the summer.

Whoa, that was another close call, Noelle thought to herself as the group readily followed down the alternate path and began chatting about future summer plans.

I'd better call mother in advance of our visit to ensure she doesn't bring the subject up like Grandmere just inadvertently did. Who'd have ever thought it would be so challenging to maintain a little privacy? Sheesh.

"Well, I guess you four should get settled," Celeste said as the conversation waned and the last bit of lemonade was consumed. "I have dinner planned for seven o'clock. That should give you a little time to go out and explore a bit if you want to beforehand."

"That's perfect, Grandmere," Noelle replied. "Would you like to come with us? I thought we'd drive around the city a bit and then maybe walk in the downtown historic district."

"No, thank you, dear, I think I'll stay here and sneak in a little rest after I call Aubert. You four go on ahead and have a good time."

***

Following dinner, Celeste invited the group to once again sit outside at the patio table overlooking the garden, and she served coffee and cookies.

"Well, I was able to connect with Aubert," Celeste said as they were being seated. "He graciously invited all five of us to visit the winery tomorrow. He promised he would take you down into the caves where the wine is stored and share tastes directly from the barrels. You know, he seldom, if ever, allows the public onto the property, so this truly is an extraordinary invitation."

"That is wonderful, Celeste," Mark replied. "I did a little internet research about DuBois-Estelle, and you are right about visitors. It sounds like no one ever gets to go there without a personal invitation. I also read that their wine is quite famous as well. It sounds similar to the reputation DRC has on the other side of the valley. So, wow ... thank you, thank you, thank you!"

"Oh, you are all very welcome," Celeste said humbly. "The only thing is that I don't think I'll be coming along. The invitation is for 9 a.m., and that's a bit early for me. In fact, I'm feeling a bit tired tonight, all the excitement of meeting you I suspect, so I think I'll retire for the evening. Wello, would you mind gathering the dishes? Just put them in the sink, and I'll tend to them tomorrow. Good night all. It has been a genuine pleasure to spend time with you." And then, smiling before she turned away, she added, "Oh, and, Joshua, I think I'm learning a bit about your heart, as I said I would, and I like it as much as everything else about you."

When Celeste had departed, Noelle asked the others if they would take care of the dishes while she went to speak with her grandmother.

She knocked gently on the second-floor bedroom door to announce herself.

"Grandmere," she whispered through the wooden barrier. "It's Noelle; may I come in?"

Hearing no response, Noelle turned the doorknob and slowly opened the door.

"Grandmere? It's Noelle, are you alright?"

Celeste was sitting at an antique desk next to a window that overlooked the garden. She heard her granddaughter but said nothing as Noelle approached. Instead, with her back turned, she dabbed at her eyes with a white lace handkerchief.

"Grandmere? What is it? Are you crying? I was just coming to check on you, and to ask since when is nine o'clock too 'early' for you? You always get up long before the sun rises. By nine, you're practically ready for lunch. Are you ill?"

"No, no, my dearest one, my physical health is fine. It's my heart that is aching tonight."

"Your heart?"

"Yes, it is an ache from many years ago." Celeste sighed. Then looking up into Noelle's comforting eyes, she continued, "I've never told anyone before, but I guess now, at my age, it won't hurt to share with you. And who knows, maybe sharing the story will help me to come to terms with it finally."

"Grandmere, this sounds serious."

"Please sit down, Wello, this will take a few minutes.

"For many years after your grandpere died, Aubert DuBois continued to take care of our family and me financially. I never asked for his help, but I think even though he wasn't, he may have felt somewhat responsible for the accident, and, as I said, he is a very kind man.

"After my children were grown and had moved away, I went to see Aubert. I intended to thank him for his kindness and invite him to stop sending money since I no longer needed it to support your mother and uncle. When I arrived, he had a grand dinner set out for me in the vineyard. A table was dressed in fine linen, and a lantern was lit. It was a perfect summer evening, and the sunset was spectacular. I remember it all, every detail, like it was yesterday.

"It was a very romantic setting, and I was a bit taken aback by the sentiment. During dinner, Aubert, whose wife, Pearl, had passed away almost nine years before, expressed that his kindness toward me had been not only because of

135

Robert's accident, but also because he harbored feelings for me.

"Of course, I was shocked, to say the least, but as he explained things, it all seemed to make sense. And if I was honest, I had to admit that I felt a particular fondness for him as well, mostly due to his kindnesses. But I had always thought him a handsome man, and he was, of course, a very successful winemaker with a stellar reputation.

"So, anyway, after that evening, we started seeing each other off and on -- mostly for lunches in town and the occasional church meeting. Over time, however, our hearts began to grow closer. I'm not sure I should have ever let it go as far as it did. Frankly, I'm not sure what I was thinking. I was acting and feeling like a schoolgirl, yet I was in my late sixties."

"So, what happened?" Noelle asked when Celeste took a long breath and sighed again.

"Eventually, he asked me to marry him," Celeste answered. "Marry him! Perhaps I should have seen it coming, but I didn't. I just thought we would remain close friends, as we grew older. Sure, there was some romantic spark, but he never so much as held my hand, let alone kissed me. He was the perfect gentleman, old school, as you might say.

"And, of course, I couldn't marry Aubert; my heart will always belong to Robert in that way, and when I told him I couldn't marry him, he was crushed. I tried to maintain the relationship after that, but it became more and more awkward knowing his true feelings. Gradually we stopped seeing each other, and for the past several years, we only talk by phone now and again. We are still friends, just not like we once were.

"And so, I'm afraid that if I went to DuBois-Estelle with you tomorrow, it might dredge up all those unresolved feelings, and I don't think that would be fair to Aubert, or to me for that matter. So, I hope you can understand why I don't want to go. I know nine o'clock isn't 'early' for me. Please understand my feelings in this, Wello, will you?"

Noelle looked hard at her grandmother, and a tear formed in her eye. She had always known of Grandmere's love for family but had never seen any glimpse of the romantic love she had felt for her husband. It was hard for her to think of old people as having romance, but she saw it shining through her beloved Grandmere, and it moved her.

"Thanks for sharing with me, Grandmere, and of course, I'll honor your desire not to join us at the winery. I'm sorry this has been a private burden for you for all these years. I'm sure Mr. DuBois would be devastated if he knew his profession of love had placed such a heavy yoke on your heart.

But I won't say anything to him either. If he happens to ask about you, I'll just tell him that you are well and that you speak fondly of his kindness to our family over the years.

"Of course," Noelle went on, "I would be remiss if I didn't share my opinion privately with you that I am sure Grandpere would have no problem at all with you seeing, or even dating, Mr. DuBois. I don't know about marriage, but it seems reasonable for you two to spend time together as friends without being concerned about unintended perception. Just talk with him, honestly. We all have precious few years on this earth, and we should seize the moments for love and friendship when they are presented."

"Thank you, Wello. Spoken like someone far older than you are ... the wisdom of the ages even. I will consider your encouragement, and maybe I will reach out to Aubert after your visit. You are precious, my child."

***

The boys slept in the guest cottage behind the garage while the girls enjoyed the comforts of the oversized guest bedroom on the second floor of the main house just down the hall from Celeste's room. Noelle remembered the room as being the space where she played as a little girl. It always had two twin beds in it, but she had never noticed them much other than as places for her dolls to rest and as support for the tents she and her siblings would make by draping sheets and blankets over chairs or whatever else they could move into place to serve as imaginary castle walls.

The conversation with her grandmere had sobered Noelle's disposition just enough to make it noticeable to Elise.

"Is Grandmere alright?" Elise asked in a whispered tone as they settled into bed and doused the lights.

"Yes, she's fine. She was just pining a bit for the past and being sentimental about it. I think she is remembering herself when she was younger like we are, and how the romance of youth has now faded for her. I guess that's inevitable when you get older. You know, the struggles of life can sometimes overwhelm the simple pleasures that once preoccupied your world."

"Speaking of romance," Elise ventured, "have you and Josh picked up where you seemingly left off in Bordeaux? I'm still laughing about your antics that last morning at breakfast when you both confessed your interest in each other."

"I don't know if 'picked up' would be the right term, but I'm definitely feeling the same way. As much as I have insisted I didn't want my health situation to dampen our summer, if I'm honest, I do find myself thinking about it when it comes to Josh. If I didn't have that cloud hanging over me, I think I'd seriously pursue a relationship with him. I've never felt this way about a guy before. I mean, I've had several boyfriends, but there's something about Josh that's different. I can't exactly describe it other than to say it's very real, and I like the way it makes me feel."

"I'm enjoying Mark's company too, but I don't think I'm feeling quite the same spark you are," Elise said dreamily. "And hey, about the summer, like you always say, I think you should seize the moment while it's here. Who knows what the future might hold? I mean, maybe Josh is 'the one'?"

"I don't know about that," Noelle replied with a grin. "But he is definitely 'a one.' And maybe you're right about seizing the moment. I shouldn't worry about things I can't control. And, it's funny you remind me that I always say that because it's true, and I even said something very similar to Grandmere not more than an hour ago. I guess I should listen to my own advice, huh?"

"You should," Elise agreed. "And for what it's worth, I think you and Josh would make a perfect couple, even if he is American. And I also think 'we' should probably stop whispering like middle schoolers at a slumber party and get some sleep. It sounds like tomorrow is going to be a big day."

CHAPTER 9

Josh was awake before dawn. He listened intently to Mark's breathing pattern across the room and concluded his friend was still fast asleep. So he quietly slipped out of bed, grabbed his clothes, and snuck into the living room area to dress.

Rummaging through the small refrigerator in the kitchen, he found a bottle of fresh orange juice and some fruit. He smiled as he thought about Celeste's kindness in placing the food items there. He grabbed an apple and a banana before stepping outside into the dark orange hue of predawn.

Immediately behind the house, hills started rising quickly. Josh found a well-worn path and began walking up. The higher he got, the brighter the sky became. It felt almost as if he was climbing to greet the sun. The crisp air was refreshing, and Josh picked up his pace to the point where he began to sweat, and his breathing became heavy.

This is good, he thought, *Lord, this is very good. I love the feeling of being alive! Thank you for bringing me to this place. Thank you for Celeste and her gracious hospitality. Thank you for my health and the ability to climb this hillside. Thank you for Mark and our friendship. Thank you for pursuing me and loving me. And, Lord, thank you for Noelle. She is really something special, a gift of friendship that I never expected and wasn't even remotely looking for on this trip. I know she knows You, and that makes it even better -- almost perfect. I just pray for wisdom as we continue to get to know each other. I like her, Lord, I like her a lot.*

Josh reached a small plateau area on the hillside and found a boulder to sit on. He looked down from his perch onto the house, which was now a good quarter-mile away. The sun had finally crested the hilltop, and he enjoyed watching its light sweep gradually across the valley below. As the area around him became illuminated, he marveled at the series of man-made terraces on which vineyards had been planted. The vines were in full leaf, and when he focused, he could almost smell the musty aroma of grapes mixed with soil rising in the mist. He continued praying for another few minutes before hopping off the rock and beginning a slow descent back to the house. Still above and looking down on Celeste's property's backyard, Josh noticed the symmetry of the garden. He was aware of it but hadn't been able to fully appreciate the extent of the planned space while standing in the midst of it. Perspective is so important in life, and he made a mental note to compliment Celeste again on the beautiful landscape she had created.

Finding a small bench along the trailside about fifty yards from the property, Josh sat down again to cool off and enjoy the sights and sounds of early morning. To his right, as far as he could see, were the terraced vineyards shrouded in a low-lying blanket of moisture that was quickly burning off. His ears were filled with bird's songs. He didn't know any of the species, but it didn't matter. Their chorus was a beautiful, almost melodic, cacophony. Josh's eyes were again drawn to the garden below. As the sun lit on it, the multiple colors seemed to awaken before his very eyes. Reds, yellows, purples, oranges, and greens -- it was a veritable rainbow of life and joy.

His private musing was interrupted when he noticed the back door to the main house open. The girls emerged, both clothed in robes and seeming to be whispering to each other in an animated fashion. Josh placed his elbow on his knee and his chin on his palm and settled in to watch the action.

Elise skipped ahead, peered into the guest house window, and then hurried back to report to Noelle. The two then both slipped back into the house.

That's strange, Josh thought as he watched with interest. *I wonder what they're up to?*

Moments later, he found out. The back door swung open again, and Elise stepped out with a tray in her hand. On the tray, Josh could make out a pitcher with four glasses and a basket full of what appeared to be fruit. With her foot, Elise then held the door open for Noelle, who followed with another tray. Josh stood up and squinted to try to get a better view of Noelle.

She is beautiful even in a house robe in the early morning, he thought.

The items on her tray appeared to be a bowl of something, maybe eggs, and he saw a plate with what looked like bacon strips on it.

Oh my, gosh, they're bringing us a surprise breakfast! He suddenly realized.

Josh shot out a shrill whistle before running down the path toward the house. The girls heard the noise and looked up to see Josh coming toward them. Seeing he had gotten their attention, Josh waved and slowed his run to a jog. The girls couldn't wave back because their hands were full, but Noelle suddenly stopped, set her tray down on the ground, and finally waved toward Josh. Her smile was bright, and Josh found himself wishing he could fly down the hill to get to her side faster.

Noelle watched as Josh ran toward the garden. For a moment, she forgot what they were doing and just stood there smiling.

"Noelle, come on! The eggs will get cold," Elise urged. "Josh will be down in a second. Let's get the food inside."

"Yes, sorry, you're right. I just lost my focus there," Noelle said.

"I don't think you lost it," Elise replied. "I think your focus is right where it has been for the past few weeks. You really are in serious 'like' with that guy, aren't you?"

"I guess so. As I was saying last night, he is pretty special."

Elise knocked loudly on the guest cottage door and heard Mark invite entrance. She set her tray down to open the door and the two of them then whispered in unison, "Surprise, a little breakfast in bed for our American tourist friends."

Elise held the door while Noelle entered first. After setting her tray down on the tiny dining table, she then held the door for Elise.

The cottage was a small space, not more than 500 square feet in size. It was really just a glorified studio apartment with a moveable partition serving as a partial separation between the small sleeping area with two twin beds and the main living space, which was furnished with a love seat, rocker, coffee table, and small cabinet with a television on it.

Upon hearing the welcome, Mark quickly threw on some pants and a shirt and emerged from behind the partition.

"Wow, this is certainly a nice surprise!" he said while still buttoning his shirt. "You ladies never stop impressing us American tourists. Umm, I smell bacon!"

Noelle found small plates and silverware in the cupboard and quickly set the coffee table for four.

"I guess we'll have to all sit on the floor around the coffee table since the dining table isn't big enough, and we don't have enough chairs to sit on anyway," Noelle said after placing the silverware.

"Hey, where's Josh?" Mark said, finally realizing his friend wasn't in the room.

"Did I hear someone call for me?" Josh said as he made a grand entrance through the front door. "I smelled the bacon from all the way up on the mountain. I ran back as fast as I could. Good morning, Noelle, you are as beautiful as the sunrise. And good morning, Elise, equally as lovely, I might add. There must be something in the air that all the girls in France are so, well, so perfect. I mean, look at this spread. We haven't seen a breakfast that smells and looks this good since we left California."

Deflecting the compliments, Noelle replied, "I think that is most likely your stomach speaking, Joshua. Typical male, food has such a way of bringing out the best in guys."

The four enjoyed light banter while they all sat on the floor together, eating around the coffee table. The morning chill quickly gave way to what was going to be a warm sunny day. The boys cleaned up after the meal while the girls made quick business of getting ready for the big trip to DuBois-Estelle.

Celeste had been up even before Josh and had enjoyed the backyard show looking down from her bedroom window.

"Ah, jeune amour," she whispered to herself as she watched the four teasing each other in the garden just before they all piled into the car to leave.

The winery was on the other side of the Rhone, so the group had to drive back through Lyon to cross the river. Traffic was moderate, and they found themselves once again in the countryside in less than twenty minutes. They drove north through the river valley and then gradually veered to the west, up into the low lying hill country. There wasn't a cloud in the sky, and the temperature had already passed 70 degrees. Josh insisted they ride with the windows down and the sunroof open rather than use the air conditioning because he wanted to smell the vineyards as they drove through them.

The roads got progressively narrower as the GPS mapping system continued leading them up higher and higher into the hills. Along the way, they passed numerous wineries, all of which had excellent signage, some for several miles along the way that offered clear direction for arrival. Of course, the signs were all hoping to entice the public to stop in for a tour and a taste and maybe a purchase of wine or a trinket from the gift shop. The tourist dollar had become a mighty thing in Burgundy, and competition for it was fierce.

"Guys, are you sure we typed the right address into the GPS?" Elise asked. "I mean, I see signs for every winery in Burgundy except the one we're looking for."

"Yeah, I was beginning to wonder the same thing," Mark echoed. "It's beginning to feel like we're on a snipe hunt or something."

"What's a snipe hunt?" Noelle innocently asked.

"Ha, good question, Noelle," Josh said, joining the conversation. "It's an American prank thing. You know, a joke that you pull on someone who is clueless about something. So, a snipe is a very rare game bird. It's supposed to look something like a quail. As a rite of passage, older boys take younger boys out into the forest on a moonless night to capture the elusive prey. Everyone brings along a burlap sack to 'bag' their bird. The older boys split off and then excitedly yell like they captured one. Rather than admit they can't find any, some of the younger boys then pretend they also did. Pretty soon, everyone is yelling, 'Snipe! Snipe!' except for the few honest kids who haven't seen any birds because they don't exist, and then they end up feeling less manly. It's kind of a cruel hazing, really."

"You Americans have some bizarre ways," Noelle said, shaking her head. "But I can assure you DuBois-Estelle is no fictitious bird. And Grandmere would not have made a mistake with the address. We just need to keep going. We'll find the place."

The road turned from narrow paved to even narrower dirt, yet the GPS kept directing them higher and higher into the hills.

"At least it's a beautiful drive," Mark said with a hint of defeat in his voice.

"Hey, man, where is your spirit of adventure?" Josh responded in an effort to defend Noelle's confidence in Celeste's directions. "As Pocahontas would sing, 'it's just around the river bend!'"

"Poca -- who?" Elise laughed.

"Never mind," Mark said, putting his hand on hers. "Just a little American history mixed with some Disney magic, and another one of those strange American sayings."

A mile later, Noelle brought the car to a halt in what appeared to be a tiny village's central square. The four looked all around for the famous chateau but saw only a small stone church, a post office that was far too modern looking for the village, a tavern, what looked like a general store, and a long, nondescript wall along the west side of the square.

"You have arrived," the automated voice on the phone app announced.

"Arrived? Arrived where?" Mark protested humorously, "Snipeville?"

"I'm not exactly sure, but this is the address Grandmere gave us. But I don't see anything remotely resembling the beautiful chateau I've seen pictures of. This is weird," Noelle said.

"Well, let's get out and walk around. Someone has to live in this village. Maybe we can ask for better directions," Josh suggested.

They exited the car and randomly started down a narrow lane leading east.

"Hey, look, over there," Josh said, "a couple of women sitting out under, what's that, their laundry?"

Two octogenarian women, dressed in what could be described as classic peasant clothing, sat talking with heavy French accents. They were seated on folding lawn chairs in the center of a haphazard and significantly overgrown yard. In addition to the colorful scarves they wore on their heads, they sought shade from the morning sun under the makeshift clothesline upon which were hanging all manner of clothing, sheets, towels, and even undergarments.

"Somehow, I doubt you boys will make much progress with these ladies, so why don't I give it a try," Noelle volunteered.

"Yeah, good idea, girl," Mark said, remembering the lesson Elise taught him at Versailles about entering into a French conversation armed with only an introductory sentence.

The three watched and listened closely as Noelle approached and engaged the women. She spoke rapidly in French, pausing only once to turn around and point to the boys. Both of the older women's faces blushed as they smiled and nodded knowingly.

"What is she saying?" Josh asked Elise.

"Just that you two are from America, and that you're our boyfriends."

"Really," Mark quickly jumped in, "we are? I mean your boyfriends?"

"Well, I guess technically speaking, you are boys, and we are friends, so, whatever works," Elise chuckled.

Noelle returned to report, "They say it's over near where we parked. I didn't see anything there, but maybe we should go back and look again."

They walked back up the lane to the square and looked everywhere for a hint of the chateau but saw nothing different than they'd seen before. They checked the address typed into the GPS app one more time and then stood perplexed by the mystery. A teenage girl walking a dog came up the road the group had driven in on and headed toward the general store.

"Excuse me," Josh called out. "Do you live around here?"

"Oui, monsieur, just down that way, can I help you?"

"I hope so," Josh said, "by the way, your English is excellent."

"Oui, thank you," the girl replied, smiling at the group. Her dog, who was keeping a vigilant eye on the men, softened when Elise reached down to pet him.

"I like your dog," she said. "What's his name?"

"He is actually a she," the girl said. "Her name is Estelle."

"Estelle, as in the famous winery?" Josh perked up.

"Oui, DuBois-Estelle. It is where my Uncle works. He is the assistant winemaker there. You know of it?"

"Yes, we do," Noelle said. "My grandfather worked there many years ago. We are trying to find the chateau but seem to be lost. We have an appointment with Mr. DuBois."

The girl chuckled, "You are not lost. You are standing right in front of it."

The four all expressed wide-eyed puzzlement at the statement.

"It is there, right behind you -- behind that wall. Do you see the small wooden door there with the fleur-de-lys on it? That is the entrance. Just ring the bell, and I'm sure they will let you in if you have an appointment. Please say hello to Mr. DuBois from Adalene. Have a nice day."

The girl and her four-legged companion turned to continue their walk to the store and then disappeared inside.

"Well, I'd say this is about the most nondescript entrance to a grand chateau that I've ever seen," Mark announced.

"I'd say you are right about that," Elise agreed.

"You know," Noelle offered, "now that I think about it, it's not all that surprising. I've always heard Mr. DuBois is an intensely private man, so this actually makes sense. And we didn't see any signs along the way mentioning his vineyard because the public is not generally invited in, and he certainly doesn't need to advertise. His wine is quite famous."

"Well, come on then, let's let him know we are here. We don't want our host to think we are tardy slackers, now do we," Mark said excitedly. "Bonjour." A female voice said through the small intercom speaker connected to the doorbell.

"Bonjour," Noelle replied. "My name is Noelle LePage. I am here with friends. We have an appointment to see Mr. DuBois."

"Ah, yes," the voice responded in English, "Aubert is expecting you. Please come in."

They heard a buzz and then a click and then watched as the wooden door's latch opened and it swung inward.

Josh flashed an enthusiastic thumbs-up signal to Noelle, and the four stepped through the door and into the courtyard of the DuBois estate.

"Oh my gosh," Mark uttered. "This feels like walking through the back of the wardrobe right into Narnia."

"Ha," Elise laughed, "now that is one story we do know here in France, and I agree. This is quite a surprise. I mean, look at this place!"

The four stood still for a moment taking in the scene. The three-story chateau was set back several hundred feet from the wall, so the barrier had wholly obscured it. It was in pristine condition, painted a light tan color with white trim around the windows and parapets. The classic French Renaissance style roof was covered in grey tile, and the several chimneys poking up through the roof were all made of red brick. A small balcony extended over the grand front entrance, and a mature vine with pink flowers climbed up a trellis to reach it. Josh envisioned Romeo's Juliet calling to him from the stoop. A beautiful green lawn with a small cobble path invited them forward toward the house. Beyond the chateau, visible on both sides, was a slowly rising hillside covered in vines.

"This place is ... uh, it's ... amazing!" Josh said in awe. "Can you imagine living here? It is perfect. It's not too big or overstated like so many of the chateaus we've seen. No, this is more like a home, a very nice home, but somehow it just feels comfortable. And these grounds, oh my, I haven't seen anything this nice since, well, since this morning in Celeste's garden."

Josh smiled at Noelle, who returned the comment with a wink.

While they stood there gawking, pointing, and talking, an older man emerged from the front door of the house.

He was too far away to recognize, but Noelle assumed it was Aubert, so she grabbed Josh's hand to urge him along.

"Come on, guys; I think that must be Aubert. Let's go meet him!"

The man waited in the circular drive near the fountain for the foursome to reach him. He was wiry and fit, slightly balding, and wore small square rimmed glasses that rested low on his nose. His jaw, was strong and angular, and sported a carefully trimmed white goatee. He stood tall and erect, not hunched over like so many older adults tended to be. If you didn't know he was in his eighties, you would think he was perhaps late sixties or early seventies at the oldest.

Noelle reached out first to greet him.

"Bonjour. Mr. DuBois?" she asked.

"Oui, oui, and you must be Noelle, or as your grandmere calls you Wello, yes? You are as beautiful as your grandmere," he said in rough English as he gave her a gentle, grandfatherly side hug.

Noelle blushed a little and demurely nodded her head.

"Yes, Wello, that would be me. Funny you would know that name, Mr. DuBois."

"Ah, I know much about you, my dear, and about your family. They are all among my favorite people in the world. And please, call me Aubert. And these three, they must be your friends. You must be Elise, yes?" Aubert said, taking Elise's hand.

"Yes, sir, pleased to meet you," she said almost instinctively half curtseying.

"The pleasure is all mine, dear. And you two must be the gentlemen from America that Celeste mentioned when she called. How do you do?" Aubert said, extending his right hand.

He shook both the boys' hands. His hand felt like a rock, and his grip was vice-like and caught both young men by surprise. His eye twinkled a little upon seeing their surprise at the firmness of his handshake.

"Ah, many years on the winepresses makes a man's hand strong, yes?" he teased.

"Yes, indeed," Josh answered. "We hope someday to have experienced as many years making wine as you have, sir, I mean, Aubert."

"That's better, yes, Aubert," the old man said, grinning. "I hear you are planning to make wine in America. I'm anxious to hear about that. But first, come, let me show you around the house, and then we'll head to the cellar and talk wine.

CHAPTER 10

The inside of the house was as immaculate and impressive as the outside. The furniture was all classic French renaissance. The place could have easily passed for a museum. Elise was beside herself with interest and had difficulty holding back the flood of questions she had. The others just walked along, listening to the answers and the stories. Eventually, they made their way through the house and out into the back area, where they were greeted with a beautifully manicured garden and another fountain.

"Come along," Aubert coaxed, "the entrance to the caves is just over there," he said, pointing to their right.

They walked to what looked like a simple shed built partially into a hillside upon which perfectly aligned vines stretched as far as the eye could see. The wooden door was weathered, and the hardware on it was made of thick iron.

"Please wait here for a second," Aubert said as he walked forward the last few steps to the door.

Turning his back to the group, he reached into his pocket and pulled out a keychain with several keys hanging from it. He proceeded to unlock two different deadbolts. Then he punched a long combination of numbers into a state-of-art alarm pad, which beeped affirmatively, acknowledging the correct sequence of symbols had been entered. As he went through these motions, Mark noticed and then pointed out to the rest of the group the several cleverly concealed surveillance cameras that were watching them.

"There we go, sorry about all the security, but these days you can't be too careful. Even though we are well protected from the outside world here, the wine business has become, well, shall we say, very competitive over the past few decades, and we've had more than one breach into our cellars. But, come, now, let's go down to where it is cooler. I think you'll like what you see, especially you gentlemen -- maybe a vision of your future in California?"

The door creaked ever so slightly as Aubert pulled it open, and they were immediately met with a waft of cool air and a set of steep stairs that dropped precipitously down into the earth.

"Watch your heads here; the roof support beam is a bit low. My great-grandfather who built these caves years ago was a much shorter man than I am."

The small hanging light over the stairs only removed the darkness to about thirty feet from the landing. After that, it was almost inky black, though very faint silhouettes of stacked wine barrels could be seen, or maybe just imagined, in the distance. The smell was strong and dense. The must of earth and grapes filled their nostrils, ten times stronger than Josh had sensed on his early morning walk in the vineyard above Celeste's house.

Josh inhaled deeply and closed his eyes.

"This is wonderful, Aubert. I can't tell you how grateful we are to be invited to your home and now down to your wine cellar. This is an experience I will remember forever."

"I'm glad you are excited, Josh, but we haven't even begun yet. Please, follow."

Aubert led the way. He carried a small flashlight, and as they explored deeper and deeper into the earthen caves, about every thirty yards or so, he flipped a switch, and another small hanging light would bring the place to life. The barrels were stacked three high, side to side, and front to back, on a carpet of small pebbles, so they almost appeared as small pyramids. The lowest barrel in each cluster was accessible, and Aubert expertly removed the waxy barrel stopper called a bung and extracted the precious nectar with a glass plongeur, or what in America is commonly called a wine-thief. In anticipation of the visit, Aubert's workers had set out wine glasses near the landing at the stairs into which Aubert would deposit approximately two ounces of the stolen liquid treasure.

He offered a brief vignette about each of the four varietals they tasted: chardonnay, pinot noir, gamay, and aligote. They tasted two samples of each from different vintages and vineyard plots. To be sure not to offend inadvertently, the four observed Aubert as he sniffed and then swirled and then smelled the juice in his glass. He then took a modest sip and swooshed it politely in his mouth. The four then followed suit. Then, unlike anything they'd ever experienced in America, after each had politely sipped, Aubert held his glass out toward the four.

"Here, please pour what you did not drink back into my glass, so that I can return it to the barrel."

"Really?" Mark asked. "You're going to put it back into the barrel after we've sipped on it?"

"Yes, my grandfather told me when I was a very young boy that you never, ever, waste a drop of precious Burgundy wine."

Once they figured out the program, Josh and Mark made it a point to take bigger sips.

"Our wines are all Grand Cru," Aubert said matter-of-factly. "We are very proud of the heritage of our estate and our wines. I am a very blessed man to have been born into such a wonderful life. I only wish I had been blessed with children, so that I would be able to now enjoy grandchildren, such as you, in my old age. But, alas, the Lord did not see fit to extend such blessing to my beloved wife and me. I am content nonetheless. Contentment is the greatest gift a man can know in this world. Remember that, my young friends."

Following each sampling, and after Aubert returned whatever wine was left after the tastings, he lovingly replaced the bung atop the barrel and then reached down to the ground, picked up a small handful of pebbles, and placed them on the edge of the barrel.

"What are the pebbles for?" Elise asked.

"They are a sign to my winemaker that we tasted from this particular barrel so that he can refill it to the top. It is imperative to keep the barrels completely full to control the oxygen content as the wine ages."

"So, when do you harvest the grapes?" Josh asked.

"Excellent question, Joshua," Aubert smiled. "Unlike in America where the harvest can be driven by many outside factors, not the least of which is the market, here we harvest the old way. It is based not only on the ripening of the grapes and the sugar content called brix, but we also harvest based on the moon's cycles. Barometric pressure is critical. We wait for an ascending moon and a clear night. Most often, we begin in mid-September. We pick all the grapes by hand, and we crush by foot. We subscribe to the old ways, though we do not run through the vineyard naked as Noah did. Clothing optional is not an option here," Aubert said, laughing at his own humor.

"That all sounds a bit religious, even spiritual," Mark commented.

"Perhaps," Aubert said. "I think, in France, we see the making of fine wine as more of an art than a science. Of course, we respect the Americans' studies of the vine and certainly don't shun scientific information, but we choose to believe in the natural as much or more here. As the famous Frenchman, Louis Pasteur, once said, 'A bottle of wine contains more philosophy than all the books in the world.'"

After forty minutes in the depths of the earth, the light and heat on the surface felt almost oppressive. Once in the sunlight and after securing, locking, and re-arming the cave entrance, Aubert quickly announced the next part of their adventure.

"Miraculously, my morning today is completely unfettered, and so I have planned a walk through the vineyard and then a light lunch at a special spot in the Chardonnay section, if that would be to your liking, of course."

Knowing what the answer would be, after a glance to confirm smiling faces all around, Noelle responded with an eloquence matching their host's verbal style, "But of course, Aubert, we would like nothing more than to enjoy a stroll in the vineyard and a small bite to eat. How very kind of you. Grandmere spoke so highly of your kindness, but I must say you have exceeded even our grandest expectations."

Aubert smiled and tilted his head slightly to the left in acknowledgment of the compliment. Noelle also detected an ever so subtle lift in his countenance when she mentioned her grandmother.

He still pines for her, she thought romantically to herself. *Oh, Grandmere, you should have pursued him.*

As they walked, Aubert led the way. His pace was brisk but in no way labored. It was as if he walked these hills daily, which was probably the case. In classic French form, at least as the boys had come to observe it in every town and village they had visited, Aubert walked resolutely and erect, with his hands clasped behind his back. After a few hundred yards, the girls found themselves beginning to tire a bit. Seeing them slow, Josh hailed to their leader.

"Aubert, a question for you."

Aubert stopped on a dime and turned. Seeing the group was lagging, he walked casually back toward them while talking, not wanting the distance he had inadvertently put between them to be an embarrassment. He saw the girls appeared to be wilting and recognized that Josh's question had been more out of chivalry than genuine interest. He offered a wink communicating "well done" to the young man as he approached.

"Yes, young Joshua, anything -- all my secrets are laid bare before you today."

"Oh, I would never ask about secrets or anything proprietary. My question is only about the workers we see in the fields today. Obviously, there is no harvesting happening this time of year. What exactly are they doing?"

"Excellent question, again. It is, I guess you could say, a form of pruning, but we call it thinning. You see, Mother Nature deals her hand in the spring, and we must then adapt each year to play it. Early on, we are very busy shoot-thinning and positioning. Next comes leaf tipping, hedging, and general managing. By the summer solstice, the vines usually stop growing, and fruit begins to set. This time of year, we carefully study each plant and clean and thin within and around it to maximize the grapes' quality. The quantity is far less important. You can only make great wine with great grapes. All the mediocre grapes in the world can never produce a fine wine."

"Which of the wine varietals is your personal favorite?" Elise asked while holding her hand to her forehead to shield the glare of the fast-rising sun.

"That, my dear, is a question I am afraid I cannot answer," Aubert said mysteriously and without hesitation. Then after a brief pause, he asked. "Do you have siblings, Elise?"

"Yes," Elise answered, wondering what in the world that had to do with her question.

"What do you suppose your father would say if asked which of his children was his favorite? Would he not answer as I have? Of course, he would. He loves them all for their special uniqueness and innate beauty. And so it is with my grapes. Of course, I particularly enjoy the one I'm tasting in the moment."

"What percentage of credit would you take in the success of your wines? I mean, how much of it is owing to 'Mother Nature,' as you would say, versus your skill as the winemaker?" Mark asked.

"Ah, that is yet another imponderable question. Let me see, how can I say this? Both are 100 percent responsible. Without the grape that nature provides, there would be no wine, but the grape would wither and die on the vine unrealized without the winemaker. I don't look at it as deserving credit, but more as basking in the blessing.

"Okay, now that we've had a little respite, let's continue to the gazebo; it's not much farther," Aubert said as he spun and started back up the hill, hands once again neatly crossed behind his back.

The gazebo, as Aubert referred to it, was like a garden oasis in the midst of Eden. It sat on a small plateau at the far end of the Chardonnay section and offered an unparalleled view of the valley within which DuBois-Estelle sat.

Surrounded by vineyards, the gazebo was made of stone and covered a picnic table that could comfortably seat eight. Though they were not on because it was daytime, small lights hung from the edges of the covering, which meant electricity had been run to this extreme point as well. A young man sat waiting in a pickup parked on a single lane farm road, and when he saw the guests arrive, he hopped out and quickly set up a light lunch of cheeses, bread, fruits, and nuts along with several bottles of wine. Then, as swiftly and silently as he had appeared, he disappeared, and the pickup rumbled down the path and out of sight.

Aubert was obviously proud of the spot and took great joy in pointing out the various natural features and buildings that inhabited the viewshed. After they were all seated, he reached for Noelle's hand and then proceeded to say a blessing for the meal. The four closed their eyes and bowed their heads with appropriate reverence as they listened to Aubert address the Creator and offer thanks for healing, health, and the coming harvest.

"So, Wello," Aubert said, smiling broadly at his use of the nickname, "please tell me, how is your Grandmere, Celeste, doing these days?"

"Oh, she is very well, thank you. I had not seen her much since I went away to school in Paris four years ago, so I did not know quite what to expect when we arrived yesterday, but I must say it seems not only has she not aged, but she may actually be getting younger," Noelle smiled.

"That is so good to hear," Aubert said quietly. He then looked away for a moment, catching his breath as he did. "I miss her, you know, Celeste. I was secretly hoping she might come along with you today. You'll note there is a sixth place that I had set at the table."

None of the four knew what to say in response, so an awkward pause ensued and filled the air.

"I loved your grandmere once, Noelle. I even asked her to marry me. Did she ever tell you that?"

Now the four were not only quiet, but their mouths were hanging ajar in astonishment at such a personal revelation.

"We were sitting right here at this table, oh, it must have been 10 or 12 years ago. My wife had passed away nearly a decade before, and I was terribly lonely up here on the hill, hiding, it seemed, behind that wall in the village square. For years after your grandpere died working here in the vineyard, I took care of Celeste and her children. After my wife, Pearl, had been gone about five years, I decided I needed a companion again. I don't do 'alone' very well. I knew Celeste better than any other woman in the world, and her heart, of course, is made of pure gold. And her beauty, well, that is as obvious as the sun and the moon. Our friendship grew deep over the years,

174

and I hoped perhaps she might feel the same way about me as I did about her. So I asked for her hand one evening while we were enjoying an early dinner right here. The gazebo wasn't built yet, but there was a picnic table here, just like today.

"I was devastated when she said no, though I understood why. She still felt married to Robert. Of course, there is no marriage in heaven, so I knew it was perfectly acceptable in the Lord's eyes to remarry, but Celeste didn't share that same view. Or maybe she was just never able to get past the loss of her Robert. It had been so sudden for her, whereas my loss of Pearl had been prolonged and gradual due to the cancer. Sometimes I wonder which is better, a slow demise or a fast one. I guess only the Lord knows what is best, and we just have to trust in that."

He sighed heavily and then stopped his monologue and looked off dreamily toward Lyon.

"She is so close and yet so very, very far away," Aubert finally concluded.

"Anyway, I am sorry to burden you with an old man's feelings. I just thought, maybe you might share with Celeste when you return home that the winemaker on the hill would still very much like to renew his friendship with her. I know marriage is out of the question, of course, and to be honest, that isn't really that important to me now. I'd just like to spend time with my friend again. I'd like for Celeste to feel comfortable returning to the vineyard. The time we have remaining on this earth may be limited, and I, for one, would like to spend it with a close friend."

Sensing some response from the group needed to be said, Noelle offered, "No burden at all, and thank you for sharing your heart, Aubert. I promise, I'll mention our conversation to Grandmere."

After lunch, Aubert led the foursome back down the hill and to the chateau. He gave each a bottle of 2006 Pinot Noir as a gift and bid them farewell. Handshakes and hugs around were exchanged, with Noelle being the last. As she hugged the man she had just met but felt she had known for a lifetime, she whispered in his ear, "Thank you so much for today, Aubert."

Placing his hands lightly on her shoulders, Aubert took a step back. She could see his eyes moistening.

"And as I said, I will tell Grandmere of our chat at lunch. And I will pray that her heart is released to, as you say, renew your friendship. You are a wonderful man, and I know she would be as blessed as you."

During the drive home, the conversation in the car was subdued. All four were still reeling somewhat from the lunch conversation. The depth of honesty and expression of love had moved each of them to their core.

"So, will you say anything to your grandmother?" Elise asked.

"I think I will. You know, it's interesting that last night, when I went to check on Grandmere while you guys did the dishes, she confided to me the reason she didn't want to join us today was that she feared seeing Aubert again might be too painful. She even shared with me about the dinner in the vineyard that Aubert mentioned. I think she misses him almost as much as he misses her. I hope she'll be open to the idea of visiting him again. I could see them together, as friends or maybe even as more. It's kind of strange to think of eighty-year-old people as being romantic, but somehow it just seems like it would be natural in this case. You never know where the Lord might lead. Perhaps there is a chance for vieil amour to bloom just as jeune amour does."

"Vieil amour?" Mark asked.

"Older love," Elise interpreted. "Mature love, the kind of love that endures through time and is not dependent on youth's romance and emotion. I'm beginning to see it in my parents. It's something I long to experience someday. I think growing old together with someone would be nice, perhaps even the ultimate experience in life."

CHAPTER 11

The next morning Celeste and her four guests went to church together at La Basilique Notre Dame de Fourviere. It was located at the top of a hill overlooking Lyon and both the Saone and Rhone rivers. Although the mass was in French, the boys didn't mind as the experience of it all was still richly fulfilling. As they walked out into the early afternoon sun, the church bells announced the noon hour for the entire city to hear as had happened in Paris.

"I'm surprised there is another Notre Dame here. Is that some sort of denomination within the Catholic church?" Mark asked.

"Fair question, but no," Elise answered. "Notre Dame simply means Our Lady, and refers to the Mother Mary, who, of course, is revered in the Catholic faith. It's neither a denomination nor a place, just a reference to Mary, who is a very popular saint in our religion. Did you enjoy the service?"

"Absolutely, I missed the English translation as we had in Paris, but only a little bit. You may have noticed I had my phone out, so I was able to use my translation app a few times. I'm glad Celeste brought us here. She is such a sweet lady."

"Why, thank you, Mark," Celeste said from behind.

"I couldn't help but overhear your conversation. I'm glad you enjoyed my church. I've been attending Mass here since I was a little girl; almost 75 years, I guess it's been. The Lord always meets me here. He gives me comfort and guidance. If it hadn't been for Him, I don't think I'd have made it through this life as well as I have. And now I marvel at the abundance of blessings I am able to enjoy, including my beloved granddaughter, Noelle. And her friends, I might add."

Turning to the group, Celeste offered, "I know today is your last day visiting with me, so I'd like to invite you all to join me for lunch at my favorite café -- my treat. It's within walking distance from here. What do you say?"

"I don't think we have any lunch plans, do we, guys?" Noelle asked, looking to her friends. "So, I think that sounds like it would be fun, Grandmere. Thank you."

"Wonderful," Celeste said, clasping her hands together and holding them to her heart. "It's a beautiful day for a walk, and I'm looking forward to hearing your stories from yesterday's visit to the winery. It's been so long since I've been there. I want to hear every detail."

Noelle smiled at the comment, but then when she was behind Celeste, she looked at her friends with raised eyebrows and wide eyes. *This should be interesting,* she thought.

The cafe was only two blocks away and had a perfect view of Lyon below. As they waited for the food, Celeste shared a few anecdotes about the city's history and how it developed over the years, starting in the hill country and then gradually moving down to the rivers and beyond. Everyone was fascinated by the stories, especially Elise.

"You know, Celeste," Elise said, "I think you would make an excellent tour guide. I don't know if Noelle mentioned it, but I recently got a job as a guide at Versailles. It's a lot of fun. I enjoy meeting all the visitors, especially the tourists from other countries. And what I find the most interesting is when they ask questions that sometimes I can't answer. It forces me to do further research, so I can answer them effectively the next time they come up. It's like a constant history lesson, even for me, the purported historian."

During the meal, the conversation gradually drifted from Lyon's history, but Celeste continued to do most of the talking in the form of question

asking rather than history telling. Her focus was
on America. She had never been to the U.S. and
was keenly interested in everything from politics
to culture, parks, monuments, and landscapes. As
Noelle had mentioned about her grandfather,
Celeste also had a profound fondness for what the
United States had done to rescue France from
Germany, and she was consistent in her praise of
America. In response to questions of her, Celeste
shared a few stories about her childhood and her
years with Robert. Her memories were clear, and
her storytelling witty and concise. The group
marveled at how incredibly together the lady was
mentally and physically at 82 years of age.

After the meal, the group ordered coffees and
continued to enjoy the view from the spacious
window booth where they were seated.

"Okay, so, enough about me," Celeste finally said.
"I've been talking practically nonstop since we sat
down. I'd like to hear about yesterday and your
time at DuBois-Estelle. As I remember, it was a
stunning place -- the house, the gardens, the
vineyard, everything. Is it still that way?"

"Oh, yes, and perhaps even more so," Noelle
answered for the group. "Aubert, he insisted we
call him that, gave us a tour of everything,
including the caves where the wine is stored. It
was very cool, both literally and figuratively. He
was so gracious to us with his time and his stories.

182

You saw the wine he gave us as a gift. That was certainly unexpected. We should have been the ones giving him gifts. He was just over the top about everything."

"And then," Josh jumped in, "he took us for a walk in the vineyard. We strolled through the Chardonnay section and ended up at a gazebo up on a hill that had a spectacular view of the entire valley, and there he treated us to a wonderful lunch."

"A gazebo?" Celeste asked. "Hmm, that's something I don't remember. Maybe it's new?"

Realizing this was the perfect entree to keep her promise to Aubert about sharing their chat with her grandmother, Noelle stepped back into the conversation.

"Yes, Grandmere, a gazebo. Aubert said it was something new since you had been to the property. He asked about you, of course, and I told him you were well. He said he once brought you to the place where the gazebo is now located. He then told us a story about that time. A dinner he said he would never forget."

The four anticipated what was about to happen, and they all watched for a reaction from Celeste. Noelle paused for a moment when she saw her grandmother's eyes divert ever so slightly to the window and the view below.

Celeste suspected where Noelle was going, and the memory of that night was as fresh in her mind as the walk from church just forty minutes earlier. She had replayed the scene over in her mind a thousand times, including several within the past 48 hours because of the conversation she'd had with Noelle two nights earlier. Suddenly her heart was heavy, and Celeste felt a physical weight on her shoulders. She wanted to cry, but her tears had all been spent during scores of sleepless nights over the years. The smell of the vineyard flooded her memory, as did the sunset and the gentle summer breeze and the beautiful table and the wine. But most overwhelming was her recollection of the friendship and the fondness she had felt for Aubert.

Did you make the right decision in declining his offer of marriage? Celeste privately wondered as she continued looking at the view. *What would your life look like now? Happier? More fulfilled? Could you be any happier? Contentment is a blessed thing;* she reminded herself. *You should not wish for what you do not have. But, you could have had it in this case. Did you make a mistake?*

"Grandmere," Noelle whispered into the older lady's musing as she reached over and took Celeste's hand. "I want you to know that I said

184

nothing to Aubert about our conversation two nights ago. I said nothing to anyone, just as I promised. But while we ate lunch, he launched into the story on his own, and, of course, I couldn't stop him. So we just sat there and listened. He shared everything, Grandmere. His heart is still so full of love for you. It was everything I could do not to try to comfort him with the knowledge that you have also suffered from that night and the separation it led to. But I do think Aubert still desires your friendship, your companionship, your vieil amour. He all but said so, and I would encourage you, after we leave, to at least call him. Don't be afraid, Grandmere. I saw the love in his eyes, and I can see the love in your eyes. The Lord will guide your steps. I think you would be happy together, at least as friends, if not more. He is so lonely up there on that hillside. He loves his vines and his home, but they are not enough. They are not you. You are both healthy, and I believe you still have many more good years, and I think they could be even better if you spent them together."

Celeste looked into her granddaughter's eyes and saw herself six decades earlier, a woman full of life and future and love. Love. She saw love in Noelle's eyes. Love for her, but also love for another. She then glanced over at Josh, who had been sitting quietly while listening to the conversation between generations. Though listening, his attention was, however, focused primarily on Noelle. Celeste saw love in his eyes as well.

"Thank you, Wello," Celeste whispered. "I will pray about these things you've said. You are an angel, you know, speaking such wisdom and truth into my life. It should be me speaking such things to you, young lady. But while you are being so bold about my heart, may I offer a thought about yours?"

"Of course, Grandmere, what is it?"

Celeste pulled the girl close to her and whispered in her ear, "I can see love in your eyes too, my bien-aime. I see it in his eyes also. So, as I pray about such things, you should as well."

***

The following week seemed to drag on forever. The boys slowly made their way down the Rhone and visited several wineries and small villages along the way to Avignon. The girls returned to their jobs in Versailles, where the minutes seemed like hours and the hours like days. Finally, Friday arrived, and once again, Noelle and Elise were on a train headed south. They settled in at Noelle's mother's house and waited for the boys to arrive for dinner around six. The doorbell rang at 5:57 p.m.

Noelle ran to open the door, and when she saw Josh, she embraced him with a warm hug.

"Man, did I miss you!" she blurted out. Then a bit embarrassed by her overly enthusiastic display of affection, she released the hug and stepped back grinning, "Uh, sorry about that, Josh, it's just, well, I really did miss you, and I'm so glad you're here. Hi Mark, I missed you too, of course, come here and get your hug," she joked as she gave him a much more subdued side hug.

Her excitement continued to bubble over as Noelle said, "Both of you, please come, come, and meet my mother. I've been telling her all about you and bragging a bit as well."

Ushering the boys into the living room, she exclaimed, "Mom, these are our friends from America, Josh, and Mark. Guys, this is my mom, Chloe."

"Hello, boys," Chloe said in a voice so much calmer than her daughter's it almost sounded flat in comparison. "It's nice to meet both of you, and I promise I won't run you over like Noelle just did."

All smiled as they politely shook hands.

"I'm really looking forward to visiting with you boys, but first, please feel free to drop your bags there in the family room; that's where you'll be sleeping. You're going to have to share the pull-out couch, I'm afraid. I made up the guest room for the girls. And then you can wash up for dinner. I'll start serving in about five minutes."

During dinner, Chloe invited the boys to share about their travels over the past week. The boys jumped at the invitation and began telling about their visits to the villages of Vienne, Valence, Montelimar, and Orange. They took turns talking about the myriad things they saw and experienced until they started talking about one town in particular, and then it was almost like a competition between the two to see who could tell the story fastest. In rapid-fire succession, Mark and Josh seemed to spar for the position of storyteller.

"We heard about this one castle, not a chateau, but an actual castle, in a town called Tarascon, so we went to check it out. It was stunning, amazing, spectacular, incredible," Mark waxed on. "And this past week just happened to be the one week each year when the town gets together, and people dress in period costumes and kind of perform a 'day in the life' at the castle. I couldn't believe how cool it was."

"Yeah," Josh jumped in. "There were small groupings of people doing various things. One group of men was fashioning weapons, you know, swords and shields and arrows and the like.

Another group of women was baking and making crafts. They even let us taste the bread. It all seemed very authentic."

"And there was a courtyard where guys were practicing swordplay and other kinds of hand to hand combat," Mark edged back in when Josh stopped to take a bite of food. "They were dressed as knights. I know they were just acting, but I'll tell you, those swords were certainly real enough. The sound they made when they clanged together was almost frightening. There was also this cool display of various kinds of armor, and they even let us try some of it on. Man, that stuff was so heavy. I have no idea how anybody could fight in a battle weighed down with all that metal.

"And then, in another room that looked kind of like a chapel, there were men and women dancing to stringed instrumental music. It felt like we were on the set of some King Arthur movie or something. It was all so real. The people, who, we were told were just volunteers from the town's heritage society, really seemed to know their stuff. At times it almost felt like we had been transported back in time and were like invisible time travelers walking through the 17th century."

Mark finally stopped to take a drink of water, and Josh pounced on the opening.

"Then we began climbing these circular stone stairways. Up, up, up, I think we climbed six or seven stories. Along the way, we stopped in various rooms that had been restored to show, for example, a dining hall. One place we stopped in was a bedroom chamber. It seemed so dark and cold. Everything was, of course, stone. In addition to the main sleeping room, there was a secondary room that was described as where the guards would keep watch over the royal family. Then, each bedroom chamber had this smallish room on the castle's outside wall that faced the river. The room had a small slit window that looked like one of those openings to shoot arrows out of, which gave a bit of a view and some light. But the most interesting thing about those little rooms was the bench seat hewn out of the stone with a hole in it that you could look through and see down to the river below. The storyboard said that the little room was the royal bathroom. They called it the 'loo with a view.' I thought that was kind of creative, though I've never understood why they called a toilet a loo.

"I know," Elise offered. "You know us French history major-tour guide-types need to know this kind of important stuff," she chuckled at herself. "When people used to fling their potty waste out of the windows, they would shout 'Gardez l'eau,' which means watch out for the water. Most historians think that's where the word loo came from. I'm just so full of critical factoids, aren't I? Okay, back to your story, boys."

"Interesting piece of trivia there, Elise, maybe it'll come in handy someday during trivia night at our wine club," Mark laughed softly. "Okay, now back to our tale. As Josh said, we climbed up several stories, and we eventually got to the top of the castle. It was a spectacular view. Not quite like the Eiffel Tower, but close. The river was on one side and the town on the other. Across the river, on a hillside, we could see another big castle. One of the placards we read said it was the home of a rival family and the river was the boundary that kept them at peace for centuries. While we were standing there, I joked about a prince in one of the castles and a princess in the other and how they might have sent flashing fire light signals to each other at night, kind of like a Romeo and Juliet thing. Anyway, it was a fun, fanciful thought."

"That would be something you would imagine, Noelle," Josh added. "You're the romantic in the group. I remember how you said you liked the romance of the story about the sunset boat rides on the Grand Canal at Versailles. And I must admit, while Mark was talking about the two lovers in the rival castles, I got swept up in the idea while we were standing there. The view was amazing. While we were there on the top of the castle looking down, I also imagined what it might have been like if marauders were attacking the

191

castle. You know, soldiers shooting arrows down on attackers and boiling oil pouring down over men trying to climb the wall with ropes. I guess it was the mock sword fighting we'd seen earlier in the courtyard that was still on my mind.

"But then, as we continued to linger there on the rooftop, all of that imaginary medieval stuff faded. And then I started thinking about the present, and just how amazing our time in France has been, and all we are learning about and experiencing. And most of all, I was thankful for you two girls and how special you've made these past few weeks for us. I'm not sure we'll ever be able to thank you properly."

"That's sweet of you to say, Josh," Elise replied. "But I think I speak for both of us when I say you two have made our summer much more fun than it otherwise would have been as well. You helped us focus our schedules at work and have something to look forward to on these several weekends. But, hey, let's not get all nostalgic just yet. We have a lot in store for this weekend, starting tonight!"

"Tonight?" Mark asked.

"Yep, we are going to go down by the riverfront. There is a local artist's street fair and a farmer's market this weekend and there is a little carnival set up for families, including a giant Ferris wheel. I was thinking I might even give you a chance to win me a stuffed animal at the dart-throwing booth," Elise winked toward Mark. "The festivities started at six o'clock, and everything stays open until midnight, so we can go after dinner and wander around for a few hours. It's really a fun time."

CHAPTER 12

As the foursome approached from the river, Elise explained that the old portion of Avignon is surrounded by a giant stone wall nearly three miles long. The moats and spiked drawbridges that once accompanied the fortress are gone today, but the wall continues to remind one of the impressive fortifications that have been in place to protect the city for over 600 years. Much of the City center within the wall maintains the charm of old France with an eclectic mixture of architecture dating back to the days of Roman occupation. It is one of the most well-preserved cities in France in terms of ancient history.

The location of the fair was easy to find due to the Ferris wheel. The sound of street bands playing was also a dead giveaway. The smells of open market food being grilled and the laughter of young people at the makeshift bars, and the children playing on the carnival rides all combined to create an almost irresistible energy that captured the minds of all four friends.

"Boy, this is really something," Mark exclaimed.

"Between this fair weekend here and the renaissance week at the castle in Tarascon, we have been scoring big on the activity chart."

"Yeah, and I'm still reeling from our visit to DuBois-Estelle and meeting Aubert," Josh responded. "For me, that was a ten and a half easy. But you're right, Mark, we have been very fortunate with our dates.

"Were you girls aware of any of this going on?" Josh asked.

"They have things going on all the time during the summer, but to be honest, we don't focus much on them. If it's convenient, and we're in town, we'll check it out, but otherwise, it's kind of standard stuff for us," Noelle answered.

They stopped at one of the bars and got cold beverages to go before strolling around and watching all the activity. Mark made an effort to win Elise a prize at the dart-throw, but he gave up after three failed attepts. They found a bench, sat down to listen to a modern jazz quartet play, and grabbed two bags of kettle corn to share.

"This reminds me of going to Cal Expo as a kid," Josh said in between songs.

"What's that?" Noelle asked with interest.

"Oh, that's the name of the California State Fair in Sacramento. We used to go every year when I was younger. It was always so much fun: the rides, the food, the music, the people, the animals, the cars ... just everything. Anyway, I remember discovering one year that musicians put on 'shows' rather than just perform."

"What do you mean?" Elise asked.

"Well, that year, a famous singer-songwriter was playing at one of the small venue stages. He was one of my mom's favorite artists from the 70s. I watched his performance with my family, and it was amazing. The guy was an excellent guitarist, and I even recognized a couple of his songs. He had an amazing rapport with the audience, and his jokes were hilarious. He was like the perfect performer. I was so impressed that after we left, I couldn't stop talking about the experience. I just went on and on about it, so my mom suggested that she and I go back and watch him a second time. I was thrilled. But what happened next ruined everything for me. The second show was exactly like the first, exactly. The songs were the same, which wasn't all that unexpected, but the interactions with the audience, and even the jokes, were identical. What I originally thought had been this amazingly intimate connection with the audience turned out to be nothing more than a slick shtick. I mean, it was still professional and musically excellent, but the personal connection was missing, so the whole thing seemed flat the second time around. I guess it was kind of one of those coming of age, ah-ha moments for me, and it was kind of depressing."

"Hey, no more depressing stories. Does anyone want to ride the Ferris wheel?" Elise interjected. "It's, like, my favorite ride of all time."

The others all enthusiastically said yes, and they headed over toward the giant wheel. It was painted pristine white, and each of the seats had different colored safety bars that came down over the riders and locked into place. Mark and Elise loaded first into a blue chair. Josh and Noelle followed next and sat in a green chair. As is always the case, it took several minutes to unload and reload all the seats on the wheel. Once the ride was full of new riders, it slowly began rotating in a clockwise direction. The chairs creaked as they independently swiveled to remain upright while climbing to the top, some 50 feet into the air, and then falling slowly back to earth. The air was warm, but the cool breeze coming off the river tempered it perfectly.

Noelle heard Elise squeal with delight as the ride's speed picked up. When she tried to look up at her friend in the seat behind them, her movement caused their green chair to rock more vigorously than was usual.

"Whoa!" Noelle yelped as she instinctively grabbed onto whatever was closest to grab, which on her right happened to be Josh's leg. "That was scary. I think I'll just sit still and stop bouncing us around."

"Good idea," Josh concurred as he placed his hand on hers. "But I'll hold onto you just in case," he smiled.

Noelle accepted his invitation and scooted over closer to him. At the top of the rotation, they could still make out the last gasps of the setting sun's color show, a dark purple and orange haze emitting from just below the western horizon. They could also see the city lights below begin to twinkle and create a shadowy outline of the old town section's wall. As they slowly spun down and then back up again, Noelle told Josh about some of her favorite childhood memories living in Avignon.

"It was a great place to grow up," she concluded. "I can't imagine a better life as a little girl. God has truly been good to my family and me, and I can say that, despite the loss of my brother and father. Those were, of course, sorrowful times, but looking back at the whole timeline, I can see God's hand in it all. Some parts are still a mystery to me and always will be, but I figure I'll learn those answers when I'm in heaven someday.

"By the way, Josh, I haven't told you, but the fact that you're a Christian was important in our decision to join you and Mark this summer. Not that I was looking for anything beyond a few fun weekends, but I had this gnawing suspicion that something more might develop between us, you know, you and I. And I think it has, and I wouldn't have wanted to invite even the chance of such a thing with someone who doesn't know God. My faith is just too important to me. You know what I mean?"

"I do know," Josh replied as he squeezed her hand gently. "To be honest, I wasn't as discerning as you, but I'm sure grateful for the outcome."

As their chair approached the top of the circle again, the ride came to a sudden halt, and their chair rocked back and forth. Once again, Noelle's grip tightened, and she gasped quietly.

"Oh, I guess they're starting to unload people down below," she uttered nervously.

Peering carefully over the side and down to the bottom of the wheel, Josh announced, "Yep, that's what's happening, alright. Aren't we the lucky ones to get stuck up here for a few extra minutes?"

"I'm not sure I'd use the word 'lucky,' but okay, a few more minutes of this view will be nice, I guess.

As long as you hold onto me and don't let me fall out."

"I'll protect you with my last breath, my lady," Josh said in his now-familiar attempt at a European accent.

"You're sweet; you know that," Noelle said as she snuggled into Josh's shoulder.

He let go of her hand, lifted his arm, and placed it over Noelle's shoulders. The two gazed at each other for a moment and then turned their eyes back out to the beauty of the western horizon.

"Noelle, I'm really glad we got to come to Avignon together. The more time we spend together, the more I ...."

Josh stopped himself mid-sentence, not wanting to risk saying too much.

"... the more I find I am enjoying our time in France. Your grandmother and your mom are both such incredible ladies. I can see them in you. And what I see is an internal beauty that matches, no, even surpasses, your external beauty."

Josh paused again and refocused his attention on the girl beside him. Even though he'd only known her for six weeks, his heart was pounding with joy.

Lord, You know I want to kiss her, but I just don't know if it's right, Josh began silently praying. *We've only been together, actually together, for what, maybe ten days? And I'm going back home in another month or so, and then what? But Noelle is so different than any other girl I've ever met. I'm not even sure I can define the difference, but I know it's special.*

"Josh," Noelle interrupted his thoughts, "would you like to kiss me?"

Josh was shocked and more than a bit terrified to think Noelle was somehow able to see into his thoughts.

"Uh, well, uh, it seems like it might be a fitting way to end such a romantic ride, I guess," he stumbled. "Would you like me to kiss you?"

No more words were spoken. Noelle reached up with her right hand, put it around his neck, coaxed Josh's lips to hers, and they kissed.

He tasted the faint peppermint of her lip gloss, and then closing his eyes, he kissed her again. The chair began to rock again as another passenger unloaded below. The wheel slowly began moving, but neither of them paid any mind to the ride's groans and creaks. They were utterly lost in the moment they'd both secretly been hoping would happen for the past several weeks. At last, the unspoken had been spoken, but without words.

After their lips parted, both let the moment linger. Then Noelle said, "Josh, I don't want to say anything inappropriate, and I hope you can receive this in the way I mean it, but I have serious feelings for you -- more than just friends -- in fact, way more than that. I know this is sudden, and I've been praying about it a lot. But, something I told Grandmere last week, she turned back on me. I told her not to deny her heart, despite the circumstances. I know we don't really know each other that well, and I realize that you're heading back to the States soon, and you have a plan for your life, and I don't have any right to create expectation or any sense of burden on you. But, Josh, I think ...."

Josh put his index finger to her lips. "Noelle, I feel it too, and I can't explain it either. I wasn't looking for it. This is the last thing I would want at this time in my life. But I can't deny it. I'm feeling it, too. Noelle, I think I'm falling in love with you."

Noelle said nothing further but instead began to weep quietly.

"What? What is it? I'm sorry if ...," Josh whispered.

"No, it's not what you said, Josh, it's just that, it's just …."

Noelle couldn't bring herself to say what she needed to say. She choked back a sob and tried mightily to control herself.

Resigned to the fact that she couldn't share the whole truth with him, Noelle continued, "Josh, I love you, too. But I have no idea what we are going to do with this. I mean, you're leaving, and I'm, well, I'm …." Again, she caught herself and stopped.

"Noelle, oh gosh, Noelle, my heart is exploding right now. To know you feel the same way I do, I mean, I mean, we don't have to figure everything out right this minute. I don't have a clue what this might mean for you or me. I just know that my heart loves you, and I want to be honest about that. I want to … I want to kiss you again."

Josh leaned in and kissed Noelle again. It was passionate yet restrained— young love exploring the boundaries of giving to one another within the context of jeune amour.

***

"That drive was stunning. All those vineyards on the hillside, and that remnant castle turret, and that bridge we crossed over, it reminded me a little of Bixby Bridge in Big Sur," Mark said wide-eyed. "I had no idea southern France was so beautiful. I mean, the vineyards, sure, and the river, and the chateaus ... but this river gorge and the Doux Valley, I just had no idea."

"Wait until you see the river view from the Train de l'Ardeche that we're going to ride on. That view from the bridge was just a teaser," Elise said. "I've made this trip twice before, and it gets better every time. One thing you should know, though, is that the train is an antique, and it's powered by coal. The engine puts out this really fine soot. Because the cars are open-air, everyone tends to get a bit sooty. Are either of you asthmatic?"

Both boys shook their heads.

"Good, then at least we won't have to worry about you gasping for clean air."

At the Colombier station, the four saw a beautiful garden, peeked into a gift shop, and explored an antique locomotive museum. Inside the museum were several old rail cars and lots of information about technology's progression from coal-powered trains to today's bullet trains. The history of the rail line they were about to ride on was also told on a series of storyboards with old photos of men whose blood, sweat and tears carved the path through the mountains and along the river gorge.

The shrill whistle from the de l'Ardeche sounded as the vintage locomotive began chugging down the track. The giant stack on top of the engine belched huge puffs of grayish smoke that smelled like sulfur. The train gradually picked up speed as it headed into the river gorge. The historic bridge came into view in the distance and captured everyone's attention.

"It looks so much different from underneath," Josh noted in a loud voice. "The engineering that goes into something like that is amazing."

As the train wound its way up the gorge, the four were mostly silent, absorbing the beauty of the place. They climbed from a tranquil pool at the base of a man-made dam to several hundred feet above the rushing river. They witnessed the snake-like pattern the flow had carved through the mountains over the centuries. Around one bend, they saw a large building at the base of a log flume that had been cut through a dense hillside forest. The building was also near the entrance to a tunnel. Though they were not all that far from the city, in the canyon they could see nothing but lush green mountains and the craggy river whose banks were bordered by a rainbow of wildflower color including red, yellow, and orange poppies and pink and purple digitalis. It was almost as if they'd been transported into the deep reaches of a Jurassic forest.

As the locomotive whooshed into the tunnel, a blast of cool air swept over everyone. Oohs and awes were audible throughout the open car. Someone made a sound like a car horn honking, and everyone laughed.

"They do that in America, too," Mark said. "Honk car horns in tunnels, that is."

"We don't do that in France," Elise lightly replied. "So, that must have been one of your fellow yanks back there."

"It's getting dark in here," Josh announced. "This is a long tunnel."

"Long enough for a stealth kiss, I think," Noelle whispered secretly into Josh's ear.

He glanced down, and despite the darkness, he could see a gleam in her eye. As excited as he was at the prospect of kissing in the center of a French mountain, Josh felt oddly uncomfortable. He hadn't said anything to Mark about the Ferris wheel encounter and didn't want to make their two friends uncomfortable with such an overt display of affection.

Sensing his hesitancy, Noelle took it for boyish shyness and undertook to initiate on her own. She extended her neck and gave Josh a peck on the cheek. Josh smiled and then looked across the seating cubicle the foursome was in to gauge their companions' reaction. Mark saw the peck and offered an enthusiastic smile and raise of his eyebrows. Elise responded by blowing an imaginary kiss in their direction. Feeling thus freed from his caution, Josh turned toward Noelle and returned the gesture ... only on her lips.

"Ooh la la," Elise teased with a big grin. Then, almost as if she had sensed Josh's trepidation, she said, "It's okay, Josh, we're well aware you two are in serious 'like.'"

After emerging from the tunnel and back into the light of day, the track took a lazy sweep along a bend in the river. The waterway below them to the east was rugged and full of giant boulders. The cascading flow rushing over the rocks created a mist that rose and mingled with the steam coming from the engine's smokestack. It was a magical combination, like the breath of God coming together with the breath of man for their mutual pleasure.

Josh pulled his phone out.

"Hey, you two lean to your right a little, and I'll get your picture with the river and tunnel in the backdrop."

Mark leaned over so that his head was slightly outside the edge of the train car, and the wind blew his hair back. Elise, too, leaned over and placed her head on Mark's chest.

"Okay, on three," Josh instructed. "Un, deux, trois."

He clicked the capture button and created an instantly viewable digital image.

"Wow, this is a great shot," Josh exclaimed as he admired his own handiwork. "Here, take a look."

The picture was indeed frame-worthy. The faces were perfectly positioned just off-center, which drew the observer's eyes beyond the bright smiles and to the river and mountain scenery behind the train. The camera's focus on the two friends' faces was crisp, but the background was also clear and distinct.

"Wow, Josh, you have a hidden talent," Elise complimented. "I'd like a copy of that photo before you leave."

Then after handing Josh's phone back to him, she pulled her own out.

"Hey, let me take one of you and Noelle, too."

Josh put his arm around Noelle, and the two smiled naturally. They waited, holding their pose, until Elise interrupted.

"It'll be better if you both remove your sunglasses," she suggested.

While they did so, and unbeknownst to the couple, Elise took a series of pictures capturing the candid, unrehearsed exchange of laughter between the two. She wouldn't show those to them as she was planning to later create a collage to surprise her friends with as a memento of their time together.

Following another several twists and turns alongside the mountain slope, the de l'Ardeche came to a slow stop at a tiny village where the group watched the engine uncouple and then spin 180 degrees on a turnstile to ready for the return trip. During the turnaround break, the foursome purchased an array of fruit from a makeshift, open-air stand near the river and then found a shady spot under a yawning oak tree and sat down to eat their snack.

"These mountains are amazing. I feel like we're in the Alps or something," Mark said. "I almost expect Maria and the Von Trapp kids to descend from a peak and start singing to us."

"I did that play once when I was in lycée classique, which would be what you call high school," Elise offered. "I played the lead role of Maria."

"I didn't know that," Noelle said, surprised. "I was in the Sound of Music play, too, during my senior year. I played the role of Liesl. That's amazing. I didn't know that about you, Elise. We've been friends for all these years and are still learning things about each other."

Noelle then stood up and spun around the trunk of the great oak with school girl charm. "I am 16 going on 17, I know that I'm naive, fellows I meet may tell me I'm sweet, and I willingly believe."

Josh stood to his feet, "Bravo, bravo!" he exclaimed, clapping his hands politely.

Then, to everyone's surprise, he began to sing himself. "You are 16 going on 17; fellows will fall in line, eager young lads and rogues and cads will offer you food and wine."

Noelle clasped her hands to her chest in astonishment. "No way! You were once, Rolf?"

"Well, it was not one of my prouder moments because I can't sing very well. But yes, when I was a junior in high school, I happened to be taking a drama class for an easy elective, and not enough guys tried out for the production, so I kind of got volunteered by my teacher. It was pretty fun, though. But the Liesl I played opposite was nowhere near as pretty or talented as you, Noelle."

The train whistle blew loudly, signaling the time for the return trip was upon them.

Mark stood and, in a deep, authoritative voice with a hint of a forced European accent, said, "Well come along, Maria and children, we should be making our way to the train now."

The three stopped and stared.

"Yeah, me too," Mark sheepishly admitted. "I was the one guy who actually tried out for the play Josh mentioned, so I got the male lead of the Baron -- small world, huh?"

Even though it traversed the same path, the return trip to the main station was equally as exciting. Things always look so dissimilar when coming from an opposite direction.

After they disembarked, they wandered back into the gift shop. After a few minutes, Josh stepped outside through the back door to stroll through the garden. The flowers were all in brilliant bloom, especially the lavender patch back near the fence that separated the manicured area from the wild forest beyond. A small path of paver stones meandered into the lavender patch, and when Josh reached the middle, he sat down. The breeze had picked up to the point that the knee-high purple blooms were frolicking vigorously. Josh gently brushed his hands over the blooms and then held them to his nose and inhaled deeply. He closed his eyes and sighed as a satisfied smile creased his face.

Noelle poked her head out of the back door of the shop, looking for Josh. She saw just the top of his head peeking up in the middle of the lavender field. She stood still and observed as the stems of purple waved around him. Noelle watched in pleasant wonder as the man she was falling for seemed so content to sit alone in a field of flowers.

Lord, he is fantastic. Who would have ever imagined I would fall for someone so in love with flowers. Guys like this just don't exist, but yet, here he is. Thank you for these days we have had. I know our future is extremely unsure, but that's okay. Today is enough for me.

CHAPTER 13

Noelle's mother had dinner ready when the group returned from the day's explorations, and they took turns extolling their favorite moments. Noelle was mostly quiet, choosing instead to absorb as much as she could from the others' stories. She found herself strangely and utterly content with just listening. Having not been along, of course, her mother did the same, and more than once, the two women's eyes met with a knowing glance.

Changing the subject from the day's activities, Josh interjected, "Chole, I don't know if Noelle told you, but when we were in Lyon, we met an old family friend, Aubert DuBois. We got a tour of his vineyard and winery. It was really cool."

"She did mention it, yes, Josh. And I understand Aubert is doing well, though now in his 80s. He's been a faithful friend to our family ever since I was a little girl. I remember playing in his vineyard. There was a tree house in an old oak in the Pinot Noir section where I spent hours with my brother and sister. Those were good days."

"Mom, one thing I didn't tell you was that Mr. DuBois told us a story about how he once proposed to Grandmere," Noelle said.

"What?" Chloe exclaimed. "I've never heard about that. When in the world did that happen?"

"He said it was about 12 years ago," Noelle continued, "long after his wife had passed away. He seemed so sad when he told us the story like he still has feelings for Grandmere. It was sweet and tragic at the same time. Grandmere confirmed it to me as well. She said she couldn't marry him because she was still married to Grandpere in her heart. Again, sweet but tragic. I encouraged her to reconnect with Aubert if only to renew their friendship and be open from there. She said she'd think about it. I meant to tell you earlier but just didn't get to that part of the story. I think it would be good if you would encourage her also, Mom. I know she'd listen to you."

"Well, I don't know," Chloe hesitated. "I mean, Grandmere is 82 now, and I'm not sure romance is something she should be pursuing at her age."

"But, Mom, it doesn't have to be 'romance' necessarily. I believe they're both lonely, and what harm would there be in rekindling their friendship? Grandmere confided in me that she stopped spending time with Aubert only after he asked her about marriage. She didn't want to lead him on. But I get the sense that if he had known that would be her reaction, he probably would have never asked. His love for her was deeper than just romance. They were best friends, and now they are both alone without each other."

"Yes, I suppose you may be right, Noelle. Thank you for sharing this with me. I will pray about it, and if I feel a sense of peace, I will talk with your grandmere. I know what it's like to be alone as a widow, and it's not easy. People treat you differently. I can't really describe it, but it's almost like they think you may be so fragile that anything they might say or do could break you. It's funny, though, because what makes you fragile is the feeling of exile itself. I've never pined for another man, but close friends have been few and far between. Other than my ladies group at church, my life has been pretty sequestered. That's why I appreciate it so much when you or your sister come to visit. I am still praying that by some miracle, you'll find a job here in Avignon so that we can be closer again."

"I know that is your dream, Mom. And I miss you, too. I honestly don't know what the Lord may have in store for me after this summer. I'm just kind of taking things a day at a time, you know?" Noelle said, offering a knowing smile and shrug of resignation that her mother fully understood.

The following morning Josh and Noelle rose early and went on a walk together through the neighborhood. She showed him her favorite park as a child and her primary school, and where her best friend once lived. They walked along the tree-lined streets and enjoyed the morning chorus of birds as the sun crept into view in the east. At the end of the lane, they walked through the cemetery behind the church the family attended, and she showed Josh the resting places of her father and brother.

"I try to come here every time I visit," Noelle said softly. "I miss them both very much, but when I'm here, sometimes we talk, and somehow my heart is always lighter when I think about where they are now. My sorrow was their joy, being born into heaven, you know? I sometimes think death is maybe a bit like birth. We spend a season in the womb where everything is safe and warm and peaceful, and then we experience a traumatic transition into a very different place and begin our season of life here on earth. Then, when we die, it's almost like a repeat of the process, a traumatic event that leads to a transition to a different place to begin another season -- the ultimate season. And if one has been spiritually born again while here on earth, then that next season is indeed a glorious one, and I can only imagine it being a joy for those who make the journey. We who are left behind grieve, not for them, but for us. We are sad and alone without our loved ones here, but the truth is our sadness will only last a short time, and then we will be reunited with them in eternal joy. I look forward to that joy someday. Not that I'm in any particular hurry to go, but, I mean, we all go sooner or later. And I'm confident I'll see my brother and father again, and Grandpere, too. I have no idea how I'll recognize them, but I think somehow I will. It's all a great mystery, but one I'm confident in."

Josh said nothing in response, not having any direct experience with death. He just held Noelle's hand and listened intently to the wisdom emanating from the girl he was falling in love with.

On the way back, Noelle suggested they stop in the park and swing for a while. At first, their sense of fun incited a friendly competition of 'who can get the highest,' but then gradually, the swinging mellowed, and they slowed to an even pace so that they swung in unison and could talk.

"I hate that we have to leave today," Josh finally said. "This weekend has been perfect, this summer has been perfect, and all because Mark was bold enough to ask for directions at the metro station. It's funny how God works to bring people together, isn't it? Noelle, I don't want today to be the end. I've been thinking about it, and I'd really like to see you one more time. I wondered if perhaps we might come to Versailles for one more weekend together just before we fly home. That would be in about three weeks. Do you think we could do that?"

"Josh, I would love nothing more. I'm sure Elise would be thrilled at the idea. Let's talk about it and make plans over breakfast. This is exciting. I've been dreading today so much, but now this idea has made it almost tolerable. I'm still going to miss you, though."

"I know, I'm going to miss you, too. But let's not dwell on the time we'll be apart; let's focus on the time when we'll be together again. Come on, let's fly high in the sky one more time, and then we'll head back to the house," Josh said as he began pumping his legs in earnest to make his swing go higher.

When they had finished swinging, they strolled back to the house arm in arm, neither in a hurry nor seeking to drag out the time. Each had a happy lilt in their step at the prospect of another meeting together in the weeks to come.

Before going inside, while standing on the front porch, Josh stopped and kissed Noelle.

"I love you, you know?"

"I love you too, Josh. I'd have never dreamed I would fall in love like this, this summer, to an

American, to you. I don't really understand it. I just know it's true."

Mark and Elise were both excited about planning another weekend in Versailles, and as the girls waved goodbye to the boys at the train station, everyone was all smiles.

"I had expected to be crying this morning," Noelle said as the train disappeared from view. "But here I stand as happy as can be. I'm in love, Elise. Josh told me he loved me this morning during our walk. Can you believe that? I'm in love!" she giggled.

"Yeah, actually I can believe it," Elise said, smiling at her friend. "You two are so perfect together. And the fact that we'll see them again in a couple of weeks is just icing on the cake. Not to douse the joy of the moment, but have you mentioned anything to Josh yet about, you know?"

"No, I couldn't bring myself to. And besides, I have a doctor's appointment this afternoon, and I'm praying for some answers so that maybe I won't ever have to tell him. I'm praying for healing, Elise. I know God can do that, and so that's what I'm praying for. Why would He have brought Josh into my life right now if He was going to take me home? That wouldn't make any sense, would it? No, I don't want Josh to worry over something neither of us can control. We'll see how things are in a couple of weeks and what our future may or may not hold. Then I'll decide what to tell him; I promise."

After lunch, Elise and Chloe both accompanied Noelle to see the doctor whose office was in the southeast section of old town near the square. They walked through the carnival area by the river as they approached the east gate of the wall.

As they walked underneath the Ferris wheel, Noelle said, "Josh kissed me at the top of the wheel on Friday night. I don't think either of us was quite expecting it to happen, but looking back on it, it really was incredibly romantic."

"I like Josh a lot," Chloe said. "And I can tell he thinks the world of you, Noelle. I can see it in his eyes when he looks at you. It's that same look your father used to give me when we were dating. So beware, my little one, I think an American may be falling in love with you."

The three women giddily chatted as they walked through the square, past the local church, and then past a carousel that was full of squealing children racing their steeds to an imaginary finish line.

"I loved riding the carousel when I was little," Noelle remarked.

"We've got a few minutes before your appointment; why don't we ride it now?" Elise suggested. "I think it looks fun."

After waiting through one more round of riders, the three ladies were near the front of the line, and so could sit three abreast on the ride. As the horses bobbed up and down and the music played loudly, smiles dominated their faces. Noelle and Elise bantered about plans with the boys in Versailles, and Chloe mostly watched and listened. As she did, her vision of Noelle morphed to that of a little girl whose legs dangled loosely over the saddled beast, being far too short to reach the stirrups, and whose chubby little white-knuckled hands were gripping onto the polished bronze pole for dear life.

Lord, I pray you'll provide a miracle for Noelle, so she can enjoy love as I did once. She's such a wonderful girl, and she deserves a bit of joy on this earth before you take her home.

One of the benefits of living in a city of Avignon's size was access to excellent medical care. The hospital was one of only three teaching hospitals in the country, and it had a stellar reputation for being on the cutting edge of medical technology and experimental trials. The hospital lobby was an energetic hub of activity, with interns and residents flitting here and there while following more senior doctors on their rounds. Noelle told the front desk attendant about her appointment, who then dutifully picked up a phone and rang the office of Doctor Philip Brodeur.

"Yes, doctor, your two o'clock, Ms. Lepage, is here ... Yes, doctor, I'll send her right up," the attendant spoke into the receiver.

"He is ready to see you," the attendant said to Noelle as she set the phone back into its cradle. "But instead of his office, the doctor asks that you meet him in the diagnostic center. He has scheduled some tests as a precursor to your consultation. Please follow the hallway down to your left. The green dash marks on the floor will take you right to the center."

The three women followed the trail of green markings and found themselves being greeted by Doctor Brodeur in less than two minutes.

He was a youngish looking man with dark eyes and just a wisp of grey at the temples. He was fit and flashed a runway model's grin.

"It is good to see you again, Noelle," Brodeur said, shaking her hand. "I have some positive news to share with you, but first, we want to do a quick blood draw and get an updated MRI. Please come this way. After we get the tests done, we can chat."

"Mom, why don't you and Elise wait here, and I'll come back for you in a few minutes," Noelle suggested.

"Okay, honey. We'll be right here," Chloe said.

Noelle and the doctor disappeared down the hallway to the right, leaving the two women alone together.

"What the doctor said sounds hopeful," Elise said as she sat down on a dark green hard-shell chair.

"I know!" Chloe echoed the upbeat tone. "I've been praying for this appointment and am hoping for a miracle. I know the diagnosis remains a mystery, but I can't help but fear the worst given the history with Noelle's brother and father. That just wouldn't be fair to Noelle. She seems so alive these days, and I can see jeune amour in her eyes. She should be able to know the joy of marriage and children as I have. Please, Elise, will you join me in praying for my baby?"

The two women held hands and prayed together for God's mercy, protection, and healing. When they finished, Elise looked up and saw tears rolling down Chloe's cheeks and thought the love of a mother for her child is among the strongest emotions a human can know on this earth.

Twenty minutes later, Noelle returned, and once reunited, the three followed an orange trail of floor markings to the doctors' office wing of the hospital. Once again, Brodeur caught them as they were approaching the small lobby area, and with his pearly white grin, invited them to accompany him into his private office.

Stopping at the door, he asked, "Excuse me, Noelle, but do you wish for your friend to join us, or would you prefer that she wait in the galley across the hallway? I can have some juice or coffee brought in for her."

"Oh, no, Elise already knows everything. She is my best friend, and I would prefer that she join us. Thank you for asking, though," Noelle replied.

"Of course, as you wish. Ladies, please take a seat and let's talk," Brodeur directed as he stepped around his desk and took a seat facing the three women.

The office was relatively austere for such an important physician as Phillip Brodeur. His reputation as a diagnostician and brain surgeon was known, not just in France but also throughout Europe. He had developed a life-saving procedure at the age of 35 and was well on his way to becoming one of the most famous physicians in France. Noelle was exceedingly fortunate to be receiving care from this man.

Brodeur began, "So, I understand from your mother that you are summering in Versailles. Lovely place. I did a portion of my residency at the Hospital Mignot just outside of the town. How have you been feeling since our last visit, Noelle? Have you had any more episodes?"

"No nothing major. A few headaches and one almost fainting spell, but that may have been due to the bit of wine I drank at lunch on an empty stomach."

"Ha, yes, I'm afraid that malady can be very common to man," the doctor replied lightly. "I'm glad to hear your report because that, combined with your labs today, suggests that your condition seems to continue to be in a state of remission … non-progressing arrest.

"As we've discussed before, the markers and symptoms you are experiencing are very similar to those experienced by your father and brother, but from what little we know, even though seemingly hereditary, it seems the condition you have manifests uniquely in each patient. For example, I see a lady down south who is 54 years old and has been relatively stable and living a normal life since I first began treating her eight years ago. Also, we've had some very encouraging research breakthroughs lately. A close colleague of mine has developed an experimental drug right here at the hospital that is showing good potential to arrest fulminant meningioma's and in a few cases even to reverse it."

Brodeur paused to let the implications of what he was saying sink in.

"So, I see this as a possibility for you, Noelle. The drug seems to work more effectively on young people than old. For example, when we tried it on the 54-year old I mentioned, she had some pretty adverse reactions. We don't understand everything, and it's still experimental, but we are preparing to run a monitored trial, and I'd like to invite you to consider being a part of it. You wouldn't know if you were actually receiving the drug or just a placebo. Of course, we would know, and we would be closely monitoring everyone's progress or lack thereof. You could participate from Versailles as the doctors there are familiar with the research, and if an issue arose, you could see them immediately. The actual monitoring is fairly simple. One blood draw each week and an MRI every other week. Much the same as you did here today. And, best of all, the trial is being funded by a grant, so there would be no cost to you. What do you think?"

As Brodeur spoke, Noelle found herself leaning farther and farther forward in her chair. Her mind was swimming with the flood of new information, but the words she kept hearing over and over were reversal and normal life.

"Is there any downside?" Noelle finally spoke.

"As far as we know, just the possibility of more frequent episodes, but we'd likely see that happening early on, if it was going to happen at all, and we could alter course at that time.

"Noelle, I know you may be thinking why change course at all right now since you seem to be in remission, but I should remind you that this disease can flare up with no warning, and if it does, this drug might not be as effective, and it could be too late to stop it. The whole condition is so undefined and unknown. I think you're an excellent candidate for this trial, and I want to encourage you to consider it. We will be starting next week, so I'll need your answer by Friday."

"Doctor, this sounds very hopeful," Chloe said breathlessly. "This might even be the miracle I've been praying for."

"I'm not exactly a praying man myself," Brodeur said, "but when it comes to the mysteries of medicine, I have no problem accepting the idea of an omniscient being or God who may be greater than science. I've seen things that I cannot explain, and we have scientific evidence that hope and faith can be contributing factors in recovery from illness. So, yes, keep praying for that miracle, Mrs. LePage. And Noelle, let me know your decision as soon as you can."

During the drive home, the girls weighed the pros and cons of joining the trial. As exciting as the prospect for healing seemed, Noelle harbored an uneasiness.

"I can't put my finger on it, but something he said about increased episodes has me a little spooked, at least in the short term. I mean, I feel like things are really clicking with Josh, and I'd hate to get sick when he came back to see us in Versailles," Noelle said.

"I hear you, girl," Elise responded, "but the doctor also said your condition could flare up at any time, and then it could be too late to start the treatment. With such hope at your fingertips, do you want to take that chance for the sake of one weekend with a guy you just met? I know you like him a lot, but I think you need to put your longer-term glasses on."

"Mom, what do you think?" Noelle asked tepidly.

"I think I have to agree with Elise. The long-term is more important than the short-term, and if Josh loves you, I'm sure he would agree as well. Plus, remember the doctor said if you suffered any adverse side effects, you could stop the trial. I've been praying for a miracle, Noelle, and I think this might be it. I would encourage you to sign up, honey. Who knows when they might start another trial."

"Okay, okay, you're both right. I'll call Dr. Brodeur in the morning," Noelle said.

"Are you going to tell Josh?" Elise asked.

"No, I'd rather not. I don't want him to worry, and everything is still so up in the air. If things are going well, maybe I'll share this with him in Versailles. We'll see."

When they walked into the house, the small red message light on the phone was flashing. Chloe casually pushed the button to listen as they went about settling in.

"Hello, Chloe, this is your mother," the message machine reported.

All three women stopped what they were doing and moved in to hover over the phone and listen to what was about to be said.

"I don't remember if Wello is still there or not, but if she isn't, please make sure she hears this news.

"At Noelle's urging, I called Aubert DuBois, and he and I met for lunch in town yesterday. It was a wonderful lunch, and just as Wello had predicted, once I let my guard down, our friendship picked up right where we left it 12 years ago. We ended up talking until the dinner crowd started showing up at the cafe. We had so much to catch up on and so many stories to share. It was the best afternoon I've spent in a very long time. Anyway, I just wanted to mention the good news and thank Wello for sharing her wisdom with me. You've got quite a daughter there, hon. She takes after her mom. Love you. Call me when you can, and we'll chat. Bye."

The machine clicked off, and Noelle clasped her hands together in classic LePage style.

"Ooh! That's the best news! I'm so happy for Grandmere and Aubert, too. Maybe they'll find vieil amour after all."

CHAPTER 14

When Elise and Noelle returned to Versailles, the height of the summer heat and the summer tourist season were in full swing. Both girls worked long days and were almost too exhausted at the end of each to talk much. Both received regular texts from the guys about their continuing trek through France, but the messages gradually became less and less about what they were seeing and more about their upcoming return visit to Versailles and their planned trip back to the States.

The Monday before the weekend that the guys were scheduled to arrive, Noelle was working a late shift at the cafe. Only a few tables remained occupied as she began the nightly routine of one final surface wipe down and setting the chairs upside down on the tops of the tables so the floors would be clear for the maintenance crew to come in after midnight and machine mop and wax them. She also began restocking the condiment bar and generally readying the place for the morning rush.

Noelle had been feeling pretty good about the experimental trial drug she'd been on for two weeks and hadn't experienced any episodes. She was in regular communication with Dr. Brodeur and the team at Hospital Mignot on the outskirts of Versailles. All things seemed to be going perfectly, and her hopes were buoyed. She was even beginning to look forward to telling Josh about her condition and the optimistic outlook of the trial.

When the final customers finished paying their bill and slipped out the front door, Noelle followed them to lock up. When she turned to go back to her restocking duties, a sudden wave of nausea overtook her like a bullet train. Though it had been quite a while since she had an episode, Noelle knew what was happening, and to avoid an uncontrolled fall, which could lead to serious injury, she immediately dropped to her knees. She couldn't stop her head from spinning, and she began to feel like she might throw up. Oddly, her first thought was regret for creating a mess that the night janitorial crew would have to contend with. Then, just as fast as it came, the spinning stopped, and Noelle was able to catch her breath. She went from her knees to a seated position on the floor and dropped her head into her lap while taking deep breaths and trying to steady herself. She closed her eyes and prayed.

Lord, what is this? Things have been going so good.

In her head, Noelle did the math to calculate the time since her last pill, and then she tried to recall whether she'd missed one over the past few days.

She was desperately trying to find an answer to the unanswerable. Then, as she tried to concentrate, she felt the pain -- the pain that always presaged the migraine-like devastation that accompanied a severe episode.

Lord, no. Please hold this back. Please don't let this happen. I'm begging you.

Her frustration and pleading soon gave way to fear, and Noelle tried to stand back up.

I need to get to my phone and call Elise, she thought.

When she stood, however, the spinning wave returned. She felt like she was on the Mad Hatter's Tea Cup ride at Disneyland Paris, and some demonic seven-year-old boy wouldn't stop turning the spinner. She grabbed a chair to steady herself as she willed her way to the back room and her purse.

Her head began to pound. The suddenness of it all took her by surprise. The headaches had never come on so fast after the nausea. Something about this episode was different from previous ones. In between the waves of tumult, Noelle strained to make sense of it all, but the pain quickly taxed all the stamina she had left after the long day on her feet working at the cafe. Once she retrieved her purse, it was all she could do to control herself long enough to sit back down on the floor. Her legs wobbled, and she involuntarily put her hands to her ears in a futile effort to squeeze out the pain. Her eyes began to twitch, and she writhed in pain and pressed harder on her ears as if trying to soften a thundering noise in the room, but the only noise to be heard was a deafening silence. Finally, the pain overtook her, and she cried out audibly. The night manager heard her from the back room and came to investigate.

"Noelle, oh my God; are you alright? Noelle, what's happening? What can I do?" the manager asked anxiously.

Noelle was now hyperventilating on top of everything else that was happening to her.

"My phone," she uttered, half delirious. "Call my friend, Elise -- in my favorites."

Noelle slowly laid herself on the floor and curled up into the fetal position. Nothing she did, no position she could find, no prayer she could utter helped. It felt as if her head was going to explode.

In the hallucinatory state brought on by the intensity of the pain, Noelle imagined an explosion and the gray mass of her brain being sprayed all over the restaurant's walls and windows. She then looked down from above at herself lying on the floor. Her eyes and face were intact, frozen in a scream, but the top of her head was gone, and her skull was empty. She then saw a tiny man inside her head where her brain had been. He was dressed in a marching band uniform and was banging loudly and rhythmically on a big bass drum. He beat the instrument so hard that he was sweating all over it, and the drum was dripping wet. With each strike, the drum sprayed water out of Noelle's head, and it began dripping down into her eyes. Then the water turned to blood, and her face was covered in red. Then the crimson ooze began to cover her clothes and then the floor. Blood was everywhere. She could feel the pulse of her heart increase in an attempt to accommodate the blood loss, and suddenly she felt a constricting in her chest. She was sure it was a heart attack. She gasped for air but found none. To stem the tide of blood flowing from her empty skull, someone had put a plastic bag over her head and face. She was asphyxiating. She emitted a blood-curdling scream when the pain reached its zenith, and then everything went black.

***

When she awoke, Noelle was in the warm cocoon of a hospital blanket. She had been sleeping in a private room under the watchful eye of an intern for more than six hours. The room was painted a beige color, and the recessed ceiling lights cast a too-bright glare. Noelle squinted to shield from the light but was afraid to move any other part of her body for fear the pain would return. She was terrified the pain would return because she didn't understand exactly where it had come from in the first place. She strained to remember what had happened, but her recollection stopped at locking the front door of the cafe.

She could hear her own breathing. It sounded calm and steady, which was reassuring. The only other sounds in the room were the continuous blowing of the air conditioner and the vital sign monitors' beeping. She suddenly realized she had several contraptions connected to her arms, and there was an oxygen tube attached to her nose. She slowly released her squint as her pupils adjusted to the white light in the room. She tried again to remember what had happened to her but still came up empty. She began taking inventory of her extremities, first wiggling her fingers and toes and then slowly moving her arms and legs. She then moved her head very slowly, not wanting to bring the headache back accidentally. As soon as she did, she heard a chair move from somewhere in a corner of the room and then a person walking toward her.

"Noelle, are you awake?"

It was Elise. She had been waiting at her friend's bedside since she was admitted around midnight. The night manager had found Elise's number and hit the autodial about the same time Noelle passed out. Elise had heard her friend's scream over the phone and panicked. She called for an ambulance and met the emergency team at the restaurant ten minutes later. They found Noelle on her side, lying near a pool of vomit, soaked in sweat and pasty white. The EMTs quickly stabilized her, put her on a backboard, and whisked her away to the hospital. The whole ordeal took less than 15 minutes.

"Elise? Is that you? Where are we?" Noelle uttered.

"We're at the hospital, Noelle. I'm so glad to hear you speak. You gave us all quite a scare last night. The doctors say they don't know what happened because all the tests they've run have come back normal. Do you remember what happened?"

"I'm trying to, but I keep coming up blank. Maybe the Lord is protecting me by blocking my memory. The only thing I do remember is a mind-blowing headache. Way worse than anything I've ever experienced before. I think it was an episode related to my condition, but it was different this time. For a moment there, I thought I was going to die. Elise, it was so frightening. I think I need to talk to Dr. Brodeur. I'm confused."

"I wonder if it might have something to do with the medication you're taking." Elise commented.

"Maybe, I don't know, but I sure want to find out. That was 'the' scariest thing I've ever experienced."

As she spoke, her memory was creeping back bit by bit, and Noelle began to feel a chill come over her. Then a tear leaked from her eye. She tried to wipe it away before Elise saw it, but she was too slow.

"Hey, Noelle, it'll be alright. You've come through this, and Dr. Brodeur has taken you off the trial drugs. You weren't on the placebo; you were taking the real deal. He said there had been a few other people on the drug that this has happened to. They're going to halt the trial for now because they need to do more research. Things will normalize for you now. He said you should be feeling better by tomorrow, but they want to keep you here in the hospital for the day, just to be safe."

"They're halting the trial?" Noelle moaned. "Where's the hope in that? Where's the miracle my mother's been praying for? Things will 'normalize?' What does that even mean for me? That I'm not going to feel sick again ... until I do ... or until I die as my brother and father did?"

She began to sob, and then she started to cry. Elise took Noelle in her arms and tried to console her friend, but it was no use. Noelle was finally coming to terms with the reality that she might not live long enough to experience jeune amour, let alone vieil amour. Her world was crashing down. The agony of the unknown had finally crushed her spirit. She'd lost the battle and given up her optimism. All seemed lost. Her one hope, her miracle, had been taken away, halted. Halted was such a sterile medical term for decimated. She hadn't released her emotions until this moment. Noelle had been pressing them back, concealing them, bottling them up, and hiding them behind a facade of youthful confidence. All that was gone now and everything came spilling over like a swollen reservoir over a cracking dam -- a torrent pouring out onto the shoulder of her best friend.

Elise said nothing further. She just held Noelle close, and the two young women from Versailles cried until they were out of tears.

***

They planned to meet Mark and Josh at the same spot they had met them during their first visit to Versailles, near the turnstile at the train station. The train was running late, so the girls had a few extra minutes to chat.

"Okay, Elise, now remember your promise; if anyone says anything about what happened the other night, it will be me. I know I have to tell Josh before he leaves for home; that's only fair.

But I need to find the right time, okay? It's my life, and he's my love, so please let me do this, will you?"

"You know I will, Noelle. You know I will. You are the bravest girl I have ever known, and I know telling Josh isn't going to be easy. But once he knows, then he can join the prayer chorus for you, and it can't hurt to have America praying for you, too."

"Thanks, Elise. You are the best friend ever. I love you, girl. You know that, right?"

"Yeah, I know. And, by the way, your new beret looks too cute on you.

Before Noelle could respond to the compliment, Elise suddenly exclaimed, "Hey, the arrival light just turned green! That means their train is here! I'm so excited to see them!"

"Joining in the enthusiasm, and projecting a little of her old chipper self, Noelle added, "I know they're excited, too! Josh's texts and emails have been non-stop about seeing us. I think he quit talking about wine more than a week ago."

"If I had to venture a guess, I think his priorities may have shifted just a bit," Elise teased her friend. "And why wouldn't they? Heck, if I were a guy, I'd make you a priority over wine any day. You're quite the catch, Noelle."

"Yeah, yeah, yeah ... enough of that, here they come. Hi guys!" Noelle yelled as soon as she saw Josh and Mark.

Unlike the last time they met at the train station, this time Josh wasn't hesitant at all about showing his affection for Noelle. He dropped his backpack and gave her a warm hug and in the process knocked her beret askew.

"I missed you, Noelle. I missed you a ton. I'm so glad we have this one final weekend together. And sometime this weekend, I want to talk about you maybe coming to California at some point. I mean, I've met your entire family, so I think it's only fair that you come and meet mine. Don't you?"

Talk of such future time together caught Noelle off guard. She had purposed in her mind to only focus on the here and now while Josh was with her. Thinking about the future only led to a sense of dread and uncertainty. But now was not the time to explain that to Josh, not when he first got off the train. She'd find the time later, a private time when she could tell him the whole story.

"We'll see about that, Josh," she chuckled as if he was joking. "But I've got some huge news," Noelle said, trying to change the subject. "But it's too big to tell you here in the train station. We want to take you two out to dinner. Are you hungry?"

"I don't know about Josh, but I am," Mark answered quickly.

"Alright then, let's go," Noelle exclaimed, anxious to move the conversation along. "We discovered this new place that has outdoor seating next to a beautiful park. It is quintessential French. You're going to love it. It's a tad bit on the spendy side, but if we hurry, we can get there in time for the early bird special, and we should be guaranteed a good seat overlooking the park. Come on."

Josh was left disappointed for the seeming slight to his suggestion about California but didn't want to make a big deal about it and risk dampening the reunion, so he decided he would pursue the matter again privately at a later time. The four piled into Elise's dad's SUV and headed south, away from the town center. They parked across the street from the cafe, and seeing several tables empty, Elise suggested they take a quick stroll into the park first.

"This place is called Parc du Domaine de Madame Elisabeth, or Elisabeth's Park for short," Elise began in her best tour guide voice. "Elisabeth was Louis XVI's sister, and the park was a gift from him to her. It's not overrun by tourists like the palace is. And there is an orchard and even a herd of sheep. It's very rural and quiet and private. I've come to enjoy it very much. It's kind of a local's place."

"This land was a gift to a sister? Wow, now that's what I call brotherly love. This place is stunning. And the tourists haven't discovered it yet, huh?" Mark asked.

"Not really. I'm not sure why. It's not all that far from the palace." Elise continued. "It is such an amazing find that I've been tempted to mention it at the end of my tours, but I haven't. I guess maybe I'm a little selfish about it."

"But you're showing it to us?" Josh said.

"Of course, but you're not tourists anymore, Josh. You are friends. The best kind of friends," Elise warmly replied.

"Well, come on. Let's get a table. Maybe we can walk farther into the park after dinner. There is a beautiful chateau in the back and a lake, too. It will make you fall even more in love with Versailles."

Hard to imagine that, Josh thought to himself. *I'm already pretty much in love with this place ... and with Noelle.*

After ordering their meals, Josh sipped on his lemon water and asked, "At the train station, you said you had big news to tell us. Okay, so what is it? The suspense is killing me."

Noelle beamed as she launched into the tale. "Do you remember, just after you left Avignon, that I emailed you about what Grandmere told us -- that she was going to see Aubert?"

"Yes, I think that was the first email I opened when we got to Cannes," Josh responded. "That was huge news!"

"Well, it gets better," Noelle went on. "After their lunch, they met again at church the following Sunday, and then they started seeing each other somewhat regularly. I talked with Grandmere several times, and she seemed very upbeat and positive about it. In fact, I've never heard her so animated. You remember how gentle and polite she was. When she spoke of her dates with Aubert, she was almost giddy.

"So anyway, she called me last night to report that Aubert had invited her to dinner at the gazebo. She shared that she had some reservations about the idea given their history there, but she decided to throw caution to the wind and take a chance. She said, and I quote, 'I should do what Wello would do if she were me.' How about that!

Grandmere was channeling me," Noelle laughed out loud.

"She described the dinner as being nearly identical to the moment they had shared 12 years ago."

"No way," a spellbound Mark whispered under his breath. "Aubert was going to venture 'there' again? Risk everything again? Wow, he must really love Celeste."

"That was my reaction, too," Noelle agreed. "But then, according to Grandmere, after dinner while they sat watching the sunset, she said she was nervously awaiting the moment of truth, so to speak, but it never came. Aubert just continued talking about their past and his hope that their renewed friendship would be long-lasting. So, Grandmere said she decided to take control ... and ... 'she' popped the question!"

"Wait? What? Celeste popped what question?" Josh leaned in.

"My grandmere, the prim and proper matriarch of our family, that demure 82-year-old well-mannered lady you met in Lyon, pulled a modern woman move. She asked Aubert to marry her!" Noelle erupted.

Both boys dropped their jaws in shock.

"She asked him?" Mark said incredulously.

"Yes! And he said yes! And they're going to get married next weekend!" Noelle erupted again in glee while clasping her hands to her heart.

"Mouth still agape, Josh struggled to compose himself. "What? Next weekend? Are you serious?"

"I couldn't make this up. It's true, every single word of it. And when Grandmere called to tell me the story, she asked … she asked, if I would be her maid of honor."

At this point, Noelle began to tear up. "Me, she wants me to stand by her side at her wedding. I just can't believe it," she said, stammering.

Seeing her eyes moisten with tears of joy, Josh felt a lump begin to form in his throat. He stared intensely into her eyes, and there, in the midst of such blessed news, their souls met and interlocked. Jeune amour, far more profound than either had felt before or even dared dream of, swept through their beings and lifted them to a higher place -- a place reserved for only the truest of romance.

After a pause, during which everyone simultaneously caught their breath and wiped at their eyes, Noelle recomposed herself and asked,

"Josh, I know you have plane tickets home next Monday. But is there any way you could postpone the trip for a week so that you could come to the wedding? It's not just me asking. Aubert specifically invited all four of us to the wedding. He said that if we hadn't visited, none of this would have happened. He says he owes his happiness to us. He said he'd cover whatever cost there might be to change your tickets. Josh, Aubert practically begged us all to come. They will be married under the gazebo. Can you imagine it? It brings tears to my eyes just to think of it."

Josh sat numbly silent; trying to process the invitation they'd been extended to attend a wedding at DuBois-Estelle, a wedding at a romantic gazebo in the Chardonnay section of one of the most famous vineyards in France, a wedding that would testify to the resolution of unrequited love, a wedding of two such wonderful people, and another weekend with Noelle.

"Josh, please say yes. Please say you'll come."

"Mark?" Josh whispered to his friend.

Mark just smiled.

"Noelle, yes, yes, a thousand times yes! Tell Aubert and Celeste we wouldn't miss it for the world!"

CHAPTER 15

The next morning Josh called Elise's cell phone. She was already awake and making coffee in the kitchen when it rang. She answered quickly on the first ring so as not to disturb Noelle, who was still sleeping in the other room.

"Hello, Josh?" she said, looking at the caller I.D. on her screen. "You're up awfully early. Couldn't sleep thinking about our big day in Versailles, eh?"

"Well, kind of," Josh answered. "Elise, the reason I'm calling is that I have a favor to ask."

"Anything, Josh, of course, this sounds kind of mysterious."

"Not so much a mystery really, but a touch of romance maybe, so here's what I'm thinking ...."

***

After a leisurely morning at the farmer's market followed by lunch and then a long walk in Elisabeth's Park, the group separated, the girls went back to Elise's house and the boys to their hotel, to freshen up for an early dinner to be followed by some dancing.

"Where are we going for dinner?" Noelle nonchalantly asked Elise as she primped at her hair.

"I'm not exactly sure. Josh called me this morning and said he had a surprise for us. He said they wanted to thank us for all of our tour guide services over the summer. It sounded like he was thinking fancy, but I don't know how fancy those boys can afford. But I'm sure it will at least be nice. We're supposed to meet them at the little pub across the street from the main palace entrance, near where we parked the bikes that day. He said we should be there by five, so we can get a happy hour cocktail. That's about all I know. Sounds fun, though."

"It does," Noelle agreed. "I like mystery dates. I'm just thrilled the guys will stay an extra week and come to the wedding with us. I can't imagine a more perfect way to end the summer. It really has been an amazing summer, hasn't it, except maybe for my unexpected visit to the hospital. But that is clearly behind us. In fact, I've been feeling great the past few days. You know, I'm beginning to think it was that medicine I was taking after all, and boy, am I glad the doctor took me off of it. I don't ever want to experience anything like that again."

Looking at her watch, Noelle then exclaimed, "Whoa, it's almost 4:30. We'd better hurry if we're supposed to be there at five."

Mark and Josh had already ordered drinks for the girls and were waiting for them at an outside table on the sidewalk. Elise lagged a step behind Noelle as they approached, and when Noelle leaned in to hug him, Josh looked over her shoulder toward Elise, and the two exchanged a knowing glance and smile.

They sat and chatted over their drinks and enjoyed watching people wander out of the palace gate. Expressions of satisfaction, wonder, and exhaustion were the most common on the faces of the departing tourists. Dads carrying worn-out kids in their arms or on their shoulders, and moms snacking the little ones in the strollers trying desperately to hold them off until dinner. Teenage boys roughhousing to impress the girls they were with, and the girls pretending to ignore the antics while secretly giggling to one another when the boys weren't looking. An elderly couple strolling while holding hands made Noelle swoon inside at the thought of Grandmere and Aubert's upcoming nuptials.

"We bought you gifts," Josh announced out of nowhere. "Here, try them on. They are silk scarves we got in a little shop near our hotel. I'm told they are very popular in France."

"Ooh, they are beautiful," Elise responded first. "I like the red one. May I try it on?"

"I picked that one especially for you," Mark said proudly. "I knew you like red, and it likes you, too."

"So that must mean the multicolored one is for me then?" Noelle asked expectantly.

"Absolutely, I chose that one for you because you remind me of a rainbow of pastel. Here, let me put it on you. I think it will look perfect," Josh said.

Noelle turned her back to Josh, so he could drape the delicate accessory over her shoulder and suddenly gasped softly when he instead wrapped it around her eyes, blindfold style.

"Josh, what are you doing?" Noelle giggled. "I think it's supposed to go over my shoulders and around my neck, not my eyes, silly."

"Ah, oui, oui, Mademoiselle, of that I am aware," Josh said in an attempted French accent. "But tonight, the scarf will be used to take you on a surprise adventure. Mark, do you have Elise's eyes covered also?"

"Yep, her eyes are covered, too. I think we're ready to go." Mark confirmed.

"Elise, did you know about this?" Noelle asked blindly.

"As I said, all I knew is that they were going to surprise us with a fancy dinner. I had no idea we would be swept away like prisoners, but I think it's kind of fun. Are you guys sure you know where it is you're taking us?"

"Absolutely, mademoiselle Elise, no question about it -- we are well acclimated to the town of Versailles thanks to your excellent tour guiding services."

As Josh spoke, Elise deftly removed the scarf from her eyes, and the three smiled at each other as they looked at Noelle.

"We won't be going far, so we won't need your car. And I'll walk in front of you and Mark behind, so you'll be perfectly safe walking blindfolded. I'll let you know of any bumps or cracks in the sidewalk, and when we cross the street, I'll take your hand while we're on the cobblestones. This is an exercise in trust. Do you trust me, Noelle?"

"Of course, I do, Josh. Lead on. I can't wait to see what you have in store for us."

To disorient her a bit, Josh first walked Noelle in large circles, turning left and then right and then right and then left again, all for no reason. He

255

then took her hand and led her across the street, through a gate, and down a gravel path."

"This is an interesting walk," a perplexed Noelle said. "Elise, are you recognizing anything? I'm completely lost."

Feigning that she too was still blindfolded, Elise replied, "I'm not sure. I thought I'd be able to calculate where we are based on the distances and directions we've walked, but I haven't got a clue. I am noticing we're no longer on pavement, so that might mean we're in a park somewhere."

The girls were enjoying their guessing game, and the boys were smiling ear to ear.

"Do you think we might be on the palace grounds?" Noelle asked aloud.

"No, I thought that might be it, but the smells are all wrong, and if there's anywhere in Versailles I know like the back of my hand, it's the palace grounds," Elise said. "Nope, it's a mystery, alright. Mark, how much farther do we have to walk blindfolded?"

"We're almost there -- only another couple of blocks. Remember, good things come to those who wait," Mark replied.

"Is that a Proverb?" Elise asked in jest.

"I don't think so. I saw it on a sign at the shop where we bought your scarves."

Noelle felt a sudden breeze when they emerged from the forested path they'd been on and into a more open area. Despite the fun, she was genuinely curious about where they might be headed, and she was racking her brain trying to figure it out. Then she heard what sounded like a splash in the distance.

"What was that?" she suddenly said. "It sounded like water of some kind. Where in the world are we?"

"We're here," Josh said. "But before I remove your blindfold, let me describe it to you. First, it is magnificent, like you are. Second, it is beautiful, like you are. Third, it will be a forever memory, like you are. Finally, it is sunset ... and we all know what that means."

Josh positioned Noelle to face west and then loosed the knot in the scarf and let it gently fall from her face. Her eyes were greeted with a spectacular orange glowing sunset. The trees in the distance stood in silhouette, like soldiers at attention, and the reflection of the colors in the sky was vivid in the calm expanse of water to her left. Noelle gasped quietly in wonder at the beauty of it all, and then, as she turned to see Josh, she saw it, waiting in the water as if beckoning to her -- a lone canoe. And then behind Josh's left shoulder, the sun rays reflecting blindingly off its many windows, she recognized the palace of Versailles.

Suddenly fully aware of their location, Noelle then turned to find Elise and found her holding hands with Mark. Both were grinning broadly.

"Surprise," Josh whispered to Noelle. "Can I interest the lady in a sunset canoe trip on the Grand Canal?"

Noelle's heart skipped a beat as she realized what was happening. She glanced again to Elise, who responded with a wink. She then looked to Mark, who raised his eyebrows and smiled. She then looked back at Josh.

Swallowing hard, Noelle teased, "A sunset canoe trip on the Grand Canal? That is an extraordinary invitation, kind sir. But you must not be from around here because men seldom invite such an excursion due to the secret meaning associated with it."

Loving that Noelle was now playing along, Josh feigned ignorance.

"Secret meaning? Pray tell, mademoiselle."

"Let's just go out and see what happens, shall we?" Noelle said with a wink.

Josh helped her into the boat, and then after sitting down himself, he signaled for Mark to push the vessel containing the two out into the water, and Josh began slowly paddling southward. The breeze was even cooler out on the canal, and Noelle felt a slight chill. Josh then removed Noelle's scarf from his backpack and placed it around her shoulders.

"Dual purpose gift," he said, smiling.

The afterglow of the sunset was even prettier than the actual sunset had been. The sky exploded in yellow, orange, and blue-green hues and the billowy cumulus clouds hovering to the west and north looked like pink cotton candy.

When they reached the middle of the waterway, Josh pulled the oars into the boat and leaned back to enjoy the drift.

"Noelle, of course, I remember the story you told about sunset canoe trips on the Canal, and that is why I wanted to bring you here. To, as you said the tradition was, express my heart. Noelle, I love you. I ... love ... you. There's no getting around it. I love you. And when I mentioned yesterday about you coming with me to America, I was dead serious. I want you to come back with me, at least for a few months. And if those months are as amazing for us as these few here in France have been, well, who knows where it all might lead. I'm

here on the canal to express my, my jeune amour
to you, Noelle."

Josh leaned in to kiss Noelle, but instead of
welcoming lips, he was met with tearing eyes.

"Noelle? What is it? I thought you'd be happy, not
sad," Josh said in puzzlement.

"Oh, Joshua, I love you too, more than I can say,
but I can't go with you to America. I'd love to,
believe me, I'd love nothing more, but I can't, at
least not now."

"Oh," Josh said dejectedly. "That's okay, I guess.
Maybe we can plan for another time? But soon, I
hope. I don't think my heart will rest until we are
together."

Noelle's tears began to flow more steadily.

"You are so incredibly sweet, Josh. That's one of
the many things I love about you, how considerate
you are. But I can't commit to later either. Josh,
there's something important I haven't told you
about. I've thought about telling you at least a
dozen times, but each time I changed my mind
because I didn't want to ruin everything we were
enjoying together."

Now it was Josh's turn to look worried. He stared
deeply into Noelle's eyes, searching for an answer

to this mystery she was about to disclose. What on earth could be so important that she would have withheld it, and now it would preclude her from visiting the United States? His mind raced for a clue, a hint, some past revelation, but he could think of nothing.

"Noelle, what are you talking about? You're worrying me. What could be so important that you would hide it from me? Wait, is it your mom? Is she okay? It can't be your grandmere; she's getting married. I'm at a loss here," Josh's frustration and disappointment were now beginning to show.

"Josh, I'm so sorry. I hope you won't be angry with me. No, it's neither mom nor Grandmere; it's ... me."

Josh paused and once again stared into the eyes of the girl who had captured his heart. Suddenly he saw pain, and then he saw fear, and then he saw overwhelming sadness. His mouth went dry in response, and he felt his heart rate quicken.

"You?"

"I'm sick with something, Josh. The doctors don't know what it is. They think it's related to what killed my father and brother. They say it's hereditary. I've been in a remission period of sorts for the past several months, but I've known all along the future was uncertain."

She paused to let the revelation sink in. She saw Josh's reaction and winced at his pain.

"I would have said something when we first met, but I didn't think it would matter. I mean, we were just a couple of people who met in a Metro station. I'd have never dreamed I would fall in love with you. I honestly never saw that coming. And then, when I started having feelings for you, I didn't want to ruin our summer fun. And then, when we were in Avignon, I had a doctor's appointment and learned there was a new drug that was showing promise as a cure, and for the past few weeks, I've been on top of the world with hope."

Josh sat stoically in stunned silence.

"So, Josh, I can't go with you to the United States. I have these, well, they call them episodes that involve intensely severe headaches. They're very unpredictable, and the last one was pretty scary. It's not safe for me to travel. There is still hope that I will recover from this, or they will develop a medication to manage it, but right now, there's just no certainty. I hope you can understand."

Noelle stopped talking and waited. What could have been the most romantic moment of her life had dramatically turned into the most tragic. She bowed her head in silent grief.

Josh lifted her chin with his hand so that their eyes met, and he finally spoke.

"Noelle, are you, are you going to die like your father and brother did?"

Noelle dropped her head once again and looked at the bottom of the canoe. She looked for an answer to the question she had been haunted by for two years.

Lord, why? She prayed silently. *Why did you bring Josh into this if I'm just going to die? Why must he suffer like I am suffering, not knowing the answer to that question? I don't understand, Lord. He is innocent in all of this, yet You chose to drag him into it. Why? How does that make sense that a loving God would do such a thing?*

Noelle again began to weep.

"I don't know, Joshua. I just don't know." she managed to say through her sobs. "I love you so much, and yet I have no idea what that even means in this situation. I can't really see much further than tomorrow, and I live on the brink of horror every day. I am so incredibly sad to have to burden you with this. I'm crushed to know that you now have to suffer alongside me. I am so sorry, Josh. Please forgive me for ... for falling in love with you."

"Oh dear God, Noelle, don't ... no never apologize for that. I'm the one who fell in love with you. I'm the one who pursued, and I'm the one who is still pursuing. I'm not afraid of this. If this is some cross you have to bear, then I want to bear it with you. A two-strand cord is stronger than a single strand, and a three-strand cord is even stronger. I want to be your second strand. I want to stand beside you and help you through this. You are everything to me, and nothing else really matters at this point. This fire will test us, and we will come out of this flame as pure gold. I know it. I will be strong for you, Noelle, if you'll let me."

She wanted to smile. She wanted to take him in her arms and hold him close. But she knew the reality and that he was only speaking from the shock of the news. Noelle knew she couldn't do this to him. Take him down a path that may well lead to the valley of death. Even though she knew that the shadows there were themselves evidence of the light of the sun rising over the mountains that enshrouded the valley, she couldn't let this beautiful boy, barely a man, suffer with her. No, it just wouldn't be fair.

"Josh, I love you. And I want to be with you forever. I just don't know how long that will be. So, let's just enjoy the time we do have together —

this next week and then the wedding. And then let's worry about later after that. Can we do that together?"

"Only if forever means as long as God wills," Josh replied sorrowfully. "If we can agree to leave our love in God's hands, then I think I can be okay with that."

Noelle laid her head down in Josh's lap, and he slowly stroked her hair as the canoe sat idle in the middle of the Grand Canal.

CHAPTER 16

"Can you tell what's happening?" Elise asked Mark as the two stood on the shoreline.

"Not really; it's getting darker," Mark said, peering out toward the water. "They stopped paddling a while ago, and now the canoe is just sitting out there. It looked like they were talking about something pretty serious, but now, oddly enough, Noelle is resting her head in Josh's lap, and they're just sitting there. Neither of them seems to be moving."

"The serious talking I can understand," Elise offered. "Probably expressing their jeune amour, you know? But now, just sitting there, I don't get that. Well, I imagine they'll be back soon."

"Isn't it cool how those two have fallen in love?" Mark said as he turned his attention from the water and back to Elise. "Josh has had scores of girlfriends over the years, but I've never seen him in love. He's like a totally different person."

"Same for Noelle, only just a few past boyfriends. She is really taken with Josh. But hey, it is kind of that time in our lives, you know -- graduated from college, looking toward the future, and all of that."

"Do you think it's moving too fast? I mean for them?" Mark queried.

"Maybe, but then, under the circumstances, maybe not," Elise answered.

"What circumstances -- something other than what you just said about graduating and looking to the future?"

Elise had let her mind drift back to Monday and Tuesday, and as a result, had momentarily let her guard down. In an attempt to cover, she said, "Not really, just those things, and maybe the fact they are getting caught up in the renewed romance between Celeste and Aubert. Now there's a story you don't hear about every day."

She paused, hoping that would be the end of it, and it was. Mark didn't pursue the matter further.

"So, Elise, awkward issue, but I feel like it's almost the elephant in the room, or maybe in the park. But I wanted to ask, you know, just to be sure. While I really like you, and I've enjoyed our friendship and our summer together, I, uh, well, I don't think my feelings for you are as serious as Josh's are for Noelle."

Elise smiled and reached out for Mark's hand.

"Of course, silly, I feel the same way. But it's awfully sweet of you to care about my feelings like that. No, Mark, I think we're destined to be the best friends of the new couple. And that's totally good with me. Being co-best friends with someone who is a good friend is, well, a very friendly arrangement, don't you think?"

Mark laughed.

"I never really thought about all those friendly complexities, but if I'm following you, yes, I agree completely. And I suspect the friendly co-best friends could themselves become best friends someday, and then when we're all together, we can have this massive friend fest!"

"We should name ourselves!" Elise suggested.

"Huh? What do you mean?"

"You know, like a group name or something."

"Oh. Hmm, I suppose you named your first car too, didn't you?" Mark teased.

"Actually, I did. Her name was Buttercup. She was a little yellow Mini Cooper. Her paint was a bit faded from the sun, so I thought she looked like butter."

"And how did you know 'she' wasn't a 'he?'" Mark played along.

"She told me, of course," Elise said matter-of-factly.

The two laughed again, and then Elise continued, "So, what name should we give to ourselves?"

Mark was at a loss.

"How about the FAAFFs," Elise blurted out.

"What's a faaff?"

"It's not a thing; it's an acronym. FAAFF," Elise repeated, saying each letter individually. "It would stand for French And American Friends Forever."

Mark contemplated the idea for a second and then said, "Huh, kind of clever. I like it. FAAFFs it is! But I wonder if our 'love' birds won't want to slip an L in there somewhere?"

As the time passed, the sky grew darker, and gradually the stars began to appear and twinkle. The clouds mysteriously disappeared with the sun, and the sky above the palace grounds became crystal clear. A three-quarter moon was beginning to ascend from behind the palace, and it created an intriguing glow effect over the rooftop.

"It's getting kind of late. Do you think I should take another canoe and paddle out to check on them?" Mark asked.

"Can I come along?" Elise replied coyly. "I think it's safe for us to go out alone now that the sun has fully set," she added with a wink.

The two co-best friends hopped into another canoe and began slowly making their way to the center of the lake.

"Hey, Elise, we should probably talk a bit louder, so they'll hear us coming. I wouldn't want to interrupt them if they're, you know, kissing."

"Oh, good idea, Mark!" Elise yelled loudly.

"Whoa," Mark rocked back in jest, "we don't have to yell you goof, but now at least we can be sure they know we're coming."

The moonlight illuminated the canal just enough to enable Mark to see Josh, who looked up and waved at the approaching vessel. Noelle sat up and waved, too.

"Josh, can what we talked about be just between us for now?" Noelle whispered.

"Whatever you want, Noelle yes, of course. I do love you, you know?"

"Yes, I know, and I love you, too."

Noelle reached over and kissed Josh on the lips.

Seeing the kiss, Mark called over, "Uh, hi guys are we disturbing anything important?"

"No, that's okay, you two, come on over. We're just sharing our jeune amour," Noelle called back in fun.

When the second canoe glided up, Josh held out a hand to catch and steady it.

"Hey guys, it was getting kind of dark, so I thought maybe we should check in on you two lovebirds. Elise assured me it was safe for us to share a canoe since the sun was down," Mark said as he paddled just enough more to bring the boats side by side.

"Ah, good idea to wait," Noelle said while smiling at Elise. "These American boys seem to take our Versailles traditions quite seriously."

"So I can see," Elise said, smiling back at her friend, "as it should be."

Trying to gracefully avoid the subject of their long talk together, Josh offered, "We thought maybe we should go back into town and grab a bite somewhere since our fancy thank you dinner never quite materialized. Is anyone hungry?"

"Famished!" Mark said. "Want to race back to shore?"

The girls looked at each other and rolled their eyes. Josh saw Noelle's expression and responded to the impromptu challenge accordingly, "I don't think so, Brother. I want to enjoy every second possible out here. We'll take it slow, but you two go on ahead. We'll be along in a few minutes."

"Mark, let me translate that for you," Elise quipped. "They're not quite done kissing. Come, my trusty FAAFF, let's give them another few minutes of privacy."

As they shoved off and started paddling away, Noelle suddenly called out, "Hey, wait, what's a FAAFF?"

"Later, girlfriend, I'll explain later," Elise yelled with her back to Noelle and hand raised high in a wave.

"We have terrific friends; you know that?" Noelle sighed.

"The best, for sure," Josh agreed. "I assume Elise knows what you just told me?"

"Yes, she's known for a long time. Ever since I started having symptoms two years ago, I swore her to secrecy when we met you and Mark. As I said, I didn't want to ruin our summer adventures. You know, sometimes Elise feels more like a sister to me than my real sister does, and I know she knows more about me than Margareet does. My last episode, so to speak, was Monday night. Elise rescued me and took me to the hospital. She stayed by my side all night until I recovered. She's a gem."

"Wait, you were in the hospital this past Monday night? As in five days ago? Oh my, gosh that's recent. And you're feeling okay now? Your condition is very mercurial. I can understand why traveling to the United States would seem scary. Like, what would you do if something happened on the plane? It's an 11-hour flight from Paris to San Francisco."

"Exactly, but hey, let's leave that decision behind us, which is where it is, and let's start looking forward to Grandmere's wedding, okay? We'll enjoy the time we have together until you have to leave, and then we'll worry about what comes after that when we have to -- deal?"

"Yeah, deal. I will love you today and tomorrow and forever, but I'll keep my mind focused just on today and tomorrow for now," Josh promised.

The scenery from the train was very familiar to Noelle and Elise since they had made several rail trips south from Versailles during the past few months, but everything was new and fresh to the boys. The train tracks followed the Rhone River closely. Grand chateaus and castle ruins dotted the landscape. Terraced vineyards climbed most of the hillsides, and hundred-plus year old bridges arching over the river were common. The train stopped in most of the larger villages and the few major cities along the way. So, when all was said and done, the time it took to get to Lyon by train was about the same as if they had traveled by car. But the trip wasn't about saving time; it was about making the most of the time they had to spend.

The four caught a taxi from the train station and arrived at Celeste's house just before three in the afternoon. Chloe was already there, and the two older ladies were engrossed in preparations for the big event scheduled for the following evening at sunset. Noelle ran to the front door from the cab and burst into the house.

"We're here!" she yelled into the cavernous main room. "And ready to party with Grandmere!"

Celeste poked her head out from around the corner. "We're right here, Wello, in the dining room working on the place settings. Come in. There's plenty left to do. Where are your friends?"

"They're right behind me. We are all so excited for you, Grandmere!" Noelle exclaimed as she skipped forward and hugged her beloved grandparent. "And you look, you look ... perfect! I swear you don't look a day over 59. You are just so beautiful, Grandmere. Love looks good on you."

Blushing, Celeste clasped her hands to her heart.

"Oh, Wello, you are just the sweetest girl in the whole world. Chloe, did you know your daughter is the sweetest girl in the whole world?"

"Yes, mom, I'm aware, as I'm sure Josh is, too," Chloe replied, seeing Josh walking in behind Noelle. "Hello, Joshua; it's nice to see you again. We're so glad you and Mark were able to stay an extra week and share this blessed occasion with us."

"Yes, oh dear, yes!" Celeste added in an animated fashion. "You know, at my age, there aren't a lot of my friends left around anymore, and without you four, the bride's side of the aisle would have felt a little bit empty.

"So, Joshua, how are things with you and my little Wello? I hear very positive reports, but it's always good to get the story directly from the source," Celeste said with a mischievous gleam in her eye.

"First, Celeste, let me say that we are honored to be here," Josh said. "Your story is truly one worth telling, and that we have been invited to be a part of it, well, it means a lot. Thank you. And as to your question, everything you've heard is true. Noelle and I are doing very well, thank you. Speaking of which, do you happen to know the tradition in Versailles about sunset canoe rides on the Grand Canal?"

"Why, of course, I do, young man. Robert proposed to me on the canal 61 years ago yesterday."

"Yesterday?" Josh spoke quietly, catching his breath. "Yesterday?"

"Yes, why? You seem more surprised by the date than the place," Celeste asked, tilting her head in curiosity.

Josh's eyes started misting as his mind conjured a marriage proposal and then raced back to his yesterday on the Canal and the way he had initially envisioned the evening unfolding. He bit his lower lip in an attempt to stem the flow of tears he felt suddenly building behind his eyes.

"Jeune amour," he struggled to whisper, "Jeune amour."

"Yes, jeune amour, on the Canal," Celeste whispered back, realizing that something about the canoe tradition and the mention of Robert's proposal had touched a soft place in Josh's heart, "you know it?"

"Yes, Grandmere Celeste, I know it. I'm just afraid I, I won't …," Josh's voice broke. "Excuse me; I'm sorry, I'll be back in just a moment."

As inconspicuously as he could, Josh slipped out of the room and into the garden. He quickly scanned over the masterpiece of landscape in search of a place to hide lest anyone witness the torrent of emotion he knew he could no longer contain.

He quickly ran past the great oak and headed for the guest house. Then he remembered the view of the garden that he'd seen from up on the mountain and the lone bench to the right of the guest house that was concealed by a tall escallonia hedge.

He fell to his knees before making it to the bench and began to weep. Softly at first, but gradually the intensity grew to a shuddering cry. He laid his head on the hard bench, and his free-flowing tears stained the stone a dark gray color.

Through his tears, Josh prayed, "Jesus, oh God, Lord, help her. Please God, anything, everything I have, Lord. I'm begging you, I'm begging you. Please hear me, Lord. Please."

"Josh?" Noelle whispered as she came around the edge of the pink-flowered hedge. "Joshua, are you okay?"

Josh lifted his head violently from the bench as if he had been caught stealing a precious jewel. He stood and swiped vigorously at his eyes, but he couldn't hide his tear-streaked face. He tried to speak but then stopped when he realized he would only break down again. So he sat on the bench and hung his head in a combination of embarrassed sorrow and unwarranted shame.

"Josh, what is it? Everyone inside is so full of joy for Grandmere."

"I know. I'm sorry, Noelle. I'll be okay in a minute," Josh finally managed to say.

Noelle sat next to him on the stone bench that had been hewn for two. She leaned her head on his shoulder and took his hands in her own.

"Josh, it's okay to cry. Believe me; I've shed buckets of tears."

"I'm just so afraid, Noelle, and I feel so helpless ... so worthless," Josh muttered.

"Helpless, maybe -- there isn't anything any of us can do other than pray, but worthless -- no way. You are worth more to me than you can imagine. Josh, you have given me a real, tangible, 'now' reason to be strong. And I need you to be strong with me. Okay? Can you do that for me? Can you be my knight in shining armor?"

Josh sighed heavily as he placed his arm around Noelle.

"I can be, if that's what you need. I can be your knight if that will help you. I'll do anything, Noelle. I'd stay in France if I could, but the visa rules are forcing us to go home. But I promise I'll come back as soon as I can if you'll wait for me."

"You know I will, Joshua Morgan. I'll wait as long as our Lord gives me breath -- I'll wait for you because I love you. I didn't know if I'd ever get to experience love, but I have with you. These few weeks have meant the world to me, Josh. I feel complete now, whole. My soul is satisfied, and my heart is full. You made all that happen for me. I'll always be so grateful for this summer, and if the Lord wills, I will treasure the opportunity to tell our story to everyone who will listen. Our story is as special as Grandmere and Aubert's. All true love stories are worth telling, don't you think?"

"Yeah, I think," Josh said, beginning to cry again. "I do think, my love; no, I know. I know more deeply and with more certainty than I've ever known anything in my life. This moment, this very second, the instant of this breath, I know, is a breath of love for you. Believe me, Noelle, whatever happens, you will always be my forever...."

His voice trailed off, choked in tears. Noelle also began to weep softly. The two clutched each other as if trying to shelter one another from the uncertain cloud of the future.

CHAPTER 17

Despite the monumental effort he made to adjust his focus and maintain a celebratory facade for Celeste's sake during dinner, Josh struggled to sleep that night. He tossed and turned during a fitful five hours between 11 p.m. and 4 a.m. Finally realizing sleep was too elusive, and to avoid disturbing Mark, Josh slipped out of the guest house the same way he had the last time they were there, only this time his departure was not for adventure, but rather, divine intervention.

As he walked out into the predawn morning, Josh felt a chill sweep through him. He wrapped his arms around himself and shivered. He then stepped back inside to grab an old woolen afghan from the couch, which he draped over his shoulders. Thus clad, he struck out again. His destination was nearby, the bench behind the escallonia hedge.

He sat on the cold stone seat with his back to the house and gazed upon the vineyard-laden hillside to the north. The moon, which was nearing full, cast a gentle hue over the landscape. The first hint of sun was still a good hour away, which gave Josh confidence that he wouldn't be disturbed. As he sat, he listened to the silence. It was deep. In its own way, it was actually loud. He thought about the summer and the adventures he and Mark had experienced. He tried to soothe the hurt in his heart with joyful memories, but each time every recollection brought him back to Noelle. Even the many days they were apart, via text and phone, they had been together. No matter what memory he conjured, she was there. She was inescapably at the epicenter of everything.

Josh turned his attention from the moon glow on the hillside to the immediate environs of the bench. He didn't see it at first, nor had he noticed it the afternoon before, but as Josh closed his eyes and gave focus to his other senses, he smelled it. It was faint at first, but once he noticed it, he allowed his mind to focus singly on the alluring fragrance. Josh inhaled deeply as an addict might, seeking out an ever deeper connection with whatever drug they might be lusting for. He allowed his mind to become intoxicated with the smell, and for the first time since the canoe ride, a genuine smile fell on his face.

To fully experience the smell, he decided to remain blind and kept his eyes tightly closed as he knelt from the bench onto his knees. Deeply inhaling again, Josh allowed himself to be drawn to his right. His mind was swimming in the aromas of honey and sweet musk. He felt a release of the yoke around his shoulders and imagined himself floating on a bed ... a bed of roses. It was a rose --

that most perfect of God's garden creations. It was a rose that was entrancing him. Oblivious to how it might have looked to a witness, Josh sniffed at the air like a hound on a hunt and began to crawl gingerly toward the intoxicant. Six feet later, he stopped. The fragrance was peaking, and given his singular focus on it, almost overwhelming. He brought himself to a comfortable sitting position, eyes still tightly closed, and carefully reached forward.

His fingertips met with a cool soft cluster of silky petals. He felt the bloom gently and then traced down its stem to a grouping of three leaves, and then, as expected but nonetheless surprising, Josh found the beauty's protector. Her knight, her knight in shining armor, wasn't that the phrase Noelle had used earlier? Josh felt the thorn carefully. It was cold and smooth and had a slight curve to it. He put the flesh of his thumb on the point and began to apply pressure, lightly at first, but gradually ever more. When the prick started to hurt, he stopped.

The thought of the thorn and how it might have been what comprised Jesus's crown transported Josh to another time and place. The garden was strangely similar, but the moon was higher in the sky. A short six feet away, the bench was instead now a craggy boulder, and the nighttime insects were suddenly very loud. The temperature soared by at least twenty degrees, and Josh began to sweat. He let the afghan covering fall from his shoulders, and for a split second, felt a cool breeze waft over his sweat-soaked back.

Josh started to release the pressure of his thumb on the thorn, but when he did, the scene began to fade back to Celeste's backyard. He was, however, drawn to the alternate reality, the dream, as he perceived it, so he applied the pressure again and was instantly returned to the craggy boulder, and the heat, and the bugs. It was far less comfortable, but for that very reason, strangely all the more alluring.

He heard a faint rustling in the bushes behind him, and he turned toward it. As he did, the pressure he felt on his thumb decreased, and the rustling stopped. Frustrated by his inability to continue unfolding the mystery in his mind, Josh pushed his finger against the thorn's tip again, this time harder, and the more pain he endured, it seemed, the clearer his alternate focus became.

A man then appeared from the bushes. He was clothed in a somewhat tattered cloak. His hair was long and coarse and dark. When the man saw the boulder, he knelt before it and laid his head against it, almost seeming to caress it. The moonlight shone on the man's face, and his eyes were filled with sadness. There was no indication of fear or apprehension, just sorrow. At the same time, he was as vulnerable as a child yet brave as a lion and as strong as Samson.

Josh remained silent, not knowing how he had not been noticed by the man when he had arrived, and he watched as the man began to pray. Josh couldn't make out all the words, but he knew it was prayer. It was a gut-wrenching outreaching petition to God for deliverance, for another way, for a miracle.

The intensity of the man's petition grew, and Josh began to feel a strange sort of empathy, and he then joined in the prayer. He didn't know what the man's burden was, but he knew well his own, and Josh began praying again for Noelle.

Lord, I know you are present here. I can feel You. First, I ask that You would hear and answer this man's prayer. Grant him your Divine wisdom and show him Your will and give him the strength to follow after it. And Lord, please do the same for me as I try to minister to Noelle. I have no idea what is happening to her, and it is scaring me to death, but I know that You know. Give me a glimpse, Lord, so that I can help her. And if I'm unable, Lord, then would you please intervene. Lord, come supernaturally and heal Noelle. Perform a miracle as You did so often when You were here on earth. I promise the testimony of Your power will be proclaimed, and Your name will be blessed.

Josh paused and took a deep breath.

And, Lord, change my heart this weekend, so that I can be a blessing rather than a burden at the wedding. Give me peace, Lord, Your peace, and take my eyes off of me, and fix them on You during the celebration of marriage we are to be a part of. And, Lord, finally, I want to pray boldly for my own marriage someday, and that, according to Your will, it may be to Noelle, and that we will live together a long time and experience vieil amour together just like Celeste and Aubert are about to.

Josh looked over at the other man praying and saw droplets of red running down his face. Josh felt moved to shift the focus of his prayer again and pray instead for whatever burden the man was suffering under. The man then suddenly lifted his head and audibly cried out to heaven. In the intensity of the moment, Josh pressed too hard on the thorn, and when it pierced the flesh of his thumb, Josh too cried out.

Josh looked down and watched intently as blood began to ooze from his finger. It dripped down and pooled onto a leaf and then fell from the leaf to the ground. The instant the thick crimson droplet hit the earth, the air temperature dropped, and the coolness of the night returned. Josh looked up toward the man again but saw only the garden bench. He crawled back over to it and laid his head down on it as he had done the afternoon before. He looked for his tear stain, but it was gone. It had dried and evaporated. Josh breathed deeply, and the smell of the rose enveloped him once again. He felt a peace fall over him, and he curled up on the ground next to the bench and fell asleep.

***

His rest was disturbed by the crow of a rooster somewhere on the hillside. Josh opened his eyes slowly and felt the warmth of the sun peaking over the escallonia onto his face. He sat up and rubbed his eyes into focus. Then he got an idea. He rose quickly and ran to the guest house to wake Mark.

As the two men scurried about in the main house kitchen preparing a surprise breakfast for the girls, Mark said, "This is a great idea, Josh. And you know what they say ... turnabout is fair play ... whoever 'they' are?"

"Yep, and I think we've outdone ourselves this time, Brother," Josh said, patting his friend on the back. 'The girls are going to be blown away by our chef skills."

"Maybe," Mark said with a hint of resignation. "But I'm not sure how much skill is required to prepare scrambled eggs and bacon."

"Hey, you're selling us way short, dude. Look at this masterpiece! We're talking perfectly crisped bacon and eggs with garden herbs mixed in and aged gruyere cheese melted on top. And this brioche! Someone at the bakery must have worked all night making these babies. I tasted one earlier, and they are out of this world!"

"I smell bacon," Elise called out winsomely as she stood at the top of the stairs.

"Oh, no, go stop her," Josh whispered to Mark. "Distract her; tell her a story; ask her a question; take her out to the garden; do something! I need at least another five minutes to put everything together and set the table for our surprise."

"Umm, it smells pretty good down there," Noelle then echoed as she approached the landing just behind Elise. "Grandmere, you shouldn't be cooking on your big day."

"What was that, Wello?" Celeste said as she opened her bedroom door and stepped into the hallway behind Noelle.

Startled, Noelle turned around quickly.

"What? I thought you ... wait, if not you, then who? Mom, are you down there?" Noelle called out.

"I'm right here, Noelle," Chloe said from behind Celeste. "What in the world is all the commotion about so early in the morning?"

Hearing all the voices and questions, Josh realized Mark couldn't possibly distract them all, so he called out in his best ranch-camp cook voice, "Come and get it! Breakfast will be served in the dining room in three minutes!"

Still looking back at the two older women in her life, Noelle smiled and shrugged. "Oh, he's the early bird."

"That boy seems quite the catch, Wello. You should hold on to him," Celeste said with a wink.

"I'd like to, Grandmere. I'd like nothing better."

Hearing his friend's summons, Mark picked up right on the queue, almost as if planned. He met Elise at the bottom of the staircase and asked her to wait while the other women made their way down. Then, to buy Josh a little extra time, he launched into an impromptu shtick.

Deciding, in the moment, to shift course from the howdy-doody ranch hand approach Josh had opted for, Mark began with a low, formal bow. "Good morning, ladies. To begin this most special day of celebration, my good friend and I have deemed it only appropriate to bless the women in our lives with a proper breakfast. We have, of course, been up since dawn rummaging and foraging for just the right combination of gastronomic delights, and lucky for you, Grandmere Celeste's kitchen contained all manner of wonderful options. Chef Josh has outdone himself once again, and I must say, you are all in for quite a feast. So, without further ado, allow me, your maitre d', to usher you into the banquet hall exquisitely prepared and truly befitting such royal queens and princesses as yourselves. First, the envy of us all and the most beautiful rose in the bouquet, if I dare 'say' ... Queen Celeste ... please come this 'way.'"

Listening from back in the kitchen, Josh rolled his eyes at the cheesy rhyme, but he enjoyed it nonetheless.

Mark and I really are quite the team when the need arises, he thought to himself.

Elise and Noelle made way for the bride-to-be to slip past them at the bottom of the stairs, and Celeste, thoroughly enjoying the moment as well as the sentiment behind it, curtseyed slightly and then took Mark's extended arm.

"Good morning, Mum. And, uh, ladies, I'll return in a jiff; please wait for your escort."

Mark's eloquent soliloquy had bought Josh enough time to set the table and put the food items into serving dishes. He stood at the doorway to the kitchen as Mark and Celeste arrived. The scene had, of course, been cast in stone by now, so Josh stepped into character, and with his best French accent imitation, he picked up where Mark left off.

"Bonjour, Madame Celeste. Welcome to the first day of your new beginning, and may your future as Madame DuBois be blessed exceedingly, abundantly, beyond. Please have a seat here at the head of the table. We will be serving once all of the guests have arrived."

In turn, Mark next seated the others: first Chloe and then, with one on each arm, he escorted Elise and Noelle together. The girls were so impressed with the greeting that they completely forgot they had not readied themselves before coming down, and all appeared a bit disheveled in their robes and slippers, but it mattered not. In their minds, they had been transported to a royal castle and were being well attended by two incredibly handsome knights.

After seating the ladies, Mark disappeared into the kitchen to help Josh with the service. He emerged with a pitcher of juice in one hand and coffee in the other. Josh followed with a platter of eggs and another of bacon. He then made one more trip to the kitchen and returned with the brioche.

"A royal breakfast for the royal court!" Josh said with a touch of flair and rolling his r's. "Bon appetit!"

After breakfast, Chloe, Celeste, and Elise all headed back upstairs. Noelle asked Josh to join her in the garden for a moment. Realizing he was the odd man out, Mark volunteered to do the dishes.

"Josh, how did you sleep last night?" Noelle asked sincerely. "I was worried about you. I know you put up a good front during dinner, but are you really okay?"

"Look at you, Noelle," Josh scoffed lovingly. "You're asking me how I'm doing. Do you hear yourself? You are worried about me? I'd say, given the circumstances, that is a pretty serious showing of selflessness. Every day I see more and more why I love you. But yes, I'm okay, all things considered. I didn't sleep all that well, but the Lord and I had some solid time together here in the garden early this morning, and while I'll admit I might have been faking it a bit last night for Grandmere's sake, this morning was one hundred percent genuine. God has given me a sense of peace about this, about us, Noelle. I laid the burden before Him, and He gladly received it. My uncertainty feels more like expectation now, expectation of a life we will enjoy together. I can't explain it other than to say ... well, I just can't explain it. I prayed for peace, and I guess He's given it to me, that peace that passes understanding."

"I'm really glad to hear that, Josh," Noelle said with a soft sigh of relief. "I know it took me months to digest all of this, and I'm still struggling. But this is so sudden for you, and you were pretty distraught yesterday afternoon. It's good to lay it down, though. You know, sometimes I don't understand how people get through things without the Lord to lean on.

"So, changing subjects to today, I'm excited for you to see me in my maid of honor dress. Mother and I found it in an online catalog, and she picked it up for me in Avignon before she came. I was a little worried about the fit, but it is perfect, and it's beautiful. I'm going to go inside and get ready. I should be down in less than an hour."

As she turned to leave, Noelle paused to add an afterthought.

"Oh, and by the way, I was thinking it would be nice if you prepared a reception toast for the couple. You know, something about the vineyard and life and blessings ... just a thought."

"Way ahead of you," Josh answered with a smile. "I've been rolling an idea around in my head since yesterday during the train trip down. I think I'll

tie John 15 in somehow. I still can't believe
Aubert asked Mark and me to come to the
wedding. Today is going to be a blast."

It took the boys very little time to get ready for the
event. While waiting on the ladies, Mark decided
to go for a walk up the hillside Josh had explored
the last time they were there. Josh opted to sit in
one of the rockers on the veranda and read. A
screen door from around the corner squeaked as it
opened, and Josh heard footsteps on the creaking
wooden deck floor. He arose and walked around
the corner to see Celeste standing alone, looking
out into the untamed forest on the kitchen side of
the house. Deciding not to disturb her private
moment, Josh turned to leave, but before he could
get back around the corner, Celeste saw him.

"Oh hello, Joshua, I was just thinking about what
a blessing today is and how my heart feels so full
and free and happy. I'm so glad you are here to
share this special day with our family. Come, and
walk with me in the garden, will you?"

"Anything for the bride-to-be," Josh said, smiling
as he joined Celeste and the two walked around to
the back of the house.

"I am so in love with your garden, Celeste. It is a
beautiful work of art, and every time I enter it, I
seem to discover something new. So, I have a
question, if I may."

"But, of course, Joshua. What can I tell you about my little corner of Eden?"

Yesterday I discovered a somewhat hidden little bench over there," he said, pointing, "behind the escallonia hedge. And near the bench is a sprawling wild-looking rose that has the most amazing fragrance and huge thorns. I was wondering what kind of rose that is and what its story is. I remember you said once that every rose has a story."

Celeste said nothing in response and instead took Josh's hand and led him to the secret bench. She sat down and patted the stone next to her, bidding him do likewise.

"Can you smell it from here?" she asked.

"Yes, I can. It is so full and rich and beautiful. The blooms seem large for a wild climber like that. It is just so unique. Please tell me about it," Josh asked again.

"You are a very perceptive young man. It is a wild rose, and it does have wonderful blooms. This plant, in particular, seems to have larger blooms than one would normally expect though the petal count is minimal. It is called rosa eglanteria. Some folks call it a briar rose. Shakespeare wrote about it often. I planted this bush here by this bench the first spring that Robert and I moved into this home. This bench was our special place. There is nothing exceptional about the bench per se; it was just special to us. We would often sit here in the early morning and talk and pray and dream together."

The two occupied the stone seat quietly for another minute before Celeste said, "I like that you enjoy my garden, Joshua. It's yet another aspect of your heart that I am learning to love. I know my dear Wello is very fond of you. You must promise me you'll take good care of her, won't you?"

"Yes, Grandmere Celeste, I most certainly will. I promise with all of my heart."

The wedding was scheduled to begin at 5 p.m. and was to be followed by a short reception in the vineyard. A family-only dinner was planned in the house afterward. The bride and her entourage got into two vehicles and left Celeste's home just after 3:30 p.m.

Maybe it was the fact that it was their second visit to the estate, but the trip seemed to take mere minutes compared to the first time. They arrived at the same nondescript village square but this time knew to park near the plain westerly wall that hid the chateau so well. The only thing different about the place was a beautiful bronze relief panel secured to the small door in the wall leading into the courtyard. It was fashioned in the style of panels that adorn the Gates of Paradise at the Baptistery of Saint John in Florence, Italy. It was easily recognizable for those familiar with scripture as the scene described in the Gospel of John and commonly known as the wedding at Cana. An apt scene, Josh thought, to announce the wedding of Aubert DuBois.

In accordance with her duties as maid of honor, Noelle tended to her grandmother's dress and the small train behind as they passed through the portal and across the decomposed granite driveway. Celeste's gown was a simple satin piece that was a beautiful ivory color. She looked stunning in it, and it made her feel far younger than her years.

When the girls went inside to freshen up, Mark and Josh elected to sit outside in the rocking chairs resting on the front veranda. The two rocked and talked for several minutes before Mark suddenly stopped rocking and stood up out of his chair to interrupt the conversation.

"Hey, Josh, I don't remember seeing that the last time we were here. Do you?" he said, pointing over to their right toward the vineyard.

"What, the vineyard?" Josh sounded perplexed.

"No, 'that,' the statue over there, I'm sure I would have remembered that. It's fantastic."

In the corner of the courtyard, near a gate that enabled passage through a low stone wall out to the vineyard, stood a life-sized bronze statue of what appeared, from a distance, to be an angel of some sort.

Josh stood as well and focused his attention on the distant piece of art.

"You know, I think you may be right, Mark. I don't recognize that either, though it's entirely possible that we just didn't notice it last time. I mean, I was pretty overwhelmed by just about everything here, and it is kind of out of the way there by the wall."

A screen door behind them creaked as Aubert pulled it open and then stepped out to join the boys.

"Josh, Mark, I'm so glad you were able to come. I really wanted all four of you wonderful young people to join Celeste and me today. You're all such an important part of our story. Welcome. And, I couldn't help but overhear your conversation about the newest lady to call DuBois-Estelle her home. Well, at least she will be the newest for another hour or so," he winked. "She will then lose that short-lived status to my Celeste. But anyway, Mark, you are correct, the statue is new. Well, not new exactly, in fact, it is nearly one hundred years old, but it is new to my courtyard.

It was a gift from a dear friend who owns a vineyard on the other side of the valley. Maybe you've heard of it? It is called Domaine Romanee Conti."

"Heard of it? Of course, it is a very famous place. You know the owner of DRC?" Josh asked.

"Ah, oui, we have been dear friends for nearly 70 years. Our fathers went to school together when they were boys, and each of us inherited our family's wine business. Living only about 25 kilometers or so away, my friend and I spent much time together working the vineyards while growing up. His family would help us during our harvest, and we would help them. Back in those days, everyone helped everyone in this little valley. We were all really like one big family in some ways. Anyway, when my friend heard of my engagement, he had the statue, which had previously graced his property for several generations, delivered here to DuBois-Estelle and placed in that spot there by the gate. The statue, which is of a beautiful young woman, is called Ange de la Vigne, or in English, Angel of the Vine. In the card that came with the gift, he said the angel is, by definition, pure and benevolent, and like the beauty of wine, always in movement and embodied by heaven. He also invited me to rename the piece 'Celeste' to honor my new angel of the vine. I'm thinking about doing just that, eh?"

"I like that idea, Aubert," Josh said, smiling. "I think Celeste is an angel, and we are so happy for the two of you."

"Come along, boys," Aubert said as he put his arms around Josh and Mark, "We should make our way up to the gazebo. The guests will be arriving soon, and I want to be there to greet them as they do. The ladies will be coming along later. You know, they have many things still to attend to."

Aubert led the boys across the courtyard to an old rusting pickup truck parked in a carport out of sight on the east side of the space. He pulled the keys out of his pocket and smiled broadly.

"Boys, meet my faithful steed, 'Ole Blue.' Blue and I have been working these hills together for over 65 years. He was a gift from my father when I turned 18. He's a one-owner pickup. I've driven almost all of his three hundred thousand plus miles. He's been through three engines, and I don't remember how many sets of brakes. He is a testimony to French auto making and may well be the oldest working pickup in France for all I know. The guests will be brought up by air-conditioned van transports, and our ladies via a white limousine, but Ole Blue will serve as our transportation to the ceremony. Come, I think you'll enjoy the ride."

Aubert talked the whole way up the hill, often using his hands for emphasis, which invited the pickup to swerve back and forth along the narrow farm road. More than once, Josh could easily have picked a grape from the vine by merely reaching out the window. As Aubert ground the gears making the final turn to the south, the gazebo came into view. Josh felt a lump forming in his throat as he remembered the lunch they had enjoyed at the spot not much more than a month earlier and the story Aubert had shared about his love for Celeste. He swallowed hard and scrunched his eyes closed to steel his resolve not to get emotional because he knew if he let himself venture down that path, he might never recover.

CHAPTER 18

As much as Aubert cherished Ole Blue, he was careful to park it out of sight from the gazebo. He walked around the venue meticulously tending to any detail that might be even the slightest bit out of place. As he walked about and randomly nitpicked, he silently offered thanksgiving to the One who had sustained him through his 84 years and was now bringing him joy and companionship for whatever number of remaining years he might be blessed to have on earth. After five minutes of fidgeting with things, Aubert sat down to rest on one of the 50 chairs that had been set up for the guests. The boys were off scouting the area since they hadn't had an opportunity to do so the last time they were there. On the back side of the gazebo, Josh noticed a small inscription carved into what looked to have been the original cornerstone of the structure. It was a portion of verse five of chapter 15 from the Bible's gospel of John. It simply said, "I Am the vine ...."

Aubert smiled as he watched the boys exploring, and he mused, *Ah, if only I had had a son to whom I could give all of this, as my father gave to me. But that is obviously not going to happen, so Lord, I will continue to wait on You to instruct about the future of the vineyard. Not that I'm worried about it, Lord. It's just on my mind as I'm thinking about the future more these days. I will continue to steward that which You have entrusted to me, and I will continue to give all the glory and praise to You, as it should be. Someday, I will need a successor, but I leave that conundrum in Your good hands for now.*

Aubert's prayer was interrupted when the first shuttle bus arrived, and guests began pouring out of it. He dutifully stood and walked over to the parking area to begin greeting the close friends and family members who had come to celebrate with him.

"Beautiful day, Aubert," Jacques Solano said as he greeted the groom with a handshake followed by a brotherly hug, "I am so happy for you, my friend. We should all be so lucky to find love in our later years."

"Thank you, Jacques. I am indeed among the most fortunate of men, and my Celeste is an angel to have me. Do you remember her?"

"I do. I remember her husband Robert also. He was a very good man and a hard worker, to be sure. So, are those her grandsons over there exploring? I don't believe I've met them."

"No, well, not exactly," Aubert said. "They are Americans visiting for the summer. One of them, the fellow on the left, his name is Joshua, he is the boyfriend of Celeste's granddaughter, Noelle. The boys are aspiring winemakers from California. They are wonderful young men. You should make it a point to chat with them sometime later today."

The three shuttle buses each made four trips up the hill from the chateau. The final vehicle to arrive, the white limousine Aubert had mentioned, carried Celeste, her daughter, granddaughter, and Elise. The priest from Celeste's church in Lyon called the assembly to focus at precisely five o'clock and addressed them in French.

"Please, may I have your attention? The hour appointed by my good friend Aubert DuBois has arrived, and we would like to start. Thank you all for coming to celebrate this glorious day of union between Aubert DuBois and Celeste Moraine. Your presence here is a testimony to your importance in the lives of these two saints and their love for you."

At that moment, Aubert walked up onto the gazebo from the right and joined Father Tovier to await his bride's arrival.

A lone violinist began playing the classic French wedding song La Vie En Rose. The crowd stood respectfully and watched quietly as Noelle slowly escorted Celeste down the aisle and up onto the gazebo platform. As soon as they arrived, Aubert took his bride's hand, and Noelle slipped over to Celeste's left. When the music stopped, Father Tovier stepped down to the gazebo's front and turned his back to those seated. By stepping down the three steps from the gazebo to the ground, the guests could easily see Aubert and Celeste up on the platform. The couple then turned together, facing the assembly, and gave their attention to the priest.

Father Tovier spoke eloquently about the two, including a bit about the connection of their families. He also mentioned the role Noelle had played in rekindling the love between the two seniors, and he thanked her for it. The priest then led the bride and groom in the recital of traditional vows and invited an exchange of rings, which Noelle assisted with. Father Tovier then walked back up onto the gazebo and led the two in a private moment of Holy Communion.

"Ladies and gentlemen, it is my distinct honor this afternoon to pronounce Aubert and Celeste to be husband and wife. May the Lord bless and keep you both and enable you to enjoy each other for many years to come. Aubert, you may kiss your bride."

In an unexpected show of fun and a bit of humor, as Celeste appeared to be puckering for a romantic kiss, Aubert surprised her by giving her a traditional greeting kiss from cheek to cheek to cheek. Surprised, Celeste raised her eyebrows in a good-humored response, and everyone chuckled at the antics. Having thus achieved his goal of levity, Aubert readied for the real kiss and leaned in. But just before their lips met, figuring it was now her turn for some fun, Celeste turned her head at the last second so that Aubert's lips met her cheek again. She then reached up and took his face and firmly planted three cheek to cheek to cheek kisses on him as well. By now, the guests were clearly entertained, and the polite chuckles turned to audible laughter. Finally, the two took each other's faces in their hands and together carefully guided their lips to connect, and when they did, applause broke out. They then turned and walked down the aisle to where tables had been set up for the guest reception. Those in attendance quickly followed, and a grand party ensued with the estate's finest wines being poured.

Aubert clinked on his wine glass with the back of a spoon to get the attention of the crowd and then spoke.

"Celeste and I are most blessed by your attendance this afternoon. As Father Tovier mentioned, you are all very important to us, and we are so pleased to share this special day with you. I cannot recall, in my 84 years, ever being to a wedding of two, shall we say, such senior citizens. But, I believe with all my heart that love can thrive regardless of age, and my heart sings that truth today. Celeste and I have both been living a somewhat lonely existence for the past decade or so, and today that comes to an end. I also will finally be blessed with a family. Something I have dearly desired my entire adult life. Celeste's daughter, Chloe, is here, as is her granddaughter, Noelle. They are now my family, and I feel exceedingly blessed to be able to say that.

"God has truly been good to both Celeste and me, and we invite you to share in His goodness with us tonight. The wine at your tables is our best 2006 Pinot Noir and our 2013 Chardonnay -- the fruit of the vine to celebrate the fruit of a blessed life. Please join me in offering a toast to my beautiful bride, Celeste DuBois!"

Everyone stood and toasted the couple, and then, no sooner than Aubert and Celeste had sat down, a chorus of clinking wine classes rang out, and someone from the back yelled, "kiss the bride!" Aubert wasted no time in complying with the request and, this time, engaged in no preliminary levity.

A few others then took turns offering toasts and well wishes to the couple. When a lull arose, Josh stood.

"Hello, all. I am Joshua Morgan. I'm the boyfriend of Celeste's granddaughter, Noelle. I have been touring France this summer with my friend Mark. We are both from the United States. We are deeply honored to be here today to witness this wonderful union of two of God's most special people. Of course, I'm sure you are all aware that God holds marriage in the highest esteem. He even refers to the relationship between Himself and His church as similar to that of husband and wife. God's love is pure and selfless, as I know the love shared between Aubert and Celeste is as well. Jesus also spoke very highly of marriage, and in fact, His first miracle was performed at a wedding. You may have noticed the beautiful bronze relief on the entry door to the estate as you arrived. If you didn't, you should enjoy it on the way out. It is a depiction of that very wedding, the wedding at Cana. Jesus' miracle there was to turn water into wine, and not just any wine, but the best wine, an excellent wine. Now I'm not going to overstate things and risk embarrassing my new friend Aubert, but I'm sure we can all attest to the fact that the wine we are enjoying this evening might even rival that which Jesus made."

Polite laughter wafted through the crowd.

"Jesus also uses the vineyard as a metaphor for our relationship with God. In the Gospel of John, the 15th Chapter, Jesus says, 'I am the vine, and my Father is the vinedresser.' And He says He is the vine and that apart from Him, we can bear no fruit. I am pleased to know that both of our newlyweds here tonight abide in Jesus, so we can rest assured they will indeed bear much beautiful fruit as a couple for God.

"Please join me in congratulating and blessing Monsieur et Madame DuBois."

Though not planned, Josh's toast was the last, and after that, the assembly went back to enjoying the food, wine, and fellowship that had been set out for them. Aubert and Celeste beamed the entire time as the guests took private moments with them one by one. It was nothing less than perfect.

After a long hour, Aubert announced that the immediate family would be retiring to the chateau for a private dinner but that everyone else was welcome to stay at the reception as long as they liked. He again thanked everyone, and then the family, including Elise, Josh and Mark, departed in a single shuttle bus.

"Aubert, that was just wonderful," Celeste said as the two held hands. "Everything was so perfect. I couldn't help recalling in my mind when we had our first dinner at that spot. So much time has passed, and so many things have changed. I love you, and I am so happy."

"As am I," Aubert responded, squeezing Celeste's hand.

"So are we all!" Chloe chimed in from the back seat.

At the house, the ladies retired upstairs for a few minutes to change into more comfortable clothes. Mark sat in the library and thumbed through a book about Burgundy wines. During the down moment, Aubert invited Josh outside to the garden.

"Joshua, thank you again for taking the time to join us today, I know it meant a lot to Celeste, and it did to me as well. And I'm sure it meant the world to Noelle. She is such a beautiful child. Celeste tells me you two have expressed your love for one another. Is this true?"

Josh was a bit taken aback by the bold question, but he decided nothing bad could come from an honest answer. After all, they had been pretty public about it, and everyone important to them in France already knew.

"Yes, we have, Aubert. I told her during a sunset canoe ride on the Grand Canal at Versailles. I assume you know about the tradition?"

"Ah, yes, and so I heard. Well done, my boy, well done. You are a quick study when it comes to the romantic traditions of France. And tell me, how was your summer in terms of learning about French wine and the history of our industry here?"

"That too has gone very well. But if I'm honest, I was a bit distracted by Noelle. Nonetheless, I found the strength to muscle through my romance and still accomplish my initial purpose in coming to France," Josh said, tongue in cheek.

"And what conclusions did you reach about French wine?" Aubert continued.

"Well, I found it all very fascinating. Many things are so different here from the way they are done in the United States. I don't know that either is necessarily better; they are just different. I do think, though, that I like the older ways better. I think you referred to it as the 'art' of winemaking when we were here last. I would like to return to France someday to study more about the art of it all. And Noelle, of course, creates the perfect excuse for me to come back."

"You remember our conversation well, Joshua. And as for returning, actually, that is what I wanted to talk with you about. I know that you are leaving for home tomorrow, so I don't need an answer right away, nor would I expect one. The good Lord knows I've been thinking and praying about this issue for over 20 years."

"Issue?" Josh asked innocently.

"Joshua, do you believe in Providence?" Aubert asked.

"As in God's hand guiding our steps? Yes, I do. I don't always understand His ways, of course, which the Bible says are unsearchable, but I do believe God plays an active role in our lives."

"Yes, exactly," Aubert agreed. "So, I believe that your coming to France was Providential. In other words, I believe God brought you here. Your visit has been a catalyst for far more important events than just a post-college jaunt to Europe.

"Your visit has led to your experience of jeune amour. Your visit has lifted Noelle's spirits to new heights. Celeste and Chloe have both shared with me that they have never seen her happier or more excited about life than since she met you. And, of course, from my purely selfish perspective, but for your visit, I would not stand here before you, a married man looking forward to, rather than dreading, my remaining years on this good earth.

"Joshua, I'd like to share with you a story. Please come and sit with me over here on the bench."

Aubert put his arm around Josh's shoulder the way a grandfather might before offering sage advice. Josh willingly followed along, both out of respect and intrigue.

"Joshua, when I was 33 years old, my beloved wife, Pearl, became pregnant with a child. I cannot begin to express the sheer joy we both felt at the

315

news. We had been praying for children from the moment we were married. Family was very important to both of us, as was the idea of legacy. We had both come from good families and believed it our duty to pass on what we were learning to the next generation.

"As the pregnancy progressed, Pearl began struggling. Medicine was not nearly as advanced as today, and all the doctors could offer was hope and prayer. My wife was on strict bed rest for the final four months of her pregnancy. It was awful for her. Not being able to act on her nesting instinct just about drove her mad. I did what I could, but it was woefully inadequate. We spent those months drawing closer together, and, at least spiritually speaking, we redeemed the days.

"One of the things we decided during those long days was what we would name our baby. We sought the scriptures for names, wanting to honor God, and in a small way pass on the spiritual legacy that was so central to who we were. If the baby was a girl, we decided her name would be Ruth to honor that great biblical hero's faithfulness and devotion. However, choosing a boy's name was more difficult because there are so many male Bible heroes."

Aubert paused and looked away. Josh could sense emotion rising in the old man, so he sat quietly and waited. After a moment, Aubert collected himself, took a very deep breath, and then exhaled slowly.

"We elected to name a boy child, Joshua," Aubert whispered as his eyes moistened.

"When I earlier shared with you that Pearl and I had not been blessed with children, I misspoke. We were, but just no children that survived. Our baby was stillborn. It was a boy. God indeed blessed us with a son. But He chose, in His unknowable and unsearchable will, to take our boy to heaven before we had a chance to meet him."

Aubert paused again as a few tears began to roll down his cheeks.

"We were never able to get pregnant again after that, and thus you see no children or grandchildren or great-grandchildren frolicking in these vineyards. What I had hoped would be the greatest joy of my life never came to pass. Then when the Lord took my Pearl too, well, for me, life was pretty much empty from that point on.

"I know some have called me a recluse for hiding behind these walls, but I just didn't have sufficient joy to share with anyone, and I certainly didn't want to be a burden to anyone. The one exception to my self-exile was Celeste, and, of course, you know that story.

"I share all of this with you, Joshua, because I am thinking that perhaps God has brought you into our lives, into my life, to answer the question I have been asking myself for these many years. Namely, who will care for DuBois-Estelle when I am gone? Who will love God and the soil and the vine and its fruit, as I have? Who will carry on my legacy -- if not blood, then perhaps a trusted friend?

"That is why I would like to ask if you would be willing to return, here to DuBois-Estelle, to work with me for a season. So together, we can see if you, Joshua, might be the Joshua I always dreamed of. If you are the man that God has perhaps appointed to take the reins and lead DuBois-Estelle into the future. Like Joshua of the Bible who led Israel's children across the Jordan River into the Promised Land, the man who would continue the generations of tradition here at the vineyard and the art of winemaking. And if, and of course I understand it would be a significant 'if,' and I say this in no way to influence anything ... no, no, a hundred times no, such things are left to God and Him alone. But if the jeune amour between you and Noelle were to one day lead to marriage and the blessing of progeny, then my legacy would, at least in part, be carried on by 'family,' my second family, but family nonetheless. Not so terribly unlike the lineage of Christ. Again, I mention Ruth as an example. Her children were from a second family. And even King David's legacy, indeed the lineage of Jesus himself, was passed through the son of a second wife.

"Of course, I understand those examples are different in their specifics, but I am content to entrust such details, indeed all the details, into God's loving and all omniscient hands.

"And there you have it, Joshua. My heart and my dreams all lay bare before you. Please pray with me, will you, my friend?"

Josh's mind was swimming with the rawness of the story and revelation, and he felt a tear of his owning welling, but before he could speak, Aubert reached over and took both of his hands as he bowed his head to pray.

"Father God. You who created and inhabit heaven and earth, may Your name be praised above all others. Lord, we pray Your will be done in all things pertaining to our lives, and we trust in Your benevolent hand of Providence. Lord, we thank Thee for Your protection and provision in our lives and that You care for us, the least of these, and that You would leave the ninety-nine to seek us out and shelter and comfort us. We owe our every breath, our every substance, the very essence of our being, indeed our eternity, to You and You alone. Thank You for Your faithfulness and Your grace and mercy and hope and love. Thank You for the fruit of Your Spirit as well as the fruit of the vine. I pray for the three-strand cord You have knitted together today, and I pray a similar cord may, if it be Your will Lord, be knitted for Joshua and Noelle. You know my heart's desire, Lord. I pray You will show clearly to Joshua the path You would have Him to follow as He seeks Your will for his future. Thank you, Jesus. It is in your name that we pray. Amen."

Josh sat silent for a moment.

"Aubert, I don't know quite what to say," Josh was finally able to respond. "I'm honored and stunned by what you have shared, all of it. Of course, I mentioned that Mark and I have been planning to be partners in the wine business for many years now, and ...."

Aubert interrupted, "Oh, I'm sorry, Joshua, I didn't mean to suggest that you abandon your friendship and partnership with Mark. No, no, quite the contrary, I think the plan you two have devised for your future is admirable, and I would expect, or at least invite you to ask, Mark to be a part of what we might build together here. Of course, his connection as a secondary 'family,' so to speak, would be different than that possibility for you, but I would certainly leave it to you two to work out any details of your partnership you might feel are appropriate. And of course, should you accept my invitation, we would have very much to discuss and plan and understand together. It is only the idea that I wish to present to you tonight. And frankly, I would prefer we not spend any more time on it now. I'd rather we go back inside and celebrate. I only mentioned it because you are leaving tomorrow, and I wanted to talk with you in person."

"Yes, of course, I completely understand. Let's go back inside and celebrate. I promise I will give your invitation serious prayer and consideration. Again, Aubert, I am profoundly honored. You are a great man in the wine world, and as I am coming to understand, also in God's plans. If things can work out, I can think of no one on earth I would rather have as my mentor."

CHAPTER 19

Dinner was a shining testament to the joy of love. Stories from the past flowed, as did dreams for the future. Conspicuously absent from the conversation, at least from Josh's perspective, was any mention of Noelle's health, and while frustrated, he understood and let it go. Celeste and Aubert had decided to postpone their honeymoon until after harvest and so were staying the night in the chateau. When nine o'clock rolled around, Chloe suggested everyone but the newlyweds should be heading back to Lyon. Though they were thoroughly enjoying the company, everyone could sense the sigh of relief from the newlyweds when the group collected their things and stepped out into the cool night air to leave.

"Mom, would you mind if Josh and I rode home together, alone? We'd like to chat before they have to leave in the morning," Noelle asked.

"Sure, Noelle, that would be fine. I was going to suggest the same thing. Great minds think alike," Chloe responded with a wink.

The threesome, Chloe, Elise, and Mark, pulled away first and headed down the hill. Josh opened the passenger side door for Noelle and got her seated before running around to the driver's side. He then put his hands on the steering wheel and looked straight ahead but did not put the key into the ignition.

"Aren't you going to start the car?" Noelle asked in a jesting tone.

"Noelle, did you know Aubert had a son once?" Josh asked quietly.

"What? No. What do you mean? I thought they had no children."

"Aubert's wife Pearl had a baby boy when Aubert was 33, but he died at birth."

"Oh, my gosh, that's so sad," Noelle said softly.

"Yes and his name was ... Joshua," Josh finished.

Noelle sat speechless for a moment. Josh had a solemn tone about him, but she couldn't quite figure out why, so she decided to hold her tongue.

"I thought, just a coincidence, right?" Josh began again. "But Aubert then went on to tell me how he has longed to find someone to succeed him here at DuBois-Estelle. He then asked if I would consider returning to France to work with him to see if perhaps I might be that someone. Can you believe that?"

Noelle was now speechless for an entirely different reason.

"Wow, Josh, that's quite a revelation. He seriously asked you that question?"

"Yes, in so many words, yes," Josh replied. "Aubert also said that he would pray for us, you and me, and our relationship. He talked about you as family, which I guess technically you are now. And he talked about the importance to him of family and legacy. He didn't come right out and say it, but I got the distinct impression that he and Celeste are praying that we, you and I, might get married someday – wild, huh?"

"Maybe not so wild when you think about it, Josh. I know we have never talked about that, but I can tell you, for me anyway, the idea has crossed my mind. I love you, and you love me. I know we're young, and we have a lot of growing together to do, but I could see it happening someday, if the Lord wills."

Josh hung his head.

"Josh, you don't see marriage as a possibility?" Noelle asked, confused by his body language.

"No, I mean yes, I do. I know it may sound impetuous, but I don't just see it as a 'possibility,' I'd like to see it become a reality. We do love each other, and we do have some growing up still to do, but we could grow together as a young married couple, couldn't we?

"My grandparents married at the ages of 20 and 19, and they were together for over 50 years until my grandpa passed away. I remember their marriage being happy and fruitful. Grandpa always told me that one of the secrets to their success as a couple was getting married so young. That way, he said, neither had any baggage to bring into the relationship. Their hearts hadn't been bruised or broken by others. They were both pure and full of hope and expectation. Before he died, Grandpa encouraged me, even though I was only a boy at the time, to not be afraid to marry young if I found the right girl and she loved Jesus. That word from him always stuck with me, though I hadn't really thought much about it.

"I guess what I'm saying, Noelle, is that I kind of like the idea. And if I do come back to France, I'd like it to be not only to work with Aubert but perhaps also to ask you to be my wife. I think becoming a member of your family, so I could call you Wello, too, sounds like a great idea," Josh smiled.

Not sure exactly what Josh was saying, Noelle felt the need to clarify.

"Are you asking me now?" Noelle followed. "I mean, you're leaving tomorrow, and I think I might be a bit confused."

"I'm not exactly proposing right now, but I am saying that my intent in continuing our relationship would be to do so someday. I want to be that committed to you, Noelle. Not just dating, per se, but more like what my grandpa would have called courting. Look, there are a hundred things I've got to think through, and I'm sure you do too, but I'd like to begin thinking about them through the lens of 'us' ... because I love you."

Noelle leaned across the console between the two bucket seats and kissed Josh.

"Through the lens of us, I like that, Josh."

***

Exhausted from the wedding and having said their goodbyes the night before, everyone agreed the boys would take a cab to the train station and not disturb the girls. They had to leave Lyon very early because their connecting flight out of Paris left at 10 a.m., and besides, neither Josh nor Noelle wanted to go through the sadness of saying another goodbye.

As the plane lifted off, Mark was already napping. On the other hand, Josh was making mental notes of all the things that would have to be planned in order to return to France. During the drive to Lyon, he had discussed with Noelle targeting mid-December for the possible return trip to talk further with Aubert. If all went well, Josh would then return home for Christmas before moving to France for an extended stay on a work visa. Of course, Noelle was also on his mind -- not only their conversation about courting and possible marriage, but also Noelle's medical situation, which they had purposefully not discussed further in Lyon. There were many questions and much uncertainty about her condition. Yet, at the same time, there was so much to be hopeful about and to look forward to. It was almost too much to process, and within thirty minutes, Josh joined Mark in catching up on some much-needed sleep.

Josh was rudely awakened when a snack cart bumped into his knee, which had drifted into the aisle while he slept. He moaned quietly and rubbed at his temples, feeling a slight headache coming on. Mark was in deep rem and snoring, so Josh decided not to roust him, though the thought did cross his mind. He asked the flight attendant who was pushing the cart that bumped him if he could get some aspirin and water. While Josh waited, the reality of the headache reminded him to pray again for Noelle and specifically that God would spare her from any more severe episodes.

He'd never experienced a migraine, so he had no reference point, but what Noelle had described to him sounded more than horrible.

When the attendant returned, her voice stirred Mark.

"Hey, Brother," Josh said. "Man, you were snoozing big time. All that wedding partying took it out of you, eh?"

"Hey, Josh. Yeah, I guess so," Mark replied, yawning. "Or maybe it was the two and half months of non-stop travel and adventuring in France. Whatever, it was all good, very good. But I think it's also going to be good to get back home and start moving forward with our dream."

Mark looked out the window at the clouds for a moment before continuing. "Hey, I've been monitoring some online real estate sites and saw a small, 40-acre vineyard with a fledgling winemaking operation located in a barn all for sale near Lodi, just west of Interstate 5. There's an old 3-bed/2-bath house on the property, too. The listing says they've got water rights and the vines are only about eight years old. They're growing Cab, Merlot, Petite Verdot, and Zin."

"Wow, that's nice. What's the asking price?"

"They're asking $925,000, which, considering that it's got some going-concern value and includes the house and outbuildings, is not all that bad a price."

"No, it's not," Josh agreed.

Mark continued, his voice growing more excited as the cobwebs of sleep cleared. "If we raised enough seed money through our parents and friends, we could probably make a decent down payment, and then we'd just have to find a bank willing to roll the dice on us."

"That all sounds pretty promising. Good work scouting it out. But Mark, another possible idea has come up that I want to talk through with you," Josh said calmly.

"What? Have you been hawking real estate sites, too? I'm all ears, man!"

"Well, not exactly, no. This would be a major game change. I know we've always dreamed about becoming California wine kings, but would you be open to France instead?"

"Huh? What do you mean?" Mark asked while sitting up straighter in his seat. "France? You've been pricing vineyards in France?"

"Excuse me. Would either of you gentlemen like a beverage before we begin the meal service? We have juices and sodas, all complimentary, of course," a flight attendant interrupted.

"Sure, thanks. I'll have some orange juice," Josh answered.

"Make that two," Mark echoed.

As the boys waited for their juice to be poured, Josh shot up a quick silent prayer, *okay, Lord, help me to explain this well. If Mark doesn't get on board with the idea, I don't think I'll pursue it.*

Over the next hour, Josh carefully relayed everything he knew to Mark. He had gotten Noelle's permission to share about her condition as well, so there was a lot to discuss.

"Man, that's a lot to take in," Mark finally said. "I'm so sorry about Noelle; that must really be hard on you, friend. To learn the girl you have just fallen in love with is seriously ill. I will be praying for you both. And the offer Aubert has extended, not only to you but to 'us.' I mean that is incredible. To learn from a man like that, a legend like him, how can we not do it? Even if things don't ultimately work out long-term at DuBois-Estelle, any amount of time we could spend there would be invaluable. I would almost think that a year being mentored by Aubert might be more valuable to us than the five years we just spent in college.

"We're not really in a place to buy a winery right now anyway, plus we don't have any practical, hands-on experience, except for our six-week internships last summer. I guess I could say I'm pretty good at washing down tanks and cleaning up around a winery, but somehow I just don't see that translating all that well into the ability to make great wine."

"Yeah, that was kind of my initial reaction as well," Josh concurred. "I'm glad to hear the same general sentiment from you. It is a huge decision, though, so we don't want to rush into anything. The last thing Aubert said was that he probably wouldn't be ready for us until after the harvest this fall, so we've got some time to think and pray about it. I'd like to talk to my folks and maybe Professor Jordan at school and seek their counsel. I also did a little research, and it can take two to three months to get a work visa for France anyway. Maybe we can at least go ahead and make applications to get that process going. Aubert said he'd sign whatever paperwork we might need to submit regarding proof of employment."

"Wow, Josh, this is a fantastic opportunity. I'll talk to my folks, too, as soon as we get home.

"So, what are you thinking regarding Noelle?" Mark shifted the focus of the conversation. "Are you guys going to stay in touch? Are you going to pursue the relationship long-distance? I've heard that can be tough."

"Absolutely," Josh responded without hesitation. "Mark, I love her, and we even talked, you know, about the possibility of someday considering marriage. I realize that may sound sudden, but I've never been so sure of anything else in my whole life. Mark, Noelle is the one. I'm convinced of it. And I have to be honest; she would be a major factor in my decision to go back to France to work with Aubert. That's why how you feel is so important. I kind of set out a fleece with the Lord, and you are essentially my Old Testament version of Gabriel's lamb's wool."

"Whoa, dude, no one's ever called me lamb's wool before," Mark smiled. "So, am I supposed to be a wet fleece or dry one?"

"All you need to do is pray about it and be honest with me. That'll do just fine, friend."

***

After the girls finished breakfast, they cleaned and secured Celeste's house and then headed for the train station. Elise traveled north back to Versailles while Noelle and her mother went south to Avignon.

"Elise, I'll see you in a few days. Mom suggested that I should see Dr. Brodeur in person while I'm down this way, and I agreed. I made an appointment for tomorrow. I called my work, and they're okay with it. Say hi to your parents for me. I should be back to Versailles by Wednesday," Noelle said.

"Sounds good," Elise responded cheerfully. "Call me if anything newsworthy comes from your appointment. I'll be praying for you."

Elise's train left first, and Noelle and Chloe found a table at a cafe at the station to sit at while awaiting their train to arrive. The station was busy, and the two sat quietly sipping their drinks while people-watching. Chloe's mind was reflecting on the wedding and what it might portend for her mother's future. Noelle mused about what her future with Josh might entail. Both were in their own worlds until they were interrupted by a voice from an overhead speaker announcing their train would be delayed for an hour.

"Ugh. Well, that's classic. What would Sunday in France be without some kind of delay on the train system," Chloe said sarcastically. "At least we don't have anything pressing to get back to in Avignon today. So, I guess we'll just consider this a bit of bonus mother-daughter time, eh?"

"Sure, mom, shall we grab something to eat since we've got this table anyway?"

"I think I'd rather walk, if it's all the same to you. We've got a whole hour, so why don't we step outside and get a little sunshine?"

"Yep, that sounds even better," Noelle agreed.

The two held hands as they strolled along the relatively quiet residential streets they discovered three blocks west of the train station.

"Mom," Noelle began. "Josh told me last night that he and Aubert talked yesterday and that Aubert has invited him to return to France to work with him at the winery."

"Wow, that's quite an opportunity for a young man interested in the wine business. What did Josh say?"

"He's going to pray about it, but I think he's interested. Mom, Josh also said he wants to talk someday about marriage. We are very serious about each other, and I encouraged the idea. What do you think? I know it may seem sudden. But we really do love each other. I miss him already and can't stop thinking about us."

"I like Josh, honey. I really do. Of course, marriage is a huge step, a forever step. I think it would make sense to spend some more time together before committing, but if, after that, you two still feel the same way about each other, then you'll have my blessing. I trust your judgment, Noelle. The only thing ...."

Chloe paused briefly to gather her thoughts.

"The only thing that might cause me to pause would be, well, it might be whatever we may learn from the doctor. Your last episode was pretty scary for all of us. Of course, I believe the Lord will bring you through this, but until you have some certainty, I would just wonder a little about getting married. Adjusting to life with a man is hard enough. Adding the burden of this illness and its lack of certain prognosis or treatment might not be fair to either of you, if you know what I mean."

"I do, mom; believe me, I've thought the same thing, and that's my only hesitation. I love Josh too much to want to be a burden to him. He seems okay with the whole thing, but I'm not sure he fully understands it or can see things clearly through the picture his heart has created. He's a romantic like I am. I think if left to our own devices, in our minds we'd already be living happily ever after in Queen Antoinette's hamlet or something."

"What?" Chloe smiled.

"Oh, it's just a pretend place Marie Antoinette had built near the Versailles palace. It's a quaint little country village with a dozen or so Hansel and Gretel cottages and a farm and a lake. But none of it's real. It's mostly all facades. It was just a place where the queen would walk and dream.

***

"I'm glad you made the trip down, Noelle," Brodeur began. "How was the wedding? Your mother told me about the big news for your grandmere. I'm very happy for her and your family."

"It was absolutely perfect," Noelle replied. "Thanks for asking."

"So, how have you been feeling since your episode a week ago?" the doctor asked. "You certainly seem to have recovered quickly."

"I did recover quickly," Noelle said. "And I'm very grateful for that, given the wedding and all. As far as how I'm feeling, I'd say about average, though I have been having pretty consistent dull headaches. They seem to last almost all day. I'm getting through them okay with Tylenol, but it's just a constant reminder, you know."

"Anything else?" the doctor asked while jotting down notes.

Noelle paused and looked down, wondering whether to report the next issue with her mother in the room.

"Well," she hesitated.

"Noelle, what is it?" Chloe asked with a concerned voice. "Honey, you really need to tell the doctor everything, so that he can formulate the best course of treatment."

"I know, Mom, I know," Noelle said defensively.

"Doctor, my eyesight seems to be getting worse. It's the distances mostly. I noticed it when we were in the vineyard for the wedding. I know the grape clusters are there, I can see them up close, but they seem to blend in with the vine leaves at about ten feet away."

Brodeur stopped and put his pen down, and sighed quietly.

"That would be consistent with what I saw on today's MRI," he said soberly. "I noticed what looked like some further clouding on your occipital lobe."

"Your eyes," Chloe said with worry, "your father had trouble with his eyes, too."

"I know, Mom. That's why I didn't mention it to you. I didn't want you to worry. But I've done some research around the internet, and it's not all that uncommon for kids coming out of college to need glasses. I guess four years buried in the books can affect your distance vision," Noelle said hopefully.

"That is generally true, Noelle," Brodeur followed. "But not as dramatic as what you are experiencing. Normal vision loss at a distance is much more gradual. What you're seeing is like the change usually experienced over a decade or more. No, I'm afraid it is more likely associated with your condition than too much eye strain from book reading.

"I think we should have you see an ophthalmologist here at the hospital and get you fitted for some glasses. I can prescribe some medicine that should help with the headaches. I'm glad you described them as dull, but the duration being all day is troubling.

"Noelle," Brodeur continued, "we don't think we're going to see any measurable progress on the research, at least not enough to start another trial, for probably a year or longer. I know you had placed a lot of hope in the trial, and I'm sorry it was canceled. Your remission history seemed very positive over the summer, but the episode you experienced last week in Versailles, combined with the symptoms you are now describing, is worrisome. There is no need to panic, but I believe we need to approach these circumstances with a watchful eye. Of course, continuing to pray for divine intervention, as I know you do, can't hurt." Noelle listened carefully and found herself reading between the lines.

What exactly is he saying? It almost sounds like he's giving up on me. Maybe even suggesting I resign to some inevitable bad outcome. Is he saying there's no hope and that I'm going to die? If that's the case, why doesn't he just come right out and say it? I can see mom's face has drawn that conclusion. No further trial for a year? That's a long time, but maybe I can wait that out if I can manage these headaches with medicine. But what about this eyesight thing? Now that's seemingly a big deal. It has come on awfully fast and is pretty severe.

"Doctor, if the eyesight thing is related to my condition ... could I go blind?" Noelle asked hesitatingly.

"I honestly can't say, Noelle," Brodeur replied. "As far as I know, that hasn't happened to anyone yet, but as with many things related to this condition, a lot remains uncertain. Remember I mentioned the 54-year-old woman who has been stable for years. Maybe your case will be similar to hers. I wish I had more answers for you, Noelle, but I don't. All I can suggest is that we respond to your symptoms with the medications we have and try to manage things while hoping for the best. If you're still strong in a year, when we hope to get the trial back up and running, we can reevaluate then."

"I understand," Noelle sadly said in response.

"Yes, Doctor, we understand," Chloe echoed quietly. "And we will continue praying for that miracle; you can be sure of that."

CHAPTER 20

"Noelle, it's so good to talk by phone," Josh said as their conversation began. "I love the regular emails and text messages, but hearing your voice just means so much more. I've got news about our wine plans here in the States to share with you. But first, tell me how you're feeling. Your last few emails have left me worrying some. It seems like your episodes are coming on more regularly, but at least not as severely as the one that happened the week before we left."

"That's a pretty good summary of things, Josh," Noelle said, "more frequent, but less intense. I saw Dr. Brodeur again several weeks ago, and he said all we can do is stay the course, manage the symptoms, and pray. He knows of a few patients who have been able to remain stable for years, one lady for 12 years, so I'm praying I will be one of those patients, at least until they get another drug trial started. Then, even though it's a bit scary because they think the medicine is what triggered my major episode in Versailles, I plan to volunteer for the trial again."

"How are your eyes doing?"

"That's the best news," Noelle said. "They seem to be pretty stable after that first dramatic loss of distance vision. I'm getting used to the glasses, but I'm thinking about switching to contact lenses. What do you think?"

"Ha, I think you're beautiful either way, so whatever you think is best, I'll be one hundred percent on board. And how's your mom doing?" Josh asked.

"She's good. She came up to visit last weekend and stayed here at Elise's house. Elise's parents have been so wonderful. They definitely have the gift of hospitality, that's for sure. My sister Margareet came down from Rouen the same weekend, so we had a little family reunion. She felt bad about not making it to Grandmere's wedding, and she enjoyed looking at all the photos. My sister seems to be doing well. And when Mom asked if she was experiencing any of the same symptoms I have been, she said no. So, it looks like the Lord has spared her. That's a blessing."

"That's for sure," Josh agreed. "So, now to my news. I've been talking with Aubert almost daily this past week. And Mark and I have also consulted with a dozen or so people we know here in the California wine business, and all the counsel we are getting says we should return to France. Mark is in, too! Aubert is delighted to know we are coming."

"Josh, that is great! I can't think of better news," Noelle exclaimed excitedly. "When will you come? Where will you live? What exactly will you be doing for the vineyard? How long will you stay?"

"Whoa, slow down a bit," Josh said, laughing. "I'm excited, too, but we don't have answers to all those questions quite yet. The last time Aubert and I talked about it, he thought early December would be a good timetable. I've got to talk with my folks about Christmas, though. That's a big time of year for our family, so I might put the trip off until after the holidays. Have you given any thought to your holiday plans? Are you feeling better or stable enough yet to consider a trip here to meet my family? If not, that's okay, and I don't want you to feel pressured at all, but it would be pretty cool if somehow that could happen before I move to France."

"No holiday plans as of yet, and I'm still leery of a 12-hour plane flight."

"I understand," Josh said. "Well, regardless of the timing, now at least we know we'll be back together before too long. Aubert said he has a two-bedroom guest cottage at the estate that Mark and I can stay in. The commitment we're making to each other is for one season, so we'll be staying at least through the harvest and crush next year. I think Aubert is even more excited about our coming than we are. This is still so amazing it's kind of hard to wrap our heads around, and we owe it all to you, Noelle. Sometimes I still can't believe the amazing turn my life took when I met you in June."

"I know, I feel the same way," Noelle said lovingly. "I've talked to Grandmere about all of the possibilities, and she has invited me to live at her house. She's not staying there often anymore; she and Aubert only occasionally use it when they come to town. So I'm thinking about maybe moving down permanently and getting a job in Lyon. I'll be closer to my mom that way, too. Josh, I think it will be important for us to be near each other, you know?"

"I totally agree, and, of course, I'm coming to France more for you than for DuBois-Estelle, anyway. Working with Aubert is just icing on the cake from my perspective. So, I think it sounds perfect that you might live in Lyon. Isn't it amazing how everything continues to come together for us, Noelle? I'm so excited.

"Look, I've got a few more calls to make before lunch, so I'd better be going. I'm glad we connected. I love you," Josh said in closing.

"I love you, too, Josh, more than I think you know. And I believe that anything, no everything, is possible, including my healing. You've helped me believe that, Josh. Believe with me. I miss you. Bye."

As she hung up the call, Noelle couldn't help but feel a little guilty for putting on such an upbeat show with Josh when deep down, she had a lingering foreboding about her health.

Lord, all I can do is pray and give my anxiety over to you. I know the Bible says we are to worry about nothing and pray about everything. That's what I'm trying to do here. Please hear my prayers, Lord. And thank You for all You are doing for Josh and for the blessing that all of this is to Aubert and Grandmere.

***

Christmas at the DuBois and Moraine homes had been subdued for so long it was as if Aubert and Celeste were trying to make up for lost years. The outside of the DuBois chateau was lit up like a winter wonderland, including a 30 foot tall Christmas tree in the center of the driveway turnaround that was decorated with thousands of gold and silver objects, all illuminated with seemingly endless strings of tiny sparkling white lights. Beautiful poinsettias lined the veranda railing. Inside the house, greenery was everywhere, and the entire place smelled like a fresh Christmas wreath. A smaller 15-foot tree was in the corner of the front room near the fireplace which was snapping and crackling as it emitted a wonderful natural warmth into the ample space. A 24 piece nativity elegantly graced the coffee table in front of the soft leather sofa. The baby Jesus was conspicuously absent until midnight on Christmas Eve, consistent with the Moraine tradition of awaiting the baby king's birth.

After enjoying a Christmas Eve prime rib roast dinner fit for royalty, Aubert invited the family to join him in the living room for a reading of the first Christmas account from the gospel of Luke. Standing arm in arm in front of the tree with her groom, Celeste gushed, "Aubert, darling, you've really outdone yourself. I can't remember a Christmas as beautiful and perfect as this one. Thank you so much, my love."

Aubert's eyes moistened, "Celeste, Christmas has never held such meaning to my heart. Of course, celebrating Christ coming to earth as a helpless babe in a cattle stall is the true reason for the season, but this year my heart also explodes with joy over you, my sweet. I have never been happier."

The two seniors kissed affectionately and then sat down together on the sofa.

Chloe looked over to Noelle to share a smile about the love they were witnessing, but suddenly her smile was replaced with a look of concern. "Noelle, are you feeling alright? You don't look ...."

Before she could finish her sentence, Chloe watched as Noelle's eyes seemed to roll back in her head, and she slumped to her right and then slipped from her seat down onto the floor.

"Noelle!" Chloe yelled.

Aubert immediately ran to the girl's side and cradled her head carefully, trying to protect it from the small convulsions shaking Noelle's body.

"I think we should get the car ready and take her to the hospital. She feels icy cold, and she doesn't seem lucid at all," Aubert directed hastily.

Celeste called for the houseman to bring the car around, and they were on the road to Lyon in less than three minutes.

***

The hospital in Lyon was similar in size to Avignon's facility, but it did not have the teaching and research arm of practice. Staffing was light due to the holiday, as was the demand, so there was no problem getting Noelle admitted via the emergency room. Chloe did the best she could to explain Noelle's medical history to the attending physician and asked him to please try to reach Doctor Brodeur in Avignon. Fortunately, she had his cell phone number, and the ER doctor connected with Brodeur. After the phone consultation, the ER doctor, whose name was Ballett, ordered an MRI and blood draw. Noelle remained mostly unresponsive, though her convulsions calmed.

"Mom, I'm so sorry this is happening on Christmas Eve. I know how special this holiday time with the family was for you and Aubert," Chloe said sadly. "I think you two should head back home and rest. There's no reason for you to spend the whole night sitting in these uncomfortable chairs. I promise I will call you if anything happens."

"Dear, of course, no one can control the timing of such things, so don't worry about that," Celeste said reassuringly, "But I think you may be right about us not serving much purpose here in the waiting room. To be closer, though, we will spend the night at my house across the river. And promise me you'll call no matter what time it may be."

"I promise, Mom. And please be praying for my baby."

After Aubert and Celeste left, Chloe sat alone in the Emergency Room waiting area. She grabbed a coffee from a vending machine and slowly sipped on it while trying to control her emotions and fend off the flood of memories that were threatening to drown her.

Lord, this is so reminding me of the last days with Paul and Michael. I'm scared. I know she is in Your hands, but I so want her to be in mine as well. She is such a wonderful girl and with so much promise and hope, and love. Please save her so that she can enjoy more of life and love. In so many ways, she is just getting started. She and Josh, that is.

"Oh no, I should call Josh," Chloe whispered to herself, interrupting her own prayer.

After she pulled the cell phone from her purse, Chloe realized she didn't have Josh's cell number in her contacts list, and she hadn't thought to grab Noelle's phone before they left the house. She wasn't even sure what time it was in California, not that it mattered, because she had no way of reaching Josh.

Perfect, she scolded herself angrily. *This night is just one disaster after another.*

Even though she was blameless, the weight of the moment overwhelmed her, and her frustration about not being able to call Josh was the tipping point that led to tears. Chloe's tears of fear,

351

sadness, and frustration, blended into a brief but powerful torrent that stained her cheeks and reddened her eyes.

When she regained control of her emotions, Chloe sat stoically, as if in a trance, and began processing the memories. Although her previous experiences had been in the Avignon hospital, the Lyon emergency room waiting area was strangely similar. Maybe all waiting rooms had the same bland colored, uncomfortable furniture, generic watercolor pictures on the wall, and aged vending machine in the corner? The smell was the same also. It was almost antiseptic, like everything was too clean. As Chloe looked down, she wondered how many gallons of tears had been mopped up from the gray and white speckled tile floor. The silence was eerily similar as well. It sounded alone, vacant, sad. Paul's final hospital stay had only been two days, and with Michael, it was only three.

Lord, could the end for Noelle be that close? Again, Lord, please intervene. At least let me talk with my baby again. Lord, if nothing else, at least let us talk.

Chloe began to weep again … this time softer, but the accompanying moaning ache came from deeper in her soul.

***

"Mrs. LePage," a nurse's assistant whispered while gently nudging Chloe's shoulder. "Ma'am, your daughter is awake, and she's asking for you. She is in room 14, just down the hall, that way."

Chloe stirred, not knowing how long she'd been asleep, and instinctively raised her hands to clear her eyes while squinting into the bright light beaming from the recessed fixture in the ceiling.

"Thank you, yes, room 14?" she muttered as she stood up and groggily headed down the hall in the direction the assistant had pointed.

Chloe steadied herself before walking through the open door into emergency room 14. Noelle's eyes were closed, and she looked to be peacefully resting. Chloe's eyes involuntarily did a quick reconnaissance of the space, and again she was reminded of the numerous and striking similarities to her previous ER visits. That antiseptic odor persisted, as did the sterile-looking excuses for furniture. The sound was different from the waiting room, though. Room 14 emitted the low steady hum of busy monitoring equipment along with the metronome-like beep coming from the cardiac cuff.

"Mom, I'm awake; you can come in," Chloe heard her daughter say.

"Noelle, honey, how are you feeling?"

"Tired, Mom -- really tired. What exactly happened? The last thing I remember was sitting around the Christmas tree in the living room. Then I just blacked out, and when I woke up, I was here. Did I have an episode of some sort?"

"Yes, dear, that appears to be the case," Chloe answered while scooting the hard plastic chair closer to the bedside.

The screech of the chair legs across the starkly clean tile floor caused Noelle to wince in pain.

"I've got a killer headache," she offered to explain the facial expression.

"Sorry, honey, I'll try to be more careful," Chloe whispered, as if reduced vocal volume might somehow make amends for the chair screech.

"Are Grandmere and Aubert here?" Noelle whispered back.

"No. I sent them home to Grandmere's house to get some sleep. But they said to call them any time if there was a reason for them to come back. Shall I?"

"No, that's okay; they should rest. I feel bad I messed up Christmas Eve for everyone. Speaking of which, what time is it?"

"It's actually Christmas Day now -- it's a bit after 2 a.m. I think they'd love to see you, so maybe I'll call them around seven. You know Grandmere, I'm sure she'll be up by then."

"Yes," Noelle said with a slight grin, "you're right about that. Have the doctors said anything?"

"Not yet; I think they were waiting to talk with you directly. I do know they spoke with Dr. Brodeur, and he filled them in on everything."

"Have you called Josh?" Noelle continued her questioning.

"I wanted to, but I don't have his number. You wouldn't happen to know it off the top of your head, would you?"

"Yes, I have it memorized. Maybe I can call him when we're through talking. Could you leave me your phone?"

"Absolutely, hon. I think that's best -- for you to call Josh directly. It will mean way more to him than me calling."

Mother and daughter chatted for ten more minutes. Chloe shared her memories and fears but also her hope and confidence in God. In turn, Noelle confessed her own fears and recollections of the final days with her father and brother.

"Mom, this seems awfully familiar to me, and that's what scares me," she said.

"I know, honey, me, too. But we can rest in God's hands, right? He knows our yesterdays, todays, and tomorrows, so whatever happens, we know He'll be there to care for us all."

"Yeah, I know, Mom. That's really the only comfort I have right now. The assurance of heaven, and if it's my time that I'll be reunited with Dad and Michael, but ...," her voice broke, "... I'd rather stay, you know? It's not that I'm afraid it's just, well, I want to grow old with Josh and have children and be a mom like you and a grandmere someday. I want to know what vieil amour is like," Noelle pleaded as tears began rolling down her cheeks.

"Shh, my sweet baby," Chloe said, stroking her daughter's hand and gasping to temper her own emotions. "Shh. Hey, why don't you give Josh a call now? I'm sure his voice will put a smile on your face."

Noelle took her mom's cell phone and blew a thank you kiss. "Thanks, Mom I'll only be a few minutes. You can stay if you want."

"No, I'll step out and go get a cup of coffee. Take your time, dear. Take your time."

After closing the door to room 14, Chloe walked away, down the hall. After turning a corner, she saw an empty room to her right. She glanced furtively about and then slipped inside, closing the door behind her. The room was dark and silent and cold. Chloe began to weep quietly and then knelt on the hard floor surface and prayed.

CHAPTER 21

"Josh, hi, it's Noelle. It's so good to hear your voice. Happy Christmas Eve, love, are you at your folks' house?" Noelle said, mustering all her strength to sound cheerful.

"Hey, Noelle, yes, and your timing is perfect; we just finished dinner and, uh, wait, it's like three in the morning there, isn't it? Why are you calling at such an odd time? Isn't it kind of early for a Christmas morning greeting?"

"Yeah, I guess it is. I hadn't thought about that, so, Merry Christmas, too. I love you, Josh."

"I love you ... more," Josh replied, employing the private lover's quip that had developed between the two. "I don't imagine anyone else is up yet, are they? It's even too early for Grandmere. How was Christmas Eve at the chateau? That's where you are, right?"

Noelle sighed and closed her eyes tightly, willing the headache pain to go away, if only for a few minutes. Then, after taking a deep breath, she continued. "Yes, the chateau is where we were, yes. Aubert prepared the most amazing dinner for us, and the decorations were spectacular.

Everything about it was classic and perfect. The tree was so pretty. I wish you could have seen it."

"Where you 'were?'" Josh followed. "Why didn't you stay the night? What? Are you back at Celeste's house now?"

"No, not exactly," Noelle sighed again as her upbeat facade began to falter. "Josh, I had an episode after Christmas Eve dinner. I'm at the hospital in Lyon."

The line went quiet for several long seconds.

"Josh, are you there?" Noelle asked tentatively.

"Yeah, I'm here. You're in the hospital? Are you okay? I mean, was the episode like the last one you told me about in Versailles? Noelle, I'm so sorry."

"No, Josh, this one was different. It seems they've all been different recently," Noelle said.

"All? Have you had others? You didn't mention any others. Noelle ..."

Noelle interrupted.

"I know, and I'm sorry I didn't tell you," she sighed again. "It's just, well, they weren't as severe as Versailles was, and I didn't want you to worry with

Christmas coming, and time with your family and all. I've had three small-ish episodes over the past two weeks, but nothing that required medical attention: just dizzy spells, one very short blackout, and some headaches. The headaches have been hard, but Dr. Brodeur prescribed a stronger pain med, which seems to help. And I knew you'd be here soon. But I probably should have told you. I'm sorry -- forgive me?" she said slowly.

"Noelle, of course, I do, but that's not really important right now. What is important is that you're in the hospital, and I'm nearly 6,000 miles away from you. I'm not scheduled to arrive there until the 29th. Will you be okay until then, or should I try to come earlier?"

"No, no, you should stay with your family as you planned. And besides, I wouldn't want to disrupt Mark's holiday either. I'm not going anywhere, and I'm sure I'll be back at Aubert's by the time you arrive. I can't wait to see you, Josh. I miss you so much, and I'm so excited to begin our next chapter together."

"You and me both. You sound tired, Noelle. I love you, more and most. Why don't you get some rest and we can talk again later? I'll try to call you tomorrow morning, my time. Please be careful and do exactly what the doctors say. I'll be praying for you."

'Bye, Josh, mon amour," Noelle said quietly.

***

The plane wheels chirped when they touched the tarmac. As if in a race, passengers immediately grabbed for and powered up their cell phones to check on whatever might have transpired since they left the U.S. Josh knew Chloe would be waiting for him at the luggage carousel inside, so he didn't feel the need to enter the competition. Knowing it would be several minutes before his row would be able to move forward to deplane; Josh adjusted himself in his seat and closed his eyes.

Lord, it is so good to finally be here. Thanks for a safe flight and for the great time with the family over Christmas. Lord, I'm about to start the most incredible adventure of my life: reconnecting with Noelle -- hopefully forever -- starting work with Aubert, and basically beginning a whole new life here in France. You are so good to me. Thank You. And bring Mark here safely, too, after New Year's.

Following his silent prayer, Josh let his mind wander to the adventures he had experienced the last time he was in France: meeting Noelle in the metro station outside of Paris; walking together with her through the City; enjoying wine and cheese on the boat moored beneath Pont Neuf while watching the river traffic float by; going to church at Notre Dame; cycling through the grounds and walking through the palace at Versailles; visiting the wineries in Bordeaux together; staying at Celeste's home and enjoying her garden; meeting Aubert and exploring the wine caves and vineyards of DuBois-Estelle; kissing Noelle at the top of the Ferris wheel in Avignon; riding the open-air train through the river gorge and kissing again in the tunnel; canoeing on the Grand Canal at sunset; celebrating with Aubert and Celeste at the wedding.

A smile formed on his lips, and he sighed heavily with gratefulness just before the passenger to his right nudged him to step into the aisle as it was finally their row's turn to exit. Josh grabbed his carry-on from the overhead compartment and followed a family with two pre-teen children down the narrow passageway, out of the plane, and through the boarding chute to the main airport terminal. As usual, the place was buzzing with activity, and Josh looked up for signage to direct him to the luggage area. He walked slowly, savoring the moment of arrival in this place, his new world, wanting to fix it all in his memory in the event he might decide to write the story down for his grandchildren someday. He continued breathing slowly and deeply, focusing on the sights and the sounds and the smells. Rather than anxiousness or excitement, a feeling of peace fell over him. Peace from knowing he was precisely where God wanted him to be at that very moment. Peace from having decided he would ask Noelle to marry him that very evening. Peace from knowing she would say yes and that his life with her would be happy forever.

He slipped his left hand into the front pocket of his jeans and felt the soft velvet on the small box that held the ring he would soon place on his beloved's finger. A shudder of anticipation trickled up his spine, and he chuckled to himself as he thought, *tonight is going to be the best night of my life.*

He didn't see Chloe on any of the benches near the luggage carousel, so he figured she must be running a few minutes late. His bags were among the last to emerge on the conveyor system, and after he grabbed them, he again looked for his ride. Still not seeing her, Josh walked over to a bench, pulled out his cell phone, and sat down.

"Hello, Chloe? This is Josh. I've arrived at the airport. Were you still planning to pick me up, or should I catch a cab?"

"Hi, Joshua, sorry, I'm not there. Yes, that was the plan, but if you wouldn't mind, I think it would be better if you caught a cab. I'm awfully sorry. We're here at Celeste's house. We'll have some food ready for you."

"Okay, I'll see you soon. Oh, and Chloe, give Noelle a big hug for me and tell her I've got a surprise for her!"

Half an hour later, the cab pulled into the circular driveway. Josh was a little surprised not to see Noelle come running out of the house to greet him, but then he realized she might have a headache or be resting. He collected his luggage from the vehicle trunk, paid the driver, and then began walking toward the front door. An odd quiet filled the air. Having neglected to put his jacket on, a sudden breeze caused him to shiver. The ground was hard and brown, and, of course, all the usual color from the beautiful flowers in the driveway and leading up to the house was absent as the roses were all safely asleep, as Noelle had described it, for the winter. Christmas lights were still hanging from the veranda, but they were not turned on even though the sun was setting. One of the hooks a short segment of the lights had been draped over had fallen out, and an awkward, low hanging sag disrupted the otherwise festive arrangement.

His footsteps seemed louder than usual as he walked across the wooden porch, and he set his suitcases down in preparation for his grand entry. He peeked through the glass portion of the door to see who might be in the main room but saw no one. The doorknob was painfully cold as he slowly turned it and listened for a response from inside.

"Hello, I'm here," Josh voiced tentatively as he poked his head inside. "Is everyone taking a nap?"

Celeste appeared from the dining room corner.

"Hi Joshua," she said as she approached and offered a warm hug. "Come in; we're in the back family room talking. Would you like something to drink, maybe some cocoa? I've got hot water on the stove."

"Sure, that would be nice, Celeste. It is cold out there. I'm going to have to get used to French winters, I guess. It was 73 degrees in California when I left."

"Go on into the family room, and I'll be along with your cocoa in a minute. Chloe is back there," Celeste said quietly.

Josh did as instructed and walked through the kitchen into the family room. Chloe was sitting in a rocking chair, looking into space as if planning something.

"Hi, Chloe," Josh said as he approached the lady he hoped would soon be his mother-in-law. "Where's Noelle?"

Chloe stood and embraced the young man her daughter had fallen so deeply in love with.

"Josh, sit down. Noelle isn't here," she said sadly.

Josh immediately felt uneasy, and his pulse quickened as he sat on the sofa next to the rocker. He took a deep breath and caught his eyes looking everywhere but into Chloe's. She was patient and waited for him to settle before speaking further.

"Joshua, there is no easy way to say this, but Noelle is gone. She's gone to be with her brother and father. Josh, she passed away earlier today, just before noon. I'm so sorry. Josh, she loved you so very, very much."

Josh sat frozen by the news. He wanted to speak, but his voice was numb. He wanted to cry, but his tear ducts were suddenly dry. He wanted to scream out in anguish, but his heart had abandoned him. He just sat, unmoving, and stared at Chloe. Finally, he tilted his head slightly to the left and leaned forward. His mouth was slightly agape, and he felt his tongue thickening. He deliberately focused on calming his breathing, and then all he heard was the air flowing in and out of his lungs. He closed his eyes, hoping he was in a bad dream and that when he opened them all in the world would be perfect again as it had been when he got onto the plane 12 hours earlier. But when he reopened his eyes, Chloe was still sitting in the rocker with tears rolling down her cheeks.

"Josh, I was with her. I was with her when she closed her eyes for the last time," Chloe whispered. "She said her headaches had stopped, and her vision was clear. She smiled up at me, Josh. She knew where she was going, and she was embracing the journey with joy. She told me she knew it would be difficult for me because she had sat in the seat I was in when the time came for her father and brother to leave. She pleaded with me not to think of her passing as her death but as her birth into heaven. And, Josh, the last thing she asked was that I tell you, 'yes, she would marry you.'"

Chloe broke down and began weeping freely. Josh could no longer check his emotion, and he too joined in open grief. He reached over and put his right hand on hers. With his left, he reached into his pocket and withdrew the small black velveteen box.

Through sobs and tear-stained eyes, Josh showed the box to Chloe and said haltingly, "I was going to ask her tonight."

"I think she knew that might happen. Josh, you must know how much she loved you, how much she believed in you. You made her so happy. As hard as I know this must be for you, impossibly hard, please take comfort in the truth that your presence in Noelle's life, however short, was truly a blessing to her ... and to me."

"Chloe, would you mind if I took a few minutes alone outside to think and pray?" Josh asked.

"No, not at all, take as much time as you need. I understand," she offered, trying to comfort the man her daughter had loved.

The sun was nearly down, and the pale cold of winter evening consumed the usually colorful and welcoming garden. Josh shivered, again having forgotten his jacket, but nevertheless walked directly to the secret bench. As he had in the past, he knelt before the seat and cried and prayed aloud.

"God, I don't understand. She had so much to give and could have done so much good work for You here. Why did You have to take her home? Why couldn't I have at least kissed her goodbye? Why bring me all the way back to France only to be alone? Why deprive us of vieil amour?"

Josh poured his heart and sadness and anger out to God until he had no more words to express. He then rose and sat on the bench, looking up to the vine-covered hillside as if searching for an answer. He looked over to his right at the scraggly thorny mass the wild briar rose had become in winter. It was gray and tangled and ugly and dead, just like Josh's heart.

***

By the time Mark arrived a week later, the memorial service had already taken place, and Noelle had been laid to rest in the small church cemetery in Avignon alongside her father and brother. Josh decided to stay with Chloe to provide support and comfort to her through the week and then had planned to move to the DuBois estate when Mark arrived. He borrowed Chloe's car and drove to Lyon to pick his friend up at the airport there.

The two men had spoken several times about Noelle, so Mark was fully prepared when he de-boarded the plane. Josh, too, was prepared and had steeled himself so as not to break down when he saw his friend. Their embrace was deep and genuine, but neither wanted to focus on the pain of loss. They briefly shared personal condolences, but by the time they were in the car and pulling onto the freeway, their conversation had turned to their plans for the future. Mark was abuzz with questions and ideas. They came rapid-fire, and Josh had a difficult time keeping up.

"Hey, buddy, I appreciate your enthusiasm, but I think you'd be more likely to get answers to all your questions from Aubert. He's given a lot of thought to all of this, and from what he's shared with me this past week, I think he has a good plan outlined," Josh said.

"Yeah, sure, man, sorry about the running string of questions. I know the hurt must still be heavy; I'm just so glad to see you, buddy," Mark replied, chagrined.

"Yeah, about that, Mark, I know this probably isn't going to make much sense to you, and I'm sorry to say this, but I've decided not to stay in France," Josh said sadly. "As much as I was excited about doing this together, there is just too much pain associated with this place for me right now. I can't handle it. I just need some time."

"Time, I mean, yeah, I get it," Mark responded more compassionately this time. "The loss of your love must be devastating. I have no way of even beginning to understand what you must be feeling. Take whatever time you need."

"Thanks, but the problem is, I don't know how much time I'll need, maybe a month, maybe a year, maybe more? I just can't say right now. It's just so hard even to breathe here sometimes. I know I may regret this someday, but I just don't have the strength to do this right now. I've discussed it with Aubert, and he's okay with it. He truly does understand because he knows this kind of loss. But he was insistent that I at least ask you to stay. His heart is really in this, and I think he is very sincere about wanting us to succeed him in the business eventually. I know that's a lot to ask of you, to stay here alone, that is. But, I think it does

371

make sense for both you and Aubert, and eventually, I hope, for us, too. I'm not permanently abandoning you, Mark. I'm not planning to throw away my education or my dreams. I just need to get through this overwhelming tsunami of grief I'm struggling with. It's like I'm fighting against a rip current that just won't let go, and of course, the only way out of a rip is to let it take you out until 'it' releases you, and then you slowly swim back to shore. That's what I think I need to do, let my grief take me out, and then, when it finally gives up, I will swim back in, I promise."

"Of course, man, I mean, what can I say?" Mark replied after a moment of thought. "You need space, and what kind of friend would I be if I didn't give it to you. I'm one hundred percent committed to at least a year at DuBois-Estelle, so yes, I will stay by myself. I'll do whatever I can to learn from and help Aubert. Whether we end up here long-term or not, the time spent will be worth it in the long run. But let's stay in regular touch, okay? I want to know what I can do to help you while you're caught in the rip current, and then maybe I can offer some help with your swim back to shore when the time comes."

CHAPTER 22

Winter waned, and spring burst with abundance. The vines sprang back to life, and as summer arrived the grape clusters began to take form. The weather and precipitation were the best the vineyards had experienced in over a decade, and the harvest brought in a bumper crop of excellent fruit. Mark's relationship with Aubert flourished, and the two developed a genuine friendship that extended well beyond mentor-mentee. The calm after harvest set in as November rolled into December, and the chateau was once again decorated to celebrate the holidays. Mark and Aubert had agreed to work together for a second year, and all was well at DuBois-Estelle.

"Hey, Mark. It's good to hear your voice," Josh spoke into the phone. "I know it's been a while. I've been following all the happenings over there via the website, which, by the way, I must say has been vastly improved over the past year. I see your fingerprints all over that."

"Ha, yeah, that was one of the many things Aubert has entrusted to me. In fact, the whole business plan going forward has been evolving big time, and it amazes me just how much faith he has in me, or should I say 'us'?" Mark said hopefully.

"It's been a year now, Brother. What are your thoughts about coming here to join me? I'm not trying to pressure you or anything, but I'm dying to know. And if you are coming, then we've got lots of planning to do."

"I'm aware of the anniversary coming up," Josh said solemnly. "That's partly why I called. I plan to come to France after the New Year to spend some time with you and Chloe and Aubert and Celeste. How are the newlyweds doing, by the way?"

"I swear you'd never know they were in their eighties. Those two have more energy than I sometimes do. They are here quite a bit, but it seems they are just as often off traveling somewhere. In fact, they just got back from New York. Aubert wanted to take Celeste to the United States, and they went to watch the Macy's Thanksgiving Day parade. Remember, Celeste had never been across the pond, so it was a huge deal for her. She pretty much talked non-stop about it for weeks before they left and then for another week after they got home. That lady is just so darn cute.

"So, to your comment," Mark circled back. "You're going to fly over for a visit in January, huh? That sounds great, Josh. I know everyone will be excited to see you. Any chance you might bring more than just one suitcase?"

"Yes, I think there's a good chance. I'll have my work visa by then, and I've been praying about it a lot lately. Mark, I think I'm ready to roll my sleeves up and get back into the game. It's been harder than I thought it would be, this last year, that is, but I'm coming through it and can see light at the other end of the tunnel. Ha, kind of like that tunnel we experienced on the de l'Ardeche train, remember?"

"How could I forget," Mark chuckled into the phone. "In fact, I saw Elise in October, and we took that same trip again ... kind of to celebrate the memory of two summers ago. She's doing well. Her job at Versailles has become full-time now, and she is even one of the business managers for the company. Things here have pretty much moved forward, Josh. Not that we don't all miss Noelle, everyone does, and I know the Christmas holiday is inevitably going to engender some tears, but all in all, we're doing okay here."

"That's good to know," Josh said, intending to bring the conversation to a close. "Chloe seems more upbeat in our past few conversations, and she seems excited to see me again. She says she's been invited to join the DuBois family there at the chateau for Christmas and the week following. I think that is a wonderful idea. There's nothing worse than being alone during such an important holiday, especially when it can bring with it difficult memories.

"But I've found that for me at least, alone time this past year has been very cathartic. I think my heart is finally healing, and I know my trust in God has been restored. I was in serious doubt for a while there, but that was just my anger and sadness confusing me. I connected with a grief counseling ministry at church that has been incredibly helpful. I'll tell you more when I see you. Hey, give my best to everyone, and tell them I'm looking forward to seeing them again."

***

Josh stood waiting after knocking on Chloe's front door. When there was no answer, he knocked again -- still nothing. When he turned to leave, his attention was captured by the distant sound of music coming from somewhere up the street. It was a tinny sound and a bit warbled yet strangely familiar. Drawn by it, Josh began walking down the street toward the familiar noise. As he did, he imagined the street as it might have looked 18 years earlier when Noelle was just a little girl. After thinking about it, he concluded the place probably hadn't changed all that much, maybe the trees had been a little smaller, and perhaps a few houses painted a different color. Still, overall the neighborhood seemed well established and unchanging.

Josh sat down to take in the scene from a bus stop bench under a sprawling chestnut tree that reminded him of Versailles' park-like forest. He pulled out his phone and scrolled through pictures from the summer he and Noelle met. Josh stopped on the collage of candid photos Elise sent him from their time together on the vintage train in the Doux Valley river gorge. The natural beauty of Noelle's face and the purity of joy in her eyes made him smile. As he sat, a mother pushing a baby in a stroller walked past the bench. Then two children, wholly consumed in some preadolescent conversation, pedaled by on bicycles. Next, across the street, a female jogger, probably in her early twenties, ran by. Josh sighed heavily as he thought about Chloe walking Noelle in the stroller, Noelle chatting with a friend during a bike ride, and Noelle at home during a winter break taking a run. All the while, the sound got louder until he was finally able to put his finger on its familiarity. It was an old-fashioned ice cream truck.

Josh hadn't seen such a truck since he was a small boy. It had been such a popular thing in his neighborhood he never understood why it stopped coming around. Swept up in the nostalgia of the moment, when the truck turned the corner and headed toward the bench, Josh stood and reached for his wallet. He waved at the truck driver, who dutifully waved back with a big smile and turned the volume of the music down while pulling over to the curb near the bench.

"Bonjour," Josh greeted the man, "English?"

"Bonjour, oui, oui, but of course," the man said as he hopped from the driver's seat of what appeared to be a retired mail delivery vehicle and tipped his tattered beret toward his potential customer.

"You have found a wonderful seat to enjoy the neighborhood," the man said in broken English. "The mistral winds are quiet today, and the sun is out. It is unseasonably warm, which is why I decided to bring my truck out. As you might imagine, winter is traditionally a slow time for my business, but given that it is a Saturday and sunny, I figured, why not? Besides, some of my regular customers, the children you know, they like ice cream regardless of the weather. Of course, for you, Monsieur, I also have hot coffee or tea if you prefer."

"No, I'm feeling a bit like a child myself today, so I think I'll have one of those," Josh said, pointing to one of the dozen pictures of ice cream treats pasted to the side of the vehicle.

"Ah, an excellent choice, Monsieur -- the chocolate-covered banana -- it happens to be my personal favorite!"

Josh paid the man, who then, after cranking the tinny music volume back up, proceeded on his way to search for another customer.

The ice cream treat was cold, and the banana beneath the chocolate covering was frozen. Josh bit off a piece and enjoyed feeling it warm and then melt in his mouth. He savored the mix of flavors, and once again, nostalgia flooded his mind.

When he went to adjust himself on the hard wooden bench, he put his hands down on the seat to scooch his bottom backward in order to sit more erect. He emitted a quiet yelp when he felt a sharp prick on his finger. Looking down for the culprit, Josh saw a winter weathered clump of gnarled branches that looked very similar to the briar rose in Celeste's garden. As a bit of blood oozed from his finger, Josh was reminded of his prayer experience at the secret bench the night before the wedding. He'd spent many hours over the past year ruminating about that prayer, his biggest question always being why God had chosen not to answer his plea. Gradually he came to appreciate that the man he had envisioned praying alongside him that night had been none other than Jesus himself, and the scene God had put in his mind was Gethsemane. Several months ago, Josh had heard a Bible teaching from the passage of scripture that described that scene.

"You see," the pastor had said, "Gethsemane teaches us that God's will can, and often does, differ from our own. And if this was true even for Jesus, our savior who knew God's heart so well, how much more so for us?"

Since that sermon, the pastor's words of wisdom had become inextricably woven into the fabric of Josh's faith. It had enabled him to come to grips with God's will regarding Noelle. Not that he necessarily understood it or felt any less sad about it, but only that it was, for whatever reason, God's choice. And God was God, and he was not. How unsearchable and unfathomable are His ways? Thy kingdom come, Thy will be done. Not my will, but Thine.

Josh put his hurting finger next to the cold outside of the ice cream package and held it there. He smiled as he counted the thorn a blessing, a reminder of Noelle, and of God's sovereignty. In a way, Josh found himself becoming as fond of the briar's thorn in winter as he was its bloom in spring.

He once again began walking through the neighborhood. He came upon the park where he and Noelle had sat on the swings, and then he found the little church he'd been looking for. It was silent, as might be expected on a wintery Saturday afternoon, so Josh opened the metal gate leading to the cemetery in the back without reservation.

He remembered the first time Noelle had shown him the place and how she said she loved to visit it and talk with her father and brother. What had she said? "My sorrow is their joy, being born into heaven."

Then his mind flashed to the second time he was there, the January before when he bade Noelle her final farewell.

Wanting to savor the quiet of the place, Josh walked its perimeter taking note of various epitaphs on the various markers, some stone, some bronze, and some wooden. He strolled through the yard in concentric circles until he finally arrived at the LePage family markers. An unexpected breeze blew through, and Josh shuddered slightly. To get out of the wind, he sat on the ground in front of Noelle's marker.

"Hello, my love. It's been almost a year since I was here. But I hope you know that not a single day goes by that I don't think about you. I stopped by your house to see your mom, but she was out. I'll go back and try again later. I'm moving to France to work with Aubert. Mark's been here the whole year, but I went back home. I needed to figure some things out. You were my whole reason for wanting to come back to France, you know?"

Josh's heart grew heavy, and he paused to collect himself. He glanced around and then refocused on the marker in front of him.

"Sorry I didn't bring any flowers. It's winter, and, well ... well, that's a lousy excuse. The truth is I didn't think about it. Forgive me?"

Josh paused again, this time as if waiting for an audible response.

"I'm sure you are enjoying being with your dad and brother. Say hi to them and tell them I look forward to meeting them someday. I'll watch over your mom until then. She's a wonderful lady, and I've come to love her like my own mother.

"Noelle ... Wello ... ma Cherie. I miss you, and I love you ... most. You are my precious young, jeune amour, my first, premier amour, my forever, pour toujours amour, and, someday, when I join you in heaven, I know we will finally together share vieil amour."

The End

I hope you enjoyed reading my story as much as I did writing it! If you did enjoy the story, I would appreciate it if you would please take a moment to leave a review/rating on Amazon.com to let others know.
search: johnsterlingbridges
Thank you and God bless!

A little about the author -- John lives in the Monterey Bay area of California's central coast. He is a retired attorney who has been writing novels since 2018, and, to date, has published a dozen-plus books. Writers are often counseled to "write about what they know," so John's books weave together themes revolving around adventure, suspense, mystery, the law, romance, faith, and always "place." When not writing and publishing his books, John is busy traveling and adventuring with his wife, Lorrie, hunting lighthouses (and volunteering as a docent at the one near his home), tending to his rose garden, walking his dog along the Pacific coastline, and enjoying his "Grands" (a.k.a his seven grandkids). You can chat with him at sterling.granddad@gmail.com

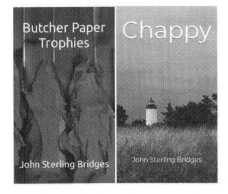

OTHER
BOOKS
BY
JOHN
STERLING
BRIDGES

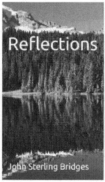

Made in the USA
Columbia, SC
15 February 2024